D1603827

OnOurBacks

Volume 2

The Best Erotic Fiction
Edited by Diana Cage

alyson books
los angeles

© 2004 BY HAF ENTERPRISES. AUTHORS RETAIN THE RIGHTS TO THEIR INDIVIDUAL PIECES
OF WORK.

MANUFACTURED IN THE UNITED STATES OF AMERICA.

THIS TRADE PAPERBACK ORIGINAL IS PUBLISHED BY ALYSON PUBLICATIONS,
P.O. BOX 4371, LOS ANGELES, CALIFORNIA 90078-4371.
DISTRIBUTION IN THE UNITED KINGDOM BY TURNAROUND PUBLISHER SERVICES LTD.,
UNIT 3, OLYMPIA TRADING ESTATE, COBURG ROAD, WOOD GREEN,
LONDON N22 6TZ ENGLAND.

FIRST EDITION: JUNE 2004

04 05 06 07 08 **a** 10 9 8 7 6 5 4 3 2 1

ISBN 1-55583-842-1

CREDITS
COVER PHOTOGRAPHY BY MICHELLE BLIOUX.
COVER DESIGN BY MATT SAMS.

Contents

Introduction

Like many people, I was introduced to sex through books—mainly in the form of cheesy best-sellers I swiped from my parents' bookshelves. I pored over Nancy Friday books, and Xaveria Hollander's *The Happy Hooker*, masturbating furiously and dog-earing favorite passages. But thinking back, my very earliest literary J/O material was an epic Shakespearean poem called "The Rape of Lucrece." In the tale, the beautiful Lucrece is ravished by one of her husband's men. Devasted, and filled with a vengeful rage, she is comforted by her handmaidens. That particular stanza—weeping, swooning handmaidens, and a ravished queen—sent my imagination aflame. The tragic queen extracts vows of revenge against her attacker from all her knights and then kills herself. That poem, with all its sex and violence, excited my budding libido over and over. My parents thought I was a Shakespeare prodigy, but really I was a blossoming pervert.

Reading erotica is such a great pleasure that I often think we should expand our roster of celebrated sexual practices to include reading smutty stories. We'd have to think of a hanky code, so queers could cruise for it. Maybe a paperback novel in the left pocket for those who like to read aloud, and one in the right for those who like to listen. Try it with this book. Stuff it in your back pocket and take it out on the town. Offer to read a story aloud to the cute girl working the cappuccino bar. It's sure to break the ice.

I'm thrilled to add a second volume of erotic writing to the *On Our Backs: The Best Erotic Fiction* series and to the rapidly growing canon of lesbian writing. The hundreds of submissions we get each year certainly indicate that lesbian erotica is thriving. And the quality of writing gets better every year. These 46 stories were originally published in *On Our Backs* magazine—and every other month we publish more sexy tales to delight and titillate queer women. This book features our very favorite stories from the past several years, along with a few sexy gems from the early days of *On Our Backs*. The stories in this volume represent the diverse terrain of lesbian sex that we cover in the magazine. I've specifically chosen stories that not only set my knickers on fire but also celebrate dyke sex in all its forms. It's all in here—vanilla sex between longtime lovers, hot spanking tales, group sex, kink, and lots more.

I'd like to thank all the wonderful contributors who made this book possible—your writing makes our lives visible. I'd also like to thank our interns past and present who transcribed stories from the early days of *On Our Backs*. This book could not have come together without the hard work of a lot of eager volunteers. I hope you love reading this book as much as I loved putting it together. And I hope this book inspires you to have lots of hot sex and maybe even pen a few smutty tales of your own.

Happy reading,
Diana Cage

Oui, Chef

Joy VanFuys

I'm a baby butch. Not that I'm so young, but I haven't been a butch long. One too many dreamy femme-fests, and I'd had it. Said goodbye, feminist vegetarian collective restaurant, and hello, New York. Changed my clothes, changed my hair, changed my head. The one thing I haven't quite changed is my pussy.

On the phone she said, "Short hair only, or hair pulled back. Short fingernails. White undershirt, black pants. Sturdy black shoes."

"You're playing my song," I told her.

"Meet me at the site at 8 A.M.," she answered, and hung up in my ear. Maybe I said the wrong thing. Maybe Pride Caterers just means she's got hubris about her hummus.

I check my look in the mirror. I still miss the swish and flow of long hair, but I love the new, cool breeze on my neck. My head is fuzzy, light, free. My pants are tight but not too tight. The black-and-red Western shirt I stole from my brother's dresser on the way out of town is perfect. Broad enough in the shoulders to hide me, funky enough to give me away. I'm going to be so late. This woman is going to kill me.

The party is at a foundation's headquarters, and I jog past tables set with china and crystal. No wheatgrass juicer in sight. It's the big time.

1

"Hey, I'm Kay," I say to the back of a white chef's coat as I swing open the door to the kitchen.

She turns; her face is a smooth mask framed by henna-red hair. She is six feet tall or more, her body lean and spare. Never trust a skinny chef, they say. Her skin is a pale ivory—Irish skin like in the soap commercial. Yeah, Irish, but not Bailey's-sipping sweet-old-lady Irish. Mean fourth-grade step-dance teacher Irish. An ice-cube shiver runs from the nape of my neck to my crotch, stopping along the way to perk my nipples hard. Down, girl.

"Good morning, Chef," she says.

"Oh, I'm not really a chef. I'm just the catering assistant. I think we spoke on the phone? My name is Kay. I'm from Connecticut. I just moved to New York, I—"

" 'Good morning, Chef' is how you will greet me. If I ask you a question, you will respond 'Oui, Chef' or 'Non, Chef.' Is that clear?"

This speech turns my guts to jelly. Her green eyes, flat and rich, conjure memories: gallons of guacamole, ruined by the collective's compromise of sprouts. Frost crystals on the avocado-green refrigerator, Mom reaching inside to pull out Popsicles for little Kay, little Brian. Pea soup, asparagus purée, spinach mousse.

"Yes. I mean, oui, Chef. Are you French? I mean, you don't sound French."

"Oui, Chef. Non, Chef."

"Oui, Chef."

"Very well." She hands me a white chef's coat with PRIDE CATERING embroidered on one side. "Change into this and begin prepping the desserts."

"Oui, Chef." I grab the jacket and bolt for the nearest door. It's not a bathroom, as I'd hoped, but a small pantry with a mirror and a sink.

I shuck off my shirt, admiring the galloping horses. Brian's going to be so pissed when he realizes I took it. I button the jacket from the bottom, transforming from Western-Wear Dyke to Caterer Dyke with a few quick movements. Then I have to stop. I move my shoulders forward and suck in my gut. The middle button buttons, but just barely. If I stand perfectly still, I'm fine. When I move, there's a definite gap. Shit.

Poking through the cabinets for an Ace bandage or some duct tape, I curse the urge that made me reach for the wife-beater this morning instead of something with a bit more support. Chef jackets aren't supposed to fit tightly. If you spill something hot on yourself, you're supposed to be able to pull it away from your skin. I'm a pretty small person, except for...well, you know. I unbutton the jacket and press my palms to my chest, willing the flesh to melt away and leave me with smooth, uncomplicated bones, muscles, skin. Instead my nipples purr, wait to be petted.

Before, all I ever wanted I had: long curly hair, curvy ass, big tits. "So lush," a tough girl whispered in my ear one night. "So Renaissance. I want to make love to your tits for the rest of my life." So I let her, till my nipples were sore, the meat of my breasts aching from the power of her suction. Let her keep me in pretty bras and panties, let her brush my hair a hundred strokes for a thousand nights. I was her girl. She would play with my pussy for hours, spreading my lips wide, examining every fold, baring my clit till it stung in the air, then bathing it with her tongue, drenching me. When I came, she blushed. When I reached for her, she froze. I should really call and tell her where I am.

There's a hard rap on the door. "I need you. Now." I button up. My stiff nipples threaten to tear tiny round holes through my undershirt, but the thick cotton jacket holds them flat. She nods her approval, but I feel like my tits are on display, served up with the pastries for general consumption. The waiters, all gay boys and straight girls, filter in and out of the kitchen, not noticing me.

I snap on latex gloves, ball melon, slice strawberries, make fruit kabobs. She watches my knife skills, studying my hands as I try not to impale my finger on a bamboo skewer. As I finish, she brings over a pan of brownies. "My specialty," she says. "Cut them into perfect one-inch squares."

I steel my knife a few times, working up the nerve to cut into the smooth surface of the chocolate rectangle. My first cut is straight and true, and I let myself breathe, begin to trust my hands. The scent is seductive, and my stomach growls. I'm dying to taste one, but I know her eyes are on me. Finally, I slip a crumb into my mouth and feel the chocolate spread over my palate, rousing each taste bud as it flows. I've never been so happy. Brownies always seemed one-dimensional before. Sweet, sure, but that's all. This melting mouthful engages my entire tongue. A dusting of flour, streaked with cocoa, speckled with espresso and studded with bittersweet chunks of chocolate, chocolate, chocolate. Yum. Jesus, am I blushing? I turn and reach for a platter in an upper cabinet. As my arm goes up, I feel a firm hand on my lower back, steadying me. Another hand slides over my armpit, and I feel strong fingers squeeze my breast. My breath stalls, then comes hard and fast. My arm is frozen in the air, the platter shuddering, as she shakes her hand up and down, back and forth. She hisses in my ear, "Finish the brownies and go to the pantry."

"Oui, Chef. Should I—"

"The pantry."

"Oui, Chef." She saw me. Eating during service. Touching my sterile gloved hand to my mouth. She's definitely going to fire me. Or something.

She carries a gold-rimmed dessert plate into the pantry, a small square of brownie in its center. I sneak a look at her face and see that her pale skin is streaked with red, a flush moving over her cheeks. I wish I knew what that meant.

"Open your jacket," she tells me. Oh, God, she noticed. I undo each button, then slide it off my shoulders. My nipples are instantly hard, whether from the change in temperature or from the scrutiny of her eyes, I'm not sure.

"Take off your undershirt. Hands behind your head."

OK, reality check. I'm in New York, in a pantry somewhere. My chef is asking me to show her my bare tits. When a chef speaks, you do what she says. Besides, I want to. She strokes my biceps, probing for muscle. Her hands are impossibly cold. Pastry hands, my grandmother called them. I have hot hands. One touch of the dough and the thin butter layers that weave through the flour melt, ruin everything.

Her hands move down to weigh each breast, lifting them from beneath. "Your breasts are very large. Why are they not properly restrained?"

"I don't know, Chef."

Her fingertips dig into my areolae, roll my nipples back and forth. "When you don't wear a brassiere, people can see your nipples. They can see the size and shape of your breasts."

I've never been so embarrassed. I've never been so hot. I am sweating, and I think my pussy is dripping down my leg. Can she smell the chocolate on my breath?

"Oui, Chef."

"Are you ashamed of these breasts? The girls all want big breasts. They pay for them, even. But you want to be a boy, don't you?"

Honestly, I'd like to sit down and talk with you about that very subject. But the way you're gripping the tips of my nipples tells me that you're not in the mood for a deep conversation on the topic of butch-femme dynamics.

"Oui, Chef."

"Take down your pants," she tells me. I'm afraid to obey, afraid not to. I don't look down, but I suspect that my memory is not wrong, that this morning I proudly put on my brand-new briefs, fresh from the boys' department at Macy's. My thighs tell me that they are soaked through.

Her palm pats my crotch gently, then harder. "Is there a dick in there? No? Then why do you need this?" she demands, pulling open the split-front.

I can't imagine an answer to this question. My response is a moan that comes from a place inside me where I've never been before.

Her fingers slip inside and work my lips apart. Is there a dick in there? Maybe. My clit is so hard that it's straining toward her touch, and I gasp as she grasps the base and pinches hard.

"Does that excite you?"

"Oui, chef."

She shifts her hand, pressing my clit down hard with her thumb, and letting two fingers curl around to probe my opening. She teases me with her fingertips, making my cunt open and close for her.

"There we are. You are a girl, aren't you? Show me."

I squeeze her fingers with all my might. "Oui, Chef."

She slips her hand from my underpants, and I whimper a little, against my will. She picks up the brownie and holds it in front of my mouth. "Would you like a bite?"

I smell my pussy, smell chocolate, on her fingers. "Oui, Chef."

"Put your hands on the counter. Your bottom in the air," she tells me.

"Open your mouth." She places the brownie between my lips. "If you bite it, or let it drop from your mouth, you'll be very sorry."

She slides down the waistband of my briefs and gives my ass a light caress.

Then I feel it—a fish spatula? a cake turner?—smack down hard. I almost let the brownie drop, but my lips hold on, even as I feel the sting again.

Tears come to my eyes, the kind of tears that in the femme old days would have left trails of black mascara running down my cheeks. Just a few, not from the pain. Not from the humiliation. From the relief.

"You will be a proper young lady." Smack. "Do you understand?"

I nod my head slowly, trying not to let a crumb drop.

"You will wear a brassiere," she tells me. Smack. Smack. "You will wear panties." Smack. Smack.

My mind is quiet, waiting for the next impact, but instead I feel her hand rubbing me, calming my sore skin.

"Do you wish to come?" she asks.

"Oui, Chef," I whimper.

"Then do it quickly. We still have guests, you know." Her fingers, now warm, slide between my legs, push deep into my pussy. I clench, flood, come and come, hard and quick, as she instructed.

"Swallow," she tells me. The brownie is a lake of chocolate saliva. I lap it with my tongue, feel it coat my teeth and soothe my throat.

"You may stand and dress." I raise my body, feeling the strain in the backs of my calves, the cool air on my butt cheeks. Afraid to look at her, I pull on my undershirt, button my pants. Finally, I look into her eyes. She smiles, and wipes my mouth with her thumb.

"I think you'll do very well. Will 40 hours a week be suitable for you?"

"Oui, Chef," I tell her. "Oui."

Orgy on Route 66

Annie Stangl

Kevin has a thing for waitresses. I think it's because they bring her coffee, which I practically never do—and then she gets to stare at their asses as they walk away. "We're staying in the motel tonight, but we're probably taking off in the morning," she says to a cute, blue-eyed, freckly girl.

This particular waitress isn't my type at all. She's very slim and girly. She seems like a cool person, but she isn't registering on my sexual radar.

But she's obviously registering on Kevin's.

"You're so sweet," Kevin says in response to an offer of sugar for her coffee. "Why don't you just stick your finger in there and twirl it around."

"Oh, Christ. I can't believe you just said that," I moan. But the waitress smiles. I try to distance myself from the cheesy pickup line by lighting a cigarette. I love that Bob's Big Boy has a smoking section. I look into the mirror next to our booth. My roots need a touch-up, my hair is getting long, and the blue streaks are a bit faded—but I'm wearing my favorite dress: It's stretchy black wool, knee-length, long sleeves, zips up the back. It has only a few holes in it. I'm probably too covered up for Kingman, Arizona, even in January. But it was the only thing clean. We've been on the road for three weeks and haven't stayed in one place long enough to do a load of wash. Kevin is wearing a threadbare Harley T-shirt and dangerously low Levi's.

The waitress is, of course, wearing her uniform. She fills Kevin's cup to overflowing and says, "I get off at 6," before walking away with an exaggerated swish.

I give Kevin a pointed look and say, "Kevin, I need something a little more substantial than pussy for dinner." But she knows I'm playing with her.

She pats my hand and says, "Drink your coffee, baby. We've got a few hours to kill. Why don't we go back to the motel?"

• • •

We picked this Best Western out of the *Damron Women's Traveler,* so I'm not really surprised to see another dyke couple in the hot tub. They are pretty cute. In fact, the butcher of the two is pretty damn good-looking.

I can tell Kevin is getting antsy for some fun. That's my girl. She's got a nonstop libido. So big, I can't keep her satisfied. I'd have to fuck her 24/7. Anyway, she's had the waitress habit since day one, so it wouldn't be fair of me to suddenly start complaining.

I give the other two gals a nod as I slide into the water. Kevin does the same and puts her hand on my shoulder so they'll know we're together. We talk a little bit about how hot it is, how odd it is to see so many dykes at a Best Western off Route 66, and other chitchatty stuff. Susan, that's the femme's name, hands me a joint, so I smoke it and hand it over to her girlfriend, whose name is Dana. She tokes up and passes it on and soon the four of us are happily making plans to head to the Grand Canyon together tomorrow.

I lean my head back and close my eyes and Dana takes the opportunity to push her foot between my thighs. I hear kissing sounds and low moans. When I pick my head up to investigate

I see Kevin and Susan entwined. My girl has a way of getting parties started.

Dana kinda looks like a surfer boy; I think this to myself as she pushes me against the side of the tub.

"We should probably go somewhere more private," she says. So I disengage just long enough to announce, "There's a king-size bed in our room."

I'm excited by the beauty of her body as I watch her walk across the parking lot. She's far bigger than I'd normally go for, the muscles I mean, and Kevin looks dwarfed as she walks alongside her.

The freckly waitress catches up to our happy little band in the parking lot. Must be 8 o'clock. She hollers, "Hey, ladies, wait up," so I sprint up the burning cement stairs and throw open the door to the room. Five sweaty dykes tumble in and fall on the bed, quickly shedding four wet bathing suits and one polyester uniform.

The waitress flops right onto her back in the middle of the bed and Susan, without so much as an introduction, dives between her freckly, tanned thighs. I hear her moan "Mmm, wet pussy." And that's the last I see of her face for the next 10 minutes.

I jump on the bed and stroke the freckly face of the waitress. She looks so happy. Before Kevin and I started this journey we call our relationship, I was living a suburban nightmare. My partner and I hadn't had sex in nearly a year. Before bed I used to hum "Love will keep us together," Captain and Tennille style, to keep from mooning over the dull ache between my legs. And then this sexy dyke named Kevin parked a fugly yellow Dodge van in front of the bookstore where I spent eight hours a day. She waltzed into my life in thrift-store threads and long stringy rock-star hair and showed me a whole lot of sex and drugs. It's just like love, but better.

Kevin and Dana kneel at the edge of the bed and watch in

admiration. But I want them to join us. "Get off your lazy asses and come over here and help us," I yell at them.

Kevin jumps up first and pushes me over onto my stomach, but I'm having none of it, so I shrug her off and push Susan out of the way and dive face first into Freckles's damp musky wetness. Her pussy is inviting, the hair neatly trimmed, big plump lips and a swollen clit to nibble on. She groans loudly as I pry apart her inner lips with the point of my tongue. Behind me someone pushes against my ass, but I don't want to break the rhythm to see who it is, so I try to guess.

From between creamy waitress thighs I say, "Dana, that must be you." But no one answers. Whoever it is makes a beeline for my ass—strokes my asshole with insistent fingertips.

I feel the fingertips pull away as Dana gets pushed down on the bed next to me. Kevin spreads her legs and slips fingers into her audibly wet cunt. "Can you take more?" she says. And Dana practically growls, "I can take whatever you can dish out."

"All right, then." Kevin reaches straight for her G spot. Dana arches her back and groans as Kevin pushes harder. "Oh yeah, fuck me," she says. "Fuck that hole, hurt it, break it."

And Kevin does. She pumps her fingers in an out, and the energy that those two create momentarily stops the rest of us. Dana yells so loud even the waitress looks up. "Oh shit, oh shit, oh shit," she says. "Oh fuck, oh God."

"Aw hell, yeah," says Susan as she takes Dana's place behind me. The thing that drives me nuts is ass-fucking, and Susan can tell, so she goes at my ass like there's no tomorrow and I can feel the tension build. "Please," I say. And then it's happening. Like something blossoming between my legs. Pure pleasure. I'm so happy at this moment. I'm always happy when I come.

I roll over and press my sweaty forehead to Dana's abdomen and laugh out loud at the bed full of naked dykes.

"I never got this much action in San Francisco. Thank God for *Damron.*"

Freckles sits up, pushes her sweaty hair away from her forehead, and says, "Do you think I'm waiting tables at Bob's Big Boy for the tips?"

Daddy

Red Jordan Arobateau

Daddy comes over smelling of cheap cologne. He wears dark trousers, shirt, boots like mine. A wan smile. He crouches on the floor, then sits. Leans back against the sofa. He's uncivilized.

Daddy's poor, but he does the best he can. Says he acts wild and crazy though he knows he'd be more effective to be proper and polite and take on the trappings of the middle class. But he can't execute it. It's too much stress.

So Daddy's an outlaw. He makes inappropriate remarks and shares his radical ideas and nasty thoughts with all who will listen—instead of hiding them.

I know soon he's going to remove his clothes, and his feet—in worn socks—will also smell of cheap cologne. He puts it in his shoes, not wanting body odor. The same scent is in his jockey shorts and T-shirt. He even puts the scent inside his hat—just to make sure, after his long day as a janitor.

He shifts his weight on the floor. I see the imprint of long cock meat in his crotch. Daddy's packing a big rod.

Daddy. I'm his boy. Identical in black trousers, T-shirt, leather jacket, and boots. But no 5 o'clock shadow like him.

I'm more feline, willowy—not being on T. I'm soon going to receive Daddy's love. Show him a good time. Nothing is going to keep Daddy from his pleasure. He's made that quite clear before.

Not the darkest night and threat of hoodlums or lack of money to take a cab. He waits for the bus in the corridor called shotgun alley, which cuts through the barrio to take him home.

I want to be in a relationship. I conveyed this to Daddy one night.

That's fine. He replied. But don't limit yourself while you are waiting. Daddy gazed at me with his sultry Daddy look. Probing deep into my eyes for so long—as if wading deep into the well of my soul for kept secrets. So long that I finally look away. When I turned back I caught Daddy's gaze resting on my chest. My tits are not very large but budding and firm. Enough for Daddy's pleasure. Daddy said the sight of my tits gets him off. To feel them and squeeze them and watch them bounce as he enjoys his stroke.

Daddy, like many transmen and butch dykes too, pisses standing up. A yellow stream into the toilet, with the seat up. Boy is fascinated. Appraises the Daddy method. A plastic disc four inches in diameter rolled into a funnel that Daddy coolly removes from his back pocket. He places the large end under his piss hole and lets it fly. Piss shoots out of the narrow end of the funnel, zizzing into the bowl.

Now Daddy comes out of his clothes. His body is hard from training with iron weights. He has a bit of fat—a small potbelly. A Daddy-style belly.

Daddy wishes he were bigger and stronger. More massive. He goes to the gym and fights in vain with the weights. A steel bar with black iron discs. Barbell and dumbbells.

Boy is in awe of Daddy's iron-hard muscles. His bulk. He's twice the size of Boy. He's macho. A powerhouse. In Boy's eyes, at least.

Daddy's body has evidently passed from that of a total woman to that of a man. Softer and more round than the former, no hips, bigger shoulders, and hairy. I didn't know him then. Just now, in his true self. Daddy's voice is changing.

Lowering week by week. But he still sneezes in a high pitch— like a girl. "I sneezed at work the other day and almost outed myself," he confides, chagrined.

Daddy wants to fuck tonight. Like all nights. I've stripped myself naked for him, and helped him out of his clothes. I sit in the middle of the bed waiting.

Daddy gouges his fingers into the can of Crisco, pushes it into Boy's butt hole. Boy's ass is upturned, waiting to be pounded. White congealed grease is smeared over his ass crack. Daddy places his big cock head at Boy's hole and begins to jiggle the shaft, vibrating, stimulating his own clit ecstatically, and simultaneously pushes past the first sphincter into Boy's rectum.

"Go slow, sir. Please, sir," Boy says breathlessly, his request laboring from his mouth; his thick stomach sucked in, tense.

Daddy's strong hands caress Boy's bottom and stroke his sides.

Daddy's strap-on dick has become a part of him—he's used it in 10,000 fuckings. Its shaft is long, slender. Nine inches of rubbery silicone. Daddy makes it pretty damn real to the person on the receiving end.

"Fuck me, Daddy! Fuck me in my little boy butt! Oh Daddy! Push your big cock up my hot little boy butt!"

"Oh, it's so good. Oh, suck. Oh, fuck. Oh, shit. Oh, baby. Oh, Jesus. Oh, God. Oh, *fuck*."

"Fuck my ass with your penis!" I shout.

"I'm giving you all my love," he shouts back, humping wildly.

"Drive your penis in my ass!"

"I'm giving you all my come."

"I could have used you during the week, Boy. I could have used your tight little ass." Boy smiles. He's growing on Daddy's heart.

"Thank you, sir."

Daddy could have used Boy's slender body to satisfy

his hard dick and his seeking spirit—both of which drive him wild.

As he readies himself to go, I mention, "Maybe we could reschedule our busy lives to meet twice a week instead of just once, sir?"

"Yeah," replies Daddy, curtly.

"Thank you, sir. I'll look at my calendar, sir. And give you a call. I could free up Wednesday or Thursday for your pleasure, sir."

As I help him on with his coat, Daddy mumbles something vague about how he, too, will consult his calendar.

How to Break a Woman
Hanne Blank

First, of course, you must find the right woman, a woman
you wish to break not only for silly, facile reasons, a woman
who presents the appropriate sort of challenge. She may be of
any proportion, any color. Only her spirit must be tall, with
powerful arms accustomed to squeezing the world in a grand
embrace.

She must be beautiful, although not necessarily pretty,
and she must know that often there is no connection between
these things. She must appreciate art, must be able to savor
with a delicate, private shiver the force that drives the sap up
and through the tree, the light that springs from a painter's
brush, the roar that fills solitude to bursting. She must be
unafraid to sing, even if she sings off-key.

She must as a matter of course be strong. But if you have
found the right sort of woman, she will be; bearing the weight
of a worthy, messy, well-ridden life will make her so. Her
smile must be unanticipated and radiant, her laugh generous
and unself-conscious. And she must want to be broken.

This last trait is most important. Not so important as to
overshadow the rest, but definitely first among equals. She
need not *know* she wants to be broken, not quite. It is enough
that she have the feeling (it usually nests somewhere between
her heart and her loins) that there is more to yielding than

being entered, more to giving up than giving out, that there is some part within her that cannot be touched by love's usual glad-hearted jiggery-pokery. Perhaps it has been brushed before and still sizzles in her memory like a fuse. Or perhaps it hasn't, and she knows it only by the shape of the mound it forms beneath the fine silt of hope.

All this is no small thing to ascertain. Flat-out asking is, of course, a possibility, but likely to generate an incomplete or wrong answer. A better response is filtered slowly out of solution: having stirred yourself into her days, watch her sighs, her asides, her unguarded, long, late-night stretches, head back and eyes shut. Note the contractions of her sadness, the burps of her laughter, the accidental intimacies she allows. As an experiment, hold her wrists when you kiss her. Bring them up far above her head, pinned against a wall. She must stare at you, nostrils flared and pupils slightly dilated, and dare you to do it again.

The longer you teach, her the better you will know when and where to begin. This is no place for your head rush, your get-rich-quick scheme. Fruit picked too green will never be sweet, and it will not be only you who suffers the days, weeks, months of pucker. Your haste will earn her disdain.

She will tell you when it is time. Eventually she will, in your presence, chain the hounds of daily survival, and she will hint that somewhere she has left a window open for the right kind of thief to find. Perhaps your hands will be entwined on a restaurant tabletop and she will overturn the grasp, her hand palm up, giving you herself with gradual, warm lassitude. She may hint with the arch of her neck, the ripe, new sigh, when you take a handful of the hair at her nape and tug her head back to kiss below her ear. Or perhaps she will simply tell you. But you must be sure. If you are not, wait. Do not hesitate to wait; longing is no enemy to the tiny fissures of need you will force open into chasms.

Longing is, in fact, what you seek: the haze, the veil, the

nimbus of desire whose presence provides the critical element of transformation. This is more alchemy than chemistry, and as for pedantry, there is to lust no greater insult. She knows this. Certain skills are simple rote, and if you have chosen well (and for your sake I pray you have) this is not a woman who will be impressed by rudiments. Your detailed knowledge of her specific feminine anatomy, for instance, is a given. To be worthy of the instrument, a virtuoso must know far more than how to play. You must know when to play, and most importantly, why.

And so when you receive the sacrament of her wrists, her strong, sweet arms given to you to tie and bind, you must understand that you bind her not to your will but away from her own. You tie her to keep her from her own resistance, from the urge to interrupt, to reciprocate. Each wind of the rope, each caress of leather takes her further from service—that career to which woman is so deeply trained—and makes it less and less possible for her to please by doing, more and more necessary that she please by being, and that her pleasure in her being, and being at your hands, be enough.

This is why you must not touch her. Hunger for touch is not the thin veneer of the need to come. It is much deeper, the hunger of a baby for the obliviating harbor of its mother's blessed arms, the gravity of flesh on flesh that can pull us to ourselves when we are furthest away. This is why touch is the thing you must withhold no matter how you want to stroke, to caress, to reassure her with gentle pressure. She may already be desiring, but desire is not sufficient. She may already be wet, her cunt weeping for want of you, but tears aren't enough either. She must yearn, keening with long-forgotten desperation, in thrall to the echoes of every time she has ever longed to be touched, to be taken, to be stolen away.

So let her feel your breath on her body, the warmth of your very life against her thigh, her ear, her neck. The currents of soft promises, of a paean to her majesty, of a rumbling threat to make her scream until her throat fails, all will rustle the infinitesimal down on the skin of her hip, her cheek. Tell the fur between her legs what you plan to do to the hungry briny goddess who hides behind it, your lips grazing the hairs as you talk to her. Tell her how she will be open for you, be filled and gorged and used for you, the vibrations of your voice dancing electrical down the wiry cables toward their destination.

Objects will come to mind as you watch her, hovering over her face as if you might at any instant kiss her. Perhaps you will plan some things you can use, like that ice cube lazily oiling your whiskey that can be held tight in your fist, chilly drops seeping between your fingers to splatter her breast, her hip, with trickling kisses. Her hairbrush can bristle a cobweb up an inner thigh. Scarf silk floats down over her face, throat, shoulder.

Make her velvet, make her leather, make her the itchy thick nubbled wool of your heavy jacket, draped over her, dragged down her, drawn up between her thighs and across her parted lips. This is a test: Do you have your number 2 pencil? Draw the featherlight maps of your lust on her skin with the sharp graphite, letting it drift over her swells and niches.

Coax close the hungry mongrel in her skin as you slip your belt off, the better to stroke her, to tease her, to catch the thick of a nipple against its doubled-over loop. Stroke her pussy with it, tease it against her clit, then part her teeth with the thick, insensible tongue that tastes of her own cunt. Learn the rhythm of her winces, the pleading of her arched back, the incantations of the wordless sounds that bubble from her mouth.

Melt her. Let her drip with the heat of your words spilling over her in bursts like Midwest thunderstorms. Make her ooze like the thick, clear lubricant in the bottle that rests quiet and complicit in a bowl of hot water, the warm liquid clinging where you drip it on her body like dreams you can't quite shake in the morning.

Listen to her sing, to her throat as it vibrates beyond sound, to the flushed rustle of her bound beauty. Give her almost enough, but never quite. Give her the glut of her own restless want, feeding it back to her. Make her measure the paradox of your delicacy and knowing, brutal force.

Sacrifice anything but her yearning, give her anything but your skin. Bear the yoke of her pleading despite the heaviness of your own desire. This is not about you, and devotion must be its own reward. Hurt her if she requires it, if you can withstand it. Go with her, bewitched, to the cross, to the lions.

And then, and only then, touch her. Call her back to the torn earth, to the shuddering grip of her longing. Touch her belly, her sides, her legs, the storm-streaked curves of her face, the terrible tenderness of cheeks and lips and forehead. Bring your skin to her skin, the weight of you to her waiting. Crush her, knead her, go into her burning and become the flame that shines through her eyes, pushing, demanding that she not stop yielding. If you are lucky, she will not.

I tell you this because your eyes were gorgeous when you flirted with me, because you eyed my dark nails and lips and reputation and you asked me if I could tell you how to break a woman. I tell you this because I liked the look of your biceps disappearing under the soft of your shirt. I liked the sharp white edge of your teeth. I tell you this because you are graceful enough, because I think you may be cruel enough, because your touch on my arm was uncompromising in just the right way to make my pussy beg like a dog for your hand, even though my face was cool and my eyes clear and steady.

So now you know. This is how you break a woman: exactly as she wants to be broken.

To Fuck a Cowboy
Rakelle Valencia

She was still there at the end of that long, dusty day as I picked up my discarded rope halter from the dirt and lashed a coiled lariat to the empty saddle of my big quarter horse gelding. She was still there. And that's how we ended up in her bed.

Everyone wants to fuck a cowboy. It's the American way, Mom's apple pie, hot dogs, and all that. Cowboys are rooted in our heritage. They're a rare breed nowadays, girl "cowboys" being even more rare. Cowboys are a daydream of the old Western heroes. They're a fantasy. Who hasn't gotten hot over the Marlboro Man and wished there was a Marlboro Woman? Who hasn't wanted a rugged, rangy body of sinuous muscles wrapped in cotton and denim, accentuated by long, worn, tight, leather chaps? Who hasn't wanted to be ensnared in a cowboy's rope?

No sooner did the gate on the round corral close than did the door of her rented double-wide trailer. And she kissed me as the lock clicked behind, me noticing that her small, soft hands rested lightly at my lean hips, not wandering from the thick, harness leather of my belt, not committing themselves like her insistent lips had promised.

I dropped my gear bag, using the thud to drive home the point that I was there, and staying, at least for one night. The contained weight of my breaking equipment and a fresh change of clothes resounded on the hollow floor. In reply, her hands tugged the embroidered Wrangler logo shirt from my leather-belted waist. I knew that in the morning the two-tone embroidered trophy shirt would be gone, a memento, a token to remind her of the time she fucked a cowboy, a real working cowboy, a filthy rendition of legends.

I took her mouth then, sucking on her lower lip with the hunger and the thirst produced by a 10-hour day in the sun, in the saddle, starting eager colts anxious to hop and bounce and throw a leg here and there, much as I was anxious to do now. She returned my fervor by mingling our tongues in a dance that grew in rhythm and strength. The pleasantries were over.

She was short, petite and cute, and I knew what to do, even if I hadn't caught her name. Shit, it's what I do, rope 'em and break 'em. But that sounds harsh. It's not. I gentle them until they're in my hip pocket. Then I like to get my legs around them, feeling the power that surges in my groin.

They say the cowboys like it rough, but that don't matter. We like the ride, any ride, and we like to ride all day, all night too if we can, and all the better if each ride is different. It don't matter, so long as it's not boring and you're not on the hell bitch.

I don't mind being bucked if she's got a little of that in her. But when I settle into the rhythm I'm there to stay, all the way to the buzzer. They call me "Stick," not referring to my physique, although it could. They say I can ride anything, and I haven't been thrown. So when I finally get a leg over, I mean business, but that's not to say it won't be fun.

I tore my mouth away to watch my finger trickle down the line of pearly white snaps along her plaid Western-yoked pink-and-purple femme dress shirt. Mesmerizing pearly white snaps, good for only one thing. I grasp each side under the collar, just above her breasts, and rip the snaps apart; I love that sound.

Her little white conservative cotton bra plopped out with a load too heavy to ignore. My tanned, weathered hand smeared dust over the pure whiteness, an alluring contrast, and I had to have my mouth on her. Suckling greedily to mewling and moans, I released her tin buckle and peeled her faded jeans open, thrusting fingers deep within a cleanly shaven crevice. Smooth flesh was hot in my hand, bypassing the hardened nodule to seek the quenching of a different thirst.

Her ready wetness gave me pause. I practically drooled down her cleave, having lost attention. I wanted her. I wanted this ride more than the last ride, more than any ride, because it was here and now, and I knew just how I wanted to saddle and mount her.

"I'm going to ride you every which way before dawn calls me back to the round corral." I grasped her hair, entangling my fingers through the cheap bottled dye job and dragged her downward to kneeling. My slickened fingers left a snail's trail of wetness from her crotch to the hollow of her pale throat. "Open the gear bag and wait."

Unbuckling my rugged leather waist belt, conservatively highlighted with silver conchos, one directly center, I wrapped slight, feminine wrists with the looped buckle end, inverting the leather length through her legs, following the seam of her untarnished buttocks until that one concho rested against her clit.

The tail of the Western working leather firmly in my grip, I liberated from my bag a worn piggin' string, the short length of which is used for tying off the legs of a roped calf, and had this waxed, thin rope knotted to the belt's tail, thrown around her pasty throat and back to hold that studded strap in place. Oh, she could release the pressure to her wrists, clit, and neck by dropping her hands, but I didn't think she would. It had never been my experience that any of them did. In fact, they all learned to pull on it, rub on it, gyrate their cunt over that silver protrusion, oiling that leather strap until it slipped into their crack and teased that eager camp follower's puckered asshole too.

But, while I could give, I was here to get. I was eager for the promise, the ride of that waiting filly I found standing at the gate all day long. I gathered and tugged the tendrils at the nape of her neck, to set her head. I wanted her to look up at me. I wanted her to search my eyes as my cunt would be searching her red, pouty lips.

Long thin fingers of my callused hands deftly plucked the brass button of my Wrangler jeans and pulled at the gritty zipper to expose the trimmed runway strip of my shaved pussy. A musky odor escaped, born of the hot day's work and an even hotter imagination that often plagued me. Denim dropped toward the unswept floor. I wanted to thrust her nose into my smell, bury her face in the erotic crease between my legs, but I would be gentler than that; I didn't want to break her too soon. I wanted her to come to me willingly, with every aching inch of her being offered for service, there for me to ride.

I showed her what she should do as I traced small circles over a stiffened clit shaft, plunging my fingers into my own wetness. She licked her lips in response, telling me that she understood, that she was thinking on it, like an eager filly during round-penning work. She wanted it too, and my will would become hers. I stepped up for that first ride.

Mounting her mouth, there at the doorway, jeans trapped on my boot tops, gear bag open at my ankles, I could find no other bliss outside of the pen. I was born to ride, compelled to ride something all of the time, anywhere. I moved my pelvis from a walking pace into that of a brisk, two-beat jog, wrapping my fingers in this filly's mane to stay with her in case she bucked or tossed around. I pulled on her hard, sinking into my seat, thrusting into her movement until we were one.

I felt a quivering beneath me, her whole body joining into

the rhythm with a creak of leather and a straining of taut rope. I had to have more. Not faster, just more of what I had now.

As if she read my thoughts, her tongue flicked into my hole with the searing force of a hot branding iron. The pointy tip of her petite nose bumped my rigid clitoris fiercely as her stiffened poker explored my cavern. Her face was sopping wet from the ride, the vision nearly ungluing me from my human saddle. I drove harder, lengthening the rhythm, the stride, into an uneven three-beat.

She bounced and jounced beneath me, her concurrent mewling turning into throaty moans, then death-defying screams like that of a rogue stallion challenging in the night.

Splashing, a tumultuous waterfall slit the air, the sound lunging at my ears, and I broke then. I was the one to buck and hop and jump, twisting and writhing from atop the saddle, forcing my mount to stay with me as I pitched and slammed through this first ride. But that was impossible.

Not one to ride 'em hard and put them away wet, I reached to release the cinch on my downed filly. She rolled to all fours. I smacked her rounded rump and drove her into the disheveled bedroom.

View From the 14th Floor
Greta Christina

Bring what you need on our first date—if we click, I'll want to do it right away. One-night stands only.

Dana read the ad on Thursday. She masturbated furiously, then called the number. They made a date, and she spent most of Saturday making arrangements.

They met in a bar on Sunday evening. Dana arrived on time and found Elizabeth already sitting in a corner booth. She was blond, with an expensive haircut, dressed in a crisp white blouse and a single strand of pearls. She already had a drink in front of her. Dana settled into the booth. "So, how long have you lived in New York?" she asked.

"Six days," Elizabeth said curtly. "Look. Here are my limits. I don't like extreme physical pain, but keep it reasonable and we'll be fine. Psychologically you can do almost anything. My safe word is 'safe word.' And I mean it about the one-night stand. After tonight, we're done." She took a sip of her drink. "You?"

Dana bit her lip. Elizabeth's tone offended her, made her want to slap the woman down. She noticed her clit thumping and wondered for a moment if she was being played, if the girl was pissing her off on purpose. She stared rudely at Elizabeth's tits and decided it didn't matter. "Your limits are fine," she said. "And mine aren't relevant to you. Do you want to do it?"

Elizabeth looked at Dana like she was appraising china. Finally she gave a small nod. "Yes. Let's do it."

"Good," Dana said calmly. "That's the last word I want to hear from you until...well, ever, I guess." She strode out the door, leaving her drink untouched, and whistled for a cab. Elizabeth followed, eyeing her suspiciously as they got in the taxi. "Lester Hotel," Dana told the cabbie. "The one in midtown." She stayed silent all the way to the hotel, where she led Elizabeth to the 14th floor and pulled a key from her pocket.

Elizabeth looked around as the door closed behind her. The room appeared untouched, except for an armchair placed at an odd angle in the dressing nook off the bedroom. The decor was elegant and unpretentious, with tall windows that took up most of the outside wall. Dana switched on all the lights, switched off the one in the dressing nook, settled into the armchair, and began to speak.

"Did you know that every week, dozens of telescopes are sold in the city of New York? Interesting statistic. Nobody seriously thinks all those people are stargazing in Connecticut on weekends. Everyone knows exactly what those New Yorkers are doing with those telescopes. And yet everyone goes on with their lives, in front of their open windows, as if they actually had privacy.

"Open the curtains."

She could see Elizabeth flinch before she obeyed. Good, she thought. This could work.

"It's Sunday night," Dana continued, "so a lot of people are home. And bored, and looking for something to do. When I scoped out the room earlier, I estimated about 5,000 windows with a direct view of this one. Probably about 50 have telescopes. More if you count binoculars. So I'm guessing we've got anywhere from 10 to 30 people in the audience tonight. Maybe more.

"Now take off your blouse and wander around the room.

28

Act like you're a normal human being who's just changing for dinner, but keep turning to face the window."

Elizabeth stopped in her tracks. She turned from the window and looked Dana in the face, dismayed, her arrogance slipping off like a discreet partygoer escaping a bad soiree.

"Don't look at me," Dana snapped. "Face the window again. Now." Elizabeth complied, her shoulders slumping, and Dana went on, calmer. "See, I placed this chair very carefully. I can see you, and your reflection in the window, but people outside probably can't see me. So don't look at me again. I don't want our audience to know I'm here. I want them to think you're doing this on your own.

"I was going to build this up nice and slow, give you some time to get used to it. But now I don't think I'm going to. Strip down to your bra and panties, and start doing jumping jacks."

This was good, Dana thought as she crossed her legs. She could see Elizabeth squeeze her eyes shut as she wriggled out of her skirt and stripped off her shoes and panty hose; she could see the reflection of the woman's blushing face as she tentatively began to jump up and down. Dana could see her butt jiggling through her panties, her breasts bouncing in her white bra, like a jiggle girl in a music video. She cleared her throat.

"Right about now," she said, "your audience should be figuring out that something's up. They're realizing that you haven't just forgotten about the curtains. By now they know you're doing this on purpose.

"Open the bedside drawer."

Elizabeth complied. She looked inside and cringed, arrogant revulsion arguing on her face with shame and disgrace. Dana hadn't picked the toys to be tacky on purpose: she just hadn't wanted to mess with condoms and stuff, so she'd picked up a few cheap things she could throw away. But now the choice seemed serendipitous. Inspired, even. She loved the thought of making this arrogant bitch put these sleazy things into her body in full view of midtown Manhattan.

"So let's get started," she said. "Lay the toys out on the bed. Take off your bra and panties. Then lie on the bed with your cunt facing the window. Put the pillows under your head so people can see your face, and spread your legs."

She could see Elizabeth breathing hard. The woman was obeying, but she was doing it slowly, hesitantly, and Dana wasn't sure if she was genuinely scared or drawing things out on purpose. Either way was fine with Dana. She pressed her thighs together as she watched Elizabeth display her new toys and spread herself out.

"So we've shown them you're an exhibitionist," Dana said. "Now let's show them that you're a pervert. Put the ball gag in your mouth. Stick the butt plug in your asshole. And then spread your cunt lips apart with your fingers. Don't touch your clit. Not yet."

Elizabeth stared fiercely at the wall as she bit down on the pink rubber ball and fiddled behind her head to buckle the straps. She turned over to insert the butt plug, but Dana snapped her fingers. "No," she barked. "Stay on your back. I know it's awkward. That's what I want." She felt a warm glow in her stomach as she watched Elizabeth struggle, groping for her asshole with her feet in the air. She could see Elizabeth fighting to regain some dignity as she settled back into place; she could see that dignity slip away again as the girl remembered her instructions, put her fingers on her pussy lips, and slowly spread them apart. Dana paused for a moment to enjoy the view: the city lights, the wall of high-rise windows shining in the night sky, with Elizabeth's debased reflection superimposed over it all. She let Elizabeth lie quietly for a minute, let her exposure sink in. Then she spoke again.

"I notice you keep your eyes away from the window. You keep focusing on something else, or else you close your eyes. So look out the window now. Think of the people watching you, and look them in the eye."

Dana waited patiently as Elizabeth squeezed her eyes shut, shuddered, and reluctantly turned to face her reflection. She caught Elizabeth's eye and saw her whimper; her pussy clenched, and she pressed on. "Now take the dildo in one hand," she said, "and the ruler in the other. Stick the dildo in your cunt and fuck yourself. Every few strokes, pull the dildo out and smack your pussy a few times with the ruler. Then do it all again. And keep your eyes on the people watching you."

"Here's the picture they're getting. They see a woman who goes into a hotel room and puts on a free sex show. They see a woman who opens her curtains, strips, jumps up and down to get their attention, then opens her legs, puts a gag in her mouth and a plug in her asshole, and spanks herself on the pussy while she fucks herself. All for them to see. And they're looking you in the eye. You can't hide from them. They know who you are."

The dildo was a squishy plastic one, a lurid pinky-tan with prominent veins. She could see Elizabeth cringe as she slid it into her visibly wet pussy; she watched her flinch as she pulled it out, gripped the ruler, and gave her clit a few hesitant smacks. It was all gone now, the arrogance, the composure, the sense of entitlement. She had stripped the woman down to a trashy slut giving a free sex show to strangers with nasty toys from a corner porn shop. Dana took a deep breath and delivered the final blow.

"I'm leaving now," she said. "I have another hotel room across the street, with my own telescope. I expect you to keep up the show for another hour. You can do any nasty degrading thing to yourself that you like, but keep the ball gag in, and keep your eyes on the window. If I don't like what I see, I'm coming back, and you won't be happy about that." She paused. "If I do like what I see, I won't be back. In an hour you can shut the curtain and do what you want. The room's paid up for the night. Checkout's at noon. It's been lovely."

31

Dana dropped the room key on the floor and left Elizabeth on the bed, violating herself, alarmed, shivering, near tears. She whistled quietly as she shut the door and rode the elevator to the lobby. She caught a cab in front of the hotel and told the driver to take her home.

Showing Billy

Shoshana Von Blankensee

"Billy?"

"Yeah, Iris?"

"We are 16 years old and in the family room of your parents house after school."

I turn to her and our eyes jump around each other. She is so young, but really handsome like River Phoenix when he was just a kid. Her mouth is a girl's mouth.

Billy is Georgia's little friend. I've been thinking about her since she got here. Georgia is my girl. She's handsome, always in a snap-up shirt and filthy Carharts. So handsome she can get away with having long black hair without looking girlie. She is half rock and roll and all Southern. She is sweet and mean, and her hands are sliding up the sides of my thighs under my skirt. I whisper, "What do you think you're doing, mister?"

When you're with the kind of girls I'm with, you walk the gender tightrope with them. If you go too far, they'll feel weird and make you stop. So you do everything you can with such carefulness and attention because you know that you're their safety net, part of the crew of girls that understands them entirely and accepts them as neither male nor female but a brilliant and gorgeous in-between. They are your safety net because they recognize you before you even speak to them, they see you and hold you to the light, and you live with them in this never-never-land, because it is magic and because it is the only way you can.

Georgia and I are doing the dishes and singing to the Dolly record we put on. I wash, Georgia dries; that's how it goes. The she gets right in my ear and says, "Baby, put your hands on the windowsill."

"No, Georgia, I'm busy," I say, waiting impatiently to hear her say it again.

"Baby, put your hands on the windowsill."

She takes the dishrag and wraps it around my neck, pulling it tight slowly. I drop the sponge and lean over an inch while I turn to look at her. She wraps one strong hand around my jaw while the other holds the rag, and she kisses me real soft and wet.

She digs two fingers into my pussy real fast, so I kind of jump. Georgia sometimes starts fucking me with a kind of urgency—like a teenage boy or a car thief—jarring and hot. I'm thinking about this when I see a little shadow moving. It's Billy. She's in the doorway of the guesthouse, and all the lights are off; I can see a little orange cigarette glow and Billy's silhouette. She has lean girl arms, a lean build, not like Georgia, who is ripped from work. I know Billy can see me bent toward her with the dishrag wrapped around my neck and Georgia's mouth against my ear.

Georgia takes her fingers out, uncovers the butter dish and scoops up a little, spreading it over her cock.

"George, you are not using butter on my ass," I laugh.

"Shh, shh." She is laughing while she shushes me, and she pulls the rag tighter as she pushes her cock into me. It makes me lose my breath, and for a minute I forget about Billy out there in the dark.

Georgia wipes the butter off her hands and starts working my pussy right in the spot that makes me shoot all over the place. I watch Billy as I gush and Georgia bites a strange part of my back I've never felt before.

Georgia is stone; I love her the way she is. Why would I want to do something to someone I love that makes her feel uncomfortable? Besides, I feel like I'm fucking Georgia when I suck her cock or pull her into my ass.

That's not to say I don't sometimes think about fucking girls the old-fashioned way, and the thought of fucking Billy makes me terrified and excited. Georgia doesn't care any-way—or maybe it's just a story she will never read.

"Lean back, Billy. Close your eyes. I want to show you something."

I push her onto the couch. She looks scared as she closes her eyes.

"Don't worry, Billy."

• • •

I slip my heels off and climb over her so my long black curls trail along her arms up to the top of her chest and then spread on either side of her face. She swallows and brings her hands up to my arms, but I take them and put them back under her head. My heart is a little torpedo or a tornado or something. I bring my mouth close to her and start unbuttoning my blouse, which I throw on the floor, and then I lean in so that my mouth is almost on hers, and I take one of her hands and bring it up to my lips, sliding two fingers in and to the back of my throat. She resists a little, like she is afraid of making me gag, but soon realizes I know my own limit. Her fingers slide deep into the back of my wet mouth, into my throat, which I open up for her. I slide her fingers out of my mouth and bring them to the back of my head and begin to move myself down, undoing her belt buckle and unzipping her pants.

"Iris—"

I look up to see her looking at me, worried.

"Billy, it's OK. Don't be scared. I'm going to show you something, OK?"

She nods. I pull her cock out of her pants and hold it in one hand and put the other one on her belly.

"Now I want you to feel my mouth on your cock the way you felt it with your fingers, and when I slide my fingers into you I want you to pretend they're your fingers sliding into me. OK, Billy?"

She looks unsure but nods anyway.

I keep my eyes on hers as I wrap my lips around the head and then begin sliding it slowly in and out of my mouth, pressing it against her clit with each downstroke. I let my mouth make that wet slurpy sound, and then I bring my hand that rests on her stomach slowly between her legs and slide it up under her boxers, under her harness, and hold it against her. She's wet, and it sends electricity around my chest. I am watching her face to make sure she's OK as I press two fingers inside her and begin moving them slowly in time with my mouth around her cock.

As I slide my fingers in and out of Billy I realize she hasn't really let girls fuck her before. I instinctively know that Billy is making an exception to the rule, just like Georgia does once a year. I am careful with her when I feel her hips begin to buck gently, and I keep my wet mouth moving in time with my drenched fingers until I felt her grip and let go and grip and let go and grip and let go and roll through a long orgasm with her hand nestled in my hair and her breath coming heavy out of her.

But Billy is in the guesthouse in the backyard, and I'm in bed with Georgia sleeping with my mouth pressed against her back the way I do. A shadow from the apple tree winds across the ceiling when cars pass on the road, and when I wake up I will kiss Georgia's mouth while she's still asleep and then get up, maybe feed the dog.

Dusty Eats Out
Lee Lynch

"Dusty, lover?" Elly asked. "Aren't you ever going to go down on me?"

It was a hot, moist, blue summer dusk. They'd been putting in 16-hour days at the diner since they'd bought it five months before. At the end of this infrequent day off, they'd begun making love early. Noisy bedding birds were a love song outside their window.

Dusty peeled her big-boned naked body away from the smaller Elly and stared anxiously through the almost smoky light at her. The last of Elly's makeup seemed like smudged dusk. "You mean...?" she asked, unable to think of the words she needed.

Elly twisted close again and smoothed Dusty's short, wavy auburn hair back, tonguing an earlobe.

"I mean with your mouth," she whispered, rubbing a sharp hip across Dusty's belly. "You know, like this," and she sucked on the earlobe, then flicked it back and forth with her tongue.

"I never did that before."

Elly stopped. Her younger body, smaller-breasted, with fragile-looking, slender shoulders, glowed, sweaty from humidity, in the dim light. The shock on her face began slowly to fade to her slow, teasing smile.

Dusty dove, belly down, under a pillow. Partly to escape that knowing smile. Mostly to hide her embarrassment. They'd been together more than a year. She'd been making love with women ever since she'd entered the Navy 22 years before, just out of high school.

"How could you never do that?" Elly asked in astonishment. "Though I can understand not wanting to with old prune-face Doris."

In the 17 years she'd been with Doris, Dusty had tried it only once, after an old Navy buddy had brought home some postcards from Denmark. She'd slid down Doris's body, getting as far as rubbing her lips across her pubic hair. Doris had stopped her. "I guess," she said to Elly, her head still under the pillow, "it just never came up."

Elly hung over her broad back so her breasts just grazed it, and said, "Do me, lover?"

It seemed to be Elly's favorite phrase, said with her Tennessee drawl exaggerated, a surefire way to turn Dusty on. But did she want to do it?

"Don't you want to?" Elly asked, her breasts tracing double patterns on Dusty's back.

She shrugged, half-hoping Elly would give up and drop the subject. The room was growing darker. Outside there was a lull in the birds' chatter and she could hear her ducks quack across the little pond that had come with her older, tiny house.

But Elly stretched against her so her slightly long brown hair tickled Dusty's neck. Again, Elly whispered into her ear. "Then let me do you."

"Elly..." Dusty complained, her tone half aggrieved, half pleased and excited.

Elly began to tickle her, giggling. "Don't hide your face from me all night, you old bear. You come out here and get yours."

Dusty twitched and held her breath to defend herself from

Elly, but the woman was unrelenting. So she heaved herself
up and pushed Elly back down on the bed. "I can't," she said,
breathless. There was nothing like a few hours alone with Elly
to make her forget her role in the world as a competent, hard-
working restaurant owner and bring out the kid in her.

"Why not?" asked Elly, apparently perfectly happy to lie
beneath her and grind her pelvis upward instead of down.
Their hot damp bodies made a sucking sound each time Elly
broke contact. "Here," she said, gripping Dusty by the buttocks, urging her forward with her hands. "Scoot up over my
mouth."

"El!"

Elly laughed at her shock. "Why not?"

"I haven't even had time for a shower today!"

Minutes later, Elly sat on the closed toilet seat as Dusty
showered.

"You sure are taking your sweet time," Elly said when
she'd finished removing her nail polish. "If we don't take
more time off, my nails are going to look like I do them with
your rose clipper."

Dusty turned off the water and dried every available inch
of herself, twice. She even passed a hand between her legs and
smelled her fingers.

Elly was laughing when she followed her back to bed in
the dark. A car started on their suburban streets. "Be home
by midnight!" called an anxious mother. Elly pulled the curtains. "You're so dry now I could start a fire with you, lover,"
Elly said, passing a hand over her skin.

Dusty narrowed her eyes, a secret half-smile on her sen-
suous face.

But Elly had become dead serious. She switched on a bedside light and slowly, deliberately untied Dusty's white terry
robe. "Yeah," Elly said, her voice deep, slow, "and that's
exactly what I'm planning to do."

In the heat she lay still, robe spread open, long fleshy legs gently urged apart, her lover's mouth breathing hotly on her skin, still warm from the shower. "Can't we turn the light off?" she asked.

Elly had parted her outer lips and was blowing between them. She looked up. "But you're so pretty to look at!" Her laugh, sometimes, was like glass wind chimes.

"Pretty?" She squirmed as Elly studied her.

Laughing, Elly said firmly, "Pretty. Even butches are pretty down there."

"You could at least close your eyes." She paused, relishing a particularly favorite fantasy of hers. "And put your heels back on."

"Why, Dusty," Elly said in surprise, but said no more. She quickly bent to the floor and slipped into her black patent leather high heels, giving Dusty time to admire their effect on her little feet, beneath her long, shaved, shapely legs. Then she nestled between Dusty's legs once more and her tongue licked, flat and hard, the length of Dusty's inner lips.

She gasped at Elly's touch. Nothing had ever felt like that.

"You like it, lover?" Elly asked, talking into her, starting a new rush of feeling.

She no longer minded the light being on. The sight of Elly's delicate fingers holding her apart, of her tongue touching her there, of her soft moisture-smeared lips pursed above her—it was as if some bright hot star shone on them, illuminating Elly for her further pleasure.

Elly pulled her inside her mouth. All of her. And Dusty felt the flood of her excitement immerse the tongue that entered her. Then the flood spilled out of her, 'till she came against Elly's soft, warm tongue.

Elly lifted her shining, smiling face and moved up beside her in the bed, kissing her all wet like that. "You've got the sweetest smell," she told Dusty. "And you taste like..."

"Sex," Dusty finished happily for her. Surely the glow she felt showed. She propped herself on one elbow and looked wondrously at Elly. "You smell like the bed after we've been doing it for hours."

Elly kissed her wetly again. "No, lover. You. This is what you smell like." Leaning back, Elly asked, "Want a cigarette?"

"No." She was wondering what Elly smelled like. "El," she began, thickly, clearing her throat, but the words were too hard. Gently, she pushed Elly back onto the bed. It was Elly's turn to grin. Slowly, she moved where she could begin to kiss Elly, as if her mouth was merely meandering over her moist skin, as if she had not a particular purpose in mind.

But by the time she'd kissed all inside her thighs, Elly's breathing had changed. "Lover," she was saying, drawling deep from her throat.

Dusty breathed deeply, through her nose. The smell of sex was everywhere. It was intoxicating. She floated on it, in it, like the ducks in their pond. She wished she'd had the privacy in the service to explore like this, the self-assurance to try again with Doris. She was resting her head on Elly's thigh, breathing her in.

"Lover, lover…" Elly repeated, twisting toward her.

The high hot flush of her contentment fled. Give her a kitchen and she could perform culinary miracles. Give her a house, a diner, what have you, and she could fix almost anything. But give her a girl and some sex—what should she do next, she wondered.

But Elly's hands pulled her head closer. All that curly hair tickled Dusty's nose. She pushed her tongue through it, found the parting of the lips, but was stuck there, couldn't get farther.

Elly reached down and opened herself to Dusty's tongue.

The boldness of the act sent another rush through Dusty. Her tongue all at once knew its way. Elly moved beneath her, already awash in a sea of her own making, her hands by now in Dusty's moist hair, twisting, curling, grasping, then falling limply to the bed as she groaned—no, cried loudly in a way Dusty had never heard a woman cry out before.

Elly pulled her up, her eyes barely open, her mouth faintly, contentedly, smiling. "You sure you never did that before?"

Dusty wrapped her sturdy arms around Elly, pressed with a hand her lover's head against her broad shoulder. The hot night trapped their fragrant heat around them, so they lay content in the flow of it. Darkness had fallen completely and with it silence. A breeze pushed past the light curtains. Dusty let her eyes close.

Some time later, Elly switched the light off. One small bird cried out in the night. Dusty, half-dreaming, wondered if stars ever fell through bedroom windows. How the white flare would glow, turning dark to dawn, waking the birds to sing their love song once more.

Stockings

Jenny Kirkpatrick

The first time I had an honest sexual experience had little to do with realizing I was a lesbian or with becoming sober. It happened at a shoe store. (How come I have the feeling I should be confessing this to the readers of *Vogue* instead of an erotica editor?) I'm just going to tell you, and I hope you let go of your prejudices about shoes and read the whole story. Oh, you don't even know what I am talking about—it went something like this.

I was 23 and had moved to St. Louis because there was a job opening for office manager at the Fashion Merchandising & Design School. I couldn't afford to go there, so I thought, *Hey, maybe this way I can take a class now and then at a discount.* So I got an apartment on the west end and was having my first little-city experiences.

I got very caught up in wearing the right thing. Impressing the gay boys and my inner Joan Rivers. Lucky for me, my best friend was a hairdresser, so at least that part was taken care of. I had auburn hair down to my chin, a bit longer in front than in the back. Supercool bangs, chopped straight across, accented my green eyes to the hilt. (Thank you, David.) I clumped it up with product, and it smelled great, if I say so myself. It didn't take long for working downtown to bore me, so I kind of started acting like I was in a movie, *starring* as a girl who worked downtown. I bought a pink fitted suit from Frederick's of Hollywood, complete with miniskirt of course. I stocked up on thigh-high stockings and camisoles. I had a few push-up bras to help Mother Nature. If I had to wear office attire, at least I would have something luxurious on underneath!

I have to mention that I was so-o-o horny and hard up. All my friends were guys or straight girls. No one seemed to be interested in me that way. And frankly, the dykes my friends introduced me to were all either married (at least for the moment) or going through a breakup longer than their "marriage" or not worth dating at all. I took to masturbating in the women's room. I would scoot up my skirt and push my hand in between my sweaty thighs (When you're at a desk typing all day with your legs together swathed in polyester or some form of nonnatural fibers, they get sweaty).

The heat from my pussy would convert the stall into a steam room. The idea of others walking in terrified me, but also turned me on so much I could come in record time.

I jacked my clit furiously. My hand a blur, my nails biting into my flesh, until I came jerking my moans into my lungs like a drunk trying to hide the hiccups. Later in the afternoon, I enjoyed the juices running down my leg, warming me, and reminding me of my naughty "coffee break."

I enjoyed my little downtown pretend life. I read detective novels from the library at lunch. Treated myself to a fancy coffee drink on Wednesdays.

One particular Wednesday with my whipped cream–topped treat in hand I wandered into Shooze, a small-ish store with a wall of shoes and clever, animal-print round racks displaying them. Shooze also sold random hip accessories like striped stockings, velvet studded wristbands, and fishnet dresses. I was wearing my pink suit and felt just a little embarrassed that I looked so officey—it took me years to realize that no one in real life wears a Frederick's suit to the office. I kind of wanted whoever might be in this righteous store to know I was really a dyke with my own studded wrist-bands at home. But I didn't worry about it too much. It was this outfit I needed shoes for anyway. I couldn't afford to get the right pair when I had gotten the suit so I was embarrassingly forced into coupling the suit with these cream pumps my cousin had demanded I get for her wedding.

No one was in the store. This sort of place was usually closer to a college or in the mall.

"May I help you?" a voice said. I turned to see a very cute woman whom I immediately wanted. She had brown hair, short around her face—the color of a perfect milk chocolate bar—and it was shiny and tousled. She wore brown vintage men's pants hanging loose on her hips and a men's undershirt, white against her tan arms with a black bra underneath. I noticed a little horn on a strip of leather around her neck.

"Yes, I need a pair of white or pink high heels to go with this suit. I'm a..."

"Size 8," she said with me.

"Yes, you can tell that?" I smiled, glad my lip gloss had been freshly applied.

"I love my job," she said simply. "Sit here. I'll take care of you."

I sat in a leopard-print '60s-era chair noticing for the first time that my skirt barely reached the top of my thigh-high stockings.

"I think you might find these to your liking," she said returning from behind a zebra-striped curtain.

"Can I put this here?" I pointed to my coffee drink.

"I can take it for you." She looked down. "Whipped cream? Right on."

Yikes, I hope I didn't have whipped cream on my lips. I licked them to confirm that raspberry was all I could taste. "Dessert in a cup," I replied.

She put some boxes on the floor, then hitched her pant leg

up just a bit before kneeling down on one knee. Her eyes were level with my thighs.

I bent over to take off my pump, but she wagged a finger between us, "No, no, no, no. That's for me to do." She cupped that place where the ankle meets the heel with one hand. I must have been frozen, because she did a gentle shake and said, "Relax, I've got you," before she slipped my shoe off. I think I groaned. I sank further into my chair, unconsciously sliding my pelvis closer to her. She wrapped her warm hand around my foot and held me there as she opened a box with one hand and pulled out a white heel that barely had any parts to it. My chest noticeably rose and fell with increased desire. My nerves flamed from her touch.

I'd worn sheer black stockings that revealed my red toenail polish. Her hand returned to the place behind my ankle and eased my foot past the thin straps of the vamp. "Voila." She looked to my face for approval.

I had to shake my head just a bit to get out of my trance. I looked at my foot. A single pearl-colored textured strap held my toes and another slunk up diagonally past my arch to the outside of my foot.

"Is that, uh, snakeskin?" My breathing was coming so hard. I was trying to say something shoe-store like. I couldn't believe I was so out of control, so quickly and so, so...*at a shoe store!*

"Alligator. But no gator died for this tiny shoe, right?" She laughed.

"Right. I mean, it is little. Not that I mind killing alligators. I mean, I haven't done that...I'm, I'm not a gator killer." I stuttered, then laughed. "OK, there's not a lot to this shoe, is there?"

"You like to leave more to the imagination?" she said but not to my face. Her brown eyes traveled up my legs to my thighs. A surge of blood swelled my clit so fast that I had to part my legs just a little for it to fit. My nipples became bullets pushing into the helpful padding of my bra. I squirmed just enough to show the lacy tops of my stockings.

My shoe sales lust-dyke brought her big eyes to mine waiting for my answer.

"Yes," I whispered. "Sometimes."

She placed her strong hand behind my knee and slipped the shoe off with the other hand. *Why would you need to touch that high to pull off a shoe?* I thought. *Have I just been horny too long? Was this in my imagination?* I have been much less aroused by a drunken lesbian grappling at my crotch than by this woman simply wrapping her warm fingers around my knee.

"Let's try another one, OK?" she asked.

"The other one," I said quickly between tense breaths.

Her eyebrow went up in question. "Ah, your partner here is feeling ignored?"

"Yes, you know you can't just do one side. I mean, not to tell you how to do it or anything."

"No offense taken. How would I know unless you tell me?"

I grinned and looked down. I had a moment then where I took conscious control over my fumbling desire. What did I have to lose, after all? A shoe store? If I let myself be swept up in passion and I was all wrong, I could still just walk out of here and never see her again, so who cared. I mean, I was sitting there wearing my Frederick's, after all. Why did I get it? Just to jack off in the bathroom? Well, yeah, actually, but, hey, why not share the wealth?

"Here, you might like this better." Going to my other foot, she tilted my leg to the outside so my thighs parted even more. Cool air hit my pussy as that last inch of steamy skin separated. I remembered my fun in the ladies' room earlier, and knew my special smell must be easing toward her. She leaned in directly between my legs. I gasped, and she leaned back with a shoehorn.

"Sorry, I had dropped this. I need to use a tool for this lovely specimen."

"I see." I gripped the arms of my chair and edged my cunt forward. "Are you sure you need to use that? I prefer your hands to the plastic."

I could see down her shirt just enough to keep me curious. I watched the muscles of her tanned arm as she moved the box closer. Mostly I felt her hand on my foot. I remembered all the friends who thought it odd that I would massage my feet at home for hours, then go to my vibrator. I finally stopped letting people know of the shoe photo shoots I'd done—just sneaking a downward peek now and then at special events. And now, it was all making sense.

She slipped on a pump that covered my heel and had an ultrapointed toe à la 1965. It gave me toe cleavage.

"What do you think?" She again put a hand behind my knee, then lifted my foot up a little more as if to show off a gem, getting it into better light, then lowered it again. Her hand didn't leave me, though, as she began to press a finger into my arch, a tight squeeze between my skin and the leather bottom. I gasped.

She looked me directly in the eye as she slid her other hand up the inside of my thigh. "Do you like that?"

"Yes." I panted.

"Do you want more?"

"Yes." I discernably and with no pretense slid all the way down on the seat and spread my legs open. My skirt hiked up on its own with the movement. My clit bulged against my black thong.

She barely even moved, pressed her mouth into me and sucked my swollen girl-knob, marrying her wet mouth with my wet cunt. She rolled my stocking down and my foot was free. Pulling from my hotness, she brought her mouth to my precious footsie and covered it with kisses, then sucked on each and every toe.

I gasped and squirmed and tried to stifle my screams, barely thinking there might be another worker or customer somewhere. "Oh, my God, this has never, ahhh, oh, oh, you," I breathed, "you're my—"

"Shh. You have the most beautiful feet I've ever seen. Your toes are perfect and so edible. I can't believe how amazing you are."

"Oh, God." I hung my head back, letting my hair swing and letting the pleasure consume me, no longer worried what anyone else thought. My dyke foot-goddess pushed her fingers into me while still holding my foot and eating and sucking and biting at me. I jammed my pussy into her hand and ripped open my shirt to get at my tits. With one motion, my bra sprung open from its front clasp. My nipples ached from being constrained for so long. I barely brushed my fingers over them for an electric jolt.

She looked at me as if she knew everything about me, as if she could read my mind. She could. "Oh, please, please." My pussy swelled so much I thought my skin would burst. Cunt juice poured down onto the leopard-print seat. I wanted to jerk my foot away from her because I didn't know if I could take it anymore. I didn't know if I was going to die or explode or both.

I tensed forward clenching the chair, then my orgasm spilled forth with me squealing and moaning as my head flew back and my chest opened. She grabbed the outside of my thighs and slammed my pussy into her mouth. I jerked her by the hair, grinding harder and harder as I came and came and came. When my screams got too loud, she shoved a shoe in my mouth but never missed a lick as she did it.

"What's your name?"

"Karla. Yours?"

"Jenny."

"Get back here, Jenny. I'm locking the doors." Karla led me and my wobbling thighs and throbbing cunt to the back of the store, where the racks of shoes loomed over us. "This will do." We fucked all afternoon in the back, while I enjoyed the occasional taste of leather in my mouth and a sharp spike on my tongue. I shocked her when I fucked myself with the heel of a stiletto while I banged the ball of the shoe into my clit. We finally collapsed only after I straddled her foot, rubbing my pussy back and forth on the vintage men's shoes she was wearing while she jacked off above me.

Newly inspired, I left St. Louis a few months later to work for a shoe designer in New York's garment district. Occasionally, my boss comments on how I never complain about working overtime and I simply tell her, "Because I love my job."

The Good Doctor
Sarah Granlund

"It looks like you have some subluxation and muscle tenderness here," she said, gently massaging the place where my neck meets my shoulders. "And here." She kneaded my lower back. "Do you have a lot of stress or tension in your life?" asked my new chiropractor, Dr. Cohen.

"Yeah, I guess I do. I just moved here, and I've been sitting at my computer all day looking for a job. My chiropractor back home always helped with my tension and headaches, so I figured you might be able to as well."

She moved over to write something in her chart, and I studied her. She was younger than I'd expected her to be, probably 27 or 28, but definitely not past 30. Her eyes were that grayish-blue color young girls dream about, and her eyebrows formed near-perfect arches. Except for her eyes, her face was rather unremarkable: lightly scarred, from adolescent acne I supposed, a nose that was almost too pointy, and lips that were rough but full. She was only an inch or two taller than me, spiked hair included. Her hands were unmanicured, but they were soft and knew where to touch me to take away the pain. She was attractive but not stunning—I definitely wouldn't have turned and followed her on the street. All the same, I hadn't been laid in ages and found myself thinking about how her skilled hands would feel on my naked body.

"Have you ever tried homeopathic remedies in addition to chiropractic care?" she asked. "Lots of chiropractors use them."

"Oh. No. I've never really believed that stuff works. A little too voodoo for me."

"OK, let me give you my spiel on homeopathy. And then I want to test some of it on you." She turned and moved to a shelf where there were dozens of small spritzer bottles. She had a nice ass. She selected a few of the multicolored bottles and proceeded to tell me that her mother was using the menopause-alleviation spray and the sleep-aid spray and that a friend of hers used the migraine spray. And that both of them felt marked improvement in their symptoms. "Are you willing to let me test the sprays on you?" She smiled, her eyes remaining on my face. She looked down when she noticed me noticing her stare.

Of course I was willing. She was a doctor and she was attractive. And I had nothing better to do that afternoon.

"OK, these are water-based, all-natural sprays. They have no taste and won't interfere with any of the medications you're on. Lift your tongue, please." She squirted the anxiety spray into my mouth, and a little dripped down my chin. I moved to wipe it off with my arm, but she motioned my hand away.

"Here, let me get that for you." She grabbed a paper towel from the counter and gently wiped the spray from my face. Her first and second fingers grazed my lower lip as her hand swept across my chin. I felt a tingle in my chest.

"OK. After I do your adjustment, we'll test your aura to see if the spray has any effect on you."

She had me lie facedown on the chiropractic table and told me she was going to adjust my hips to help with my lower back pain. Her hands roamed about my lower back and ass, lingering, then selected the point where my panties peeked out of my skirt. She pushed down with both hands and I heard a *pop*.

"How was that?" Dr. Cohen asked.

I mumbled that it was fine. I could smell her perfume, some kind of mix between flowers and citrus. Arousing. My nipples hardened. She pressed down a few more times then moved her hands along my spine to my upper back, brushing my long hair out of her way as she went. I was wearing a backless shirt held in place by a knotted string, so my entire back was exposed.

"You have such pale, soft skin," she said. "It's beautiful. And your dark hair compliments it so well. Kind of 18th-century England."

"Yeah, well," I muttered.

She undid the knot that held my shirt together. The sides fell to the table, revealing fleshy glimpses of my breasts.

"What are you doing?" I asked, rather surprised and incredibly turned on. I'd never had a chiropractor undress me before. Or tell me I had nice skin, for that matter.

"I thought it would be more comfortable for you if there weren't a knot pushing into your back while I did the adjustment." While her explanation made sense, her voice was huskier than it had been before.

She tickled my shoulders with the tips of her fingers and told me to take a deep breath, then exhale. As I did, she pushed down hard, bringing forth another loud *crack-pop*. "I'm going to turn you over, bend you into a pretzel, and jump on you now," she told me.

"Are those the technical terms, Dr. Cohen?" I asked with a smile. What the hell, why not flirt with her?

"Yep." She grinned back. She had a great smile, a toothy but not a "my, what big teeth you have" smile.

She turned me on my left side, politely but belatedly averted her eyes while I adjusted my shirt to cover my erect nipples, then had me cross my arms and bring my right knee up to my chin. Indeed a pretzel, and she did indeed jump on me. My breath escaped in a gasp, and my lower back *crack-crack-cracked*.

"There we go," she said. "That sounded good. Ready for the traction table?"

Traction tables are about the size of a single bed and have a wheel that moves up and down in waves along the spine to get the kinks out. "I've been on traction tables at other chiropractors. I didn't think they were that helpful," I told her.

"Well, this one might be different. Never hurts to try. Different doctors do it different ways, you know." She'd been reviewing her chart but looked up at me with a half-grin as she spoke. She had me get on the table, turned it on high, set the timer, and turned the radio to the local jazz station.

"These are homeopathic relaxation candles that I'm lighting," she said. She placed one near the head of the traction table and several on and around the radio. She turned the lights off and the candles let off a nice, welcoming glow. "I'll be back in a few minutes to see how you're doing."

With each pass of the wheel, a different part of my body rose toward the ceiling. First my pelvis, then my stomach, then my chest. then my neck. Reversed and repeated countless times. I began to doze off.

"How're we doing in here?" Dr. Cohen asked quietly.

"Mmm, good. This is a lot better than I remembered." I opened my eyes to look up at her. She was leaning over me, her face close to mine.

"So you're comfortable?" she asked, leaning closer, lips almost touching mine.

"Yes…" The traction table pushed my lips up to meet hers. She didn't pull away.

She put her hand behind my head and pulled me closer to her. Her tongue parted my lips and entered my mouth, cautiously exploring. I reciprocated, eager and hungry for her touch. I took hold of her shoulders and pulled her upper body tight against mine.

"I can feel your heart beating," I whispered.

"I can feel yours too."

She brushed my shirt to the side and began kissing my chest. She started near my collarbone, then worked her way down to my right nipple. She flicked it with her tongue, making it even harder. Her mouth moved to my left breast, kissing and nibbling while her hand worked my other breast. I moaned.

"Hang on," she said.

Dr. Cohen got on the traction table, straddling me. As my hips moved up toward hers, partly the traction wheel, partly me, I felt a bulge. The doctor was packing. My heart sped up at the thought. I hadn't felt anything between her legs during my adjustment, and it made me very wet to think she'd slipped into the bathroom to strap on her cock just for me.

I knew I was the last patient of the day, but there was always the possibility that someone else would come in or that the phone would ring or that she would lose interest. I pulled her face back toward mine and plunged my tongue into her mouth. She caressed the sides of my breasts with her thumbs while the wheel pushed parts of my body into hers over and over again.

I pulled her shirttail out of her pants and slid my hands into them. I grabbed her ass and pulled her against me. Her butt was firm and smooth. My fingers worked their way to her anus as she continued kissing and fondling my breasts. I teased her asshole with the tips of my nails. She sighed and her cock pressed harder against me.

"Are you OK?" she asked.

"Mmm-hmm."

Her lips moved down my body, lightly brushing my stomach on the way. "Such a firm stomach," she murmured. She licked my belly button, gently pulled on my navel ring with her teeth, and began unbuttoning my skirt. It was a wrap skirt and had only three buttons. It fell away and draped over the table as she unfastened the last one.

"Very adult underwear," she said, smiling. They were white bikinis with butterflies and flowers all over them. "Ahh, there's the woman," she said as she moved aside the damp cotton crotch and stroked my wet inner lips with a finger. I breathed faster. I tried to maneuver her finger deeper inside, but she pulled away.

She moved her body back so her chest was against mine. She kissed my neck and shoulders. My pussy was throbbing, and I felt her cock poking my thigh through her pants. I reached under her and undid her belt and fly. I shoved her pants down below her ass and grabbed hold of her cock.

"I need it," I breathed. I slid my hand up and down her shaft, rotating my hand and squeezing. Dr. Cohen moved against me, and I knew she was ready.

I held her cock, pulled aside my panties, and the next time the traction wheel thrust my pelvis up, I enveloped her.

I gasped. The first moment of penetration is always a bit painful but also the most pleasurable. I grabbed her ass with both hands and forced her deeper into me.

"Put your feet on the table with your knees up," Dr. Cohen said. She was supporting herself on the table with her elbows, her hands tangled in my hair. The position she suggested provided a better angle for both of us. I could rub my clit against her shaft and she could thrust deeper and harder. The sensation was amazing, like every possible part of my body was being stimulated: her hard cock filling my pussy and stroking my clit, her teeth and lips biting and kissing my tits and mouth, nearly every part of her body pressed against nearly every part of mine. I felt the roughness of her pants against my legs and the slight trembling of her arms against my side. I tightened around her cock, my hands still on her ass.

As she thrust down and in, I moved my hips up to meet her. And with each pass of the wheel under my ass, it was a deeper, harder, better meeting. She started breathing faster and I knew she was about to come. I pulled her harder into me, trying to reach the point that would make me explode. As I was about to climax, she gave one final, hard thrust and we managed to come at almost the same time.

Ding!

The traction wheel stopped moving. My time was up.

Dr. Cohen looked down at me and smiled. There was a little sweat on her forehead; her cheeks and neck were flushed. "Feel better now?" she asked, breathing heavily. She stood up and adjusted her clothing.

I righted my underwear and buttoned my skirt. "Definitely," I told her. I felt pleasantly used. My pussy was throbbing and my nipples still tingled. I could smell the sex in the air. She helped me tie my shirt correctly and opened the door for me.

"I thought we were going to check my aura," I said as I was walking out the door.

"You have a nice healthy glow," she told me. "You're fine."

"Thank you, doctor," I said, and walked out of the office.

Been a Long Day

Madame Pleasure

I'm tired and I'm cold. It's been a long-ass motherfucking day. I slam the door of my truck and fumble with my keys in the dark, searching with numb fingertips for the one that will unlock my house.

My house is dark. I like it like that. Dark is quiet. I shrug out of my leather jacket and leave it on the back of an arm-chair instead of hanging it in the hall closet where it usually resides. I drop clothes like bread crumbs in the hall. Marking my path to the bedroom. As if. There won't be any followers tonight. Have not been any followers to my bed in longer than I care to remember. I miss sex, frankly, but the after-shocks aren't worth the effort. I'm tired.

Naked, now. Chilblains making the hairs on my arms stand straight up, and my nipples hard as ice blocks. Nipple ring standing to attention, awaiting inspection. Crawling between the sheets is agony. Ecstasy. Cold and smooth. I am asleep almost the moment my head touches the feather pillow. The phone rings. I'm cocooned under the bedclothes. I can hear it, but it's more effort than I think it worth to put out one hand and find the phone. It rings. I ignore it. It rings again. "I'm ignoring you," I say aloud. It stops. I nod, pleased at its acquiescence. I'm asleep again. It rings. Now I'm pissed. One hand darts out from the covers, on a search and destroy mission. I pull it back under the sheets with me. What the fuck do you want? Did I actually say it aloud? Or am I dreaming?

There's a voice answering me, so it must be live. Not Memorex. I'm still snarling. The voice belongs to a woman. Which one? I mutter something unintelligible about calling when it's daylight. Click. I throw the phone into the corner. Leave me alone. This is my cave. Don't feed the animals. I'm asleep. I'm kind of asleep. I'm awake. Mostly. It's still dark. There is someone else here. My nose is awake. I wear men's cologne, and I know the difference between this smell and my smell. And I know to whom this smell belongs. The she-voice comes back to me. Am I dreaming? If I am, that fucking phone better not wake me. This is a good dream. There's a warm body next to me. And it smells like her. My still-cloudy brain registers a quick reference to "She Who Must Be Obeyed" and I am asleep again.

There's a hand on my face. Silky little fingers tipped with sharp nails. I'm groaning. Dreams are wonderfully realistic for me these days. A hand on my chest. Playing the line of muscle there like a harpsichord. Strumming one nipple lazily. Tuning an instrument. Tuning me. My throat makes the requisite sound. Somewhere in the back of my head I wonder if I'm in the right key. There's a hand between my legs. Looking for a fingerhold. In my sleep I have turned into a six-pack. I mutter this incoherently. The she-voice tells me I am sleeping and to pay no mind to her hand on my clit. Easier said than done. She's stroking it, fingers on either side of my hood, backing it up and down like learning to parallel park my old Chevy. Up and back. Little to the left. Up and back. Little to the right. I'm growling. Same as groaning. Sort of.

There's long hair brushing my chest. It tickles. I know better than to move. God forbid I wake up. A warm mouth opens on my D-ring; the cold steel is hot in seconds. Tugging. Yanking. I'm resisting, pushing my back into the mattress to heighten the tension. The warmth dissolves. Now I'm freezing. Cool breath on my still wet nipple makes me shudder. The same finely honed nails rake lazily down my abdomen. My hips thrust upward to meet them. I am moaning. I think I say her name. Must have. I'm rewarded with a stinging slap. Then another. My cheeks burn and my eyes water. The warm, wet mouth kisses it better. Sharp teeth torment my cheekbones. My jawline. I tilt my head backward into the pillow. Offering my throat. The most intimate gesture my body can make. Please. Hurt me. She does. The tiny, teasing tip of a tongue makes a warm, wet cross at the base of my neck. X marks the spot. Pointed teeth slide from my chin to the hollow of my throat. No pain, just pressure. The pressure of perfectly even, perfectly sharp incisors. I am begging. I cannot help it, have no desire to stop. Anything but. She breaks the skin. In two places at once. Two tiny punctures in the soft skin of my neck. Two fingers in my soaking wet cunt. Pleasure. Pain. My heartbeat has a new rhythm. I come. I know I am coming. The bed is wet and I am screaming. There is no cover. Nothing to warm my still-shivering body.

I do not dare to open my eyes. Soft touch on the inside of my calf. Jingling. Leather with metal. My harness. I lift my hips in response to a hard prod. Yes, my harness. It fits snugly, same as ever. One hand snakes down to touch my dick. Reassure myself that the latex has not somehow withered with lack of use. That my ever-ready dildo, my best friend, has not developed impotence in the nightstand drawer. Atrophy of the underused. A bull dyke who can't get it up. Could anything be more sad? I manage to grip the head before soft fingers turn cruel and slap away my hand. Enough to reassure me. Nope. Still rock hard. More gallant and persevering than I, my friend. In my mind, I doff my hat to my head. This thought makes me chuckle. Not for long. A tendril of hair tickles the inside of my thigh, and without nerve endings, I know her lips are closing around the tip of my cock. I stiffen. I can feel warm breath against my pubic bone and I am shuddering. In my mind, I can see her face. Reddened mouth circling my dick; hollowed cheeks; long black lashes against fair skin. Without thought, both hands come out of self-imposed restraint to grasp her hair. Pushing. Pulling. Soft and malleable beneath my hands, she yields to me. I am fucking her face. I swear to God, I feel her. The head pushing against the back of that tender throat. Warm and wet. With all my might I hold her still and thrust my hips up to meet her. Harder. I hear her moan against me, and that is more than I can stand. Every muscle in my body tenses, and I am coming again. I can almost feel the liquid sensation. One hand wraps in her hair and pulls her face away, imagining spraying that face, that exquisite neck.

Fingers still wrapped in acres of long, silky hair, I pull up to my knees and push her back in my place. Pushing velvet thighs apart to kneel between them, her ass against my knees. Letting go of that mane and pushing against her chest, that fragile breastbone, fingers splayed wide. My other hand grasps my dick, and I am stroking it. Jacking myself off between her widespread thighs. She is crying my name. Taming of the Shrew. Your turn, bitch. My hand finds her cunt. Two fingers in and she is hungry for more. The head of my cock finds her clit. None-too-gentle slaps in just the right spot. Now. I do not want to wait. It has been too long, and this is too much. All of me, all of my dick is inside her. My free hand finds her face and covers her open mouth. Go ahead, scream. Hell, bite me. I will just fuck you harder. My conversation is all in my head. The only sounds reaching my ears are muffled grunts and cries. Mine? Hers? Both? My other hand takes a full span of her ass and pulls it up, off the bed, up to me, onto me. She is coming. This sound I know. I am coming. This sound I have forgotten. Ragged breaths. She is finished. She thinks she is finished. I have another immediate aim.

I pull out to the tune of her whimpers, and push my fist against her suddenly empty pussy. Just pushing. Not going anywhere anytime soon. Maybe. The tease is as much for me as for her. My hand is covered with her. Wet. Slick. Her. No more teasing. With one hard thrust I am inside her. No slow and easy folding of the fingers, just one hard, solid fist. Take it. She does. She closes around my wrist with a welcoming scream. Too deep? Sorry, baby. Take it again. And again. The knuckle of my thumb hits her urethra and hot piss soaks my arm. That's a girl. Show me how "restrained" and "in control" you are. Now come. She does. Hard.

She is sobbing, now. Holding her. My arms cradle this woman-child. I am rocking her, soothing her. The air is cold and the blanket is too far away. I cover her with myself. The warmth is sufficient for both of us. I am asleep. At some point in the darkness, I awaken and cover both our chilled bodies with the sheet and blanket that were discarded. One arm rests protectively around her waist, curling under her and hauling her back into me. Her ass to my stomach. Stay. Good girl. It's morning. It must be morning. At no other time is intense sunlight such a pain in the ass. Eyes half-closed, I grope around in the empty bed, searching. My arms hurt. Hell, everything hurts. No, nothing there. On dead legs I stand and make my way to the bathroom down the hall. Too weary to sit, I piss standing up, one hand against the wall for support. I trudge back down the hall and stumble back to bed, pulling the covers up to my chin. Still fuzzy and numb, I roll over and reach for sleep. She'll come back. She always does.

The Arrival

Wren Marshal

Dearest Susannah,

It's been only 12 days since I saw you last, but 12 days without your touch feels like eternity. My imagination has been working relentlessly to find an erotic reverie that will satisfy my libido until I see you again. After enduring many lukewarm masturbation fantasies, I think I've finally come up with a sizzling scenario that will keep us both hot and wet for days to come. OK, Susannah, here's the scene:

You're flying down on the next plane—I've arranged to meet you at the airport at exactly noon. You step off the plane, dressed in black: jeans, turtleneck, and your boots, polished to a dangerous gleam. I am there, waiting for you, standing at a distance from the passive curiosity of the airline personnel. I too am dressed all in black; my dress is cut low, and the seams of my stockings that begin where my high heels end are visible nearly all the way up to my ass. I wear a black felt hat with feathers to match and a veil to conceal the seductive expression on my face.

Our eyes meet, accompanied by two smiles and two pounding hearts. I remain still as you approach. No smiles now, only a mutual look that sears the soul—and the cunt. I reach for you, but the glint in your eyes stops my motion in mid-air; my hands drop to my sides where they belong. I have forgotten my place in these past 12 days.

I wait until you reach for me, pull me close, and whisper how you've missed me. I return your embrace and feel your heart quicken as you squeeze me a moment before pulling back to look into my eyes once again, a moment before you wrap your fingers in my hair and bring my lips to yours. From the possession of your mouth I protest, aware of the stares—two women making out in the midst of the airport hubbub; how shocking we must seem. I attempt to pull away, more for my sake than theirs, but your hold on me is strong and the force of your kiss is making me dizzy; there is nowhere to go anyway. Your tongue searches my mouth and teases my lips until I find it hard to breathe and hold myself up at the same time. My cunt tightens in anticipation; the burning fire travels through my body to my clit, building into a pyre that burns through my whole pelvic region. I am getting really turned on...and then abruptly you push me away mid kiss, just as I am about to surrender to the intoxication of your tongue. I start to pout, but you walk away from me with a rapid stride, and I have to run to catch up. As we walk, we talk a little, chitchat about the flight and the weather. I am relieved to be quiet for the moment, because I know what will be coming very soon.

Your look turns cold. "Why are you dressed like a whore? You look like you should be out on the streets turning tricks. Maybe you need to get fucked. How 'bout it, baby, you need me to fuck you good?"

I am trembling now, aware that I'm on dangerous ground. "Don't you like it, Susannah? I played dress-up just for you."

"Yeah, me and anybody else who wants to take a look You're feeling sleazy today, huh, baby? Wantin' to show off that precious body just made for fucking. Who do you want? How about that creep who's giving you the eye? He looks likely." Your pace is even faster now, and I'm falling behind, frantically trying to maneuver through the crowd without losing you.

"Oh, no, Susannah. I swear, this is all for you. I just wanted to turn you on." Can you even hear me, I wonder?

"Don't lie to me. I know you want men to look at you. Maybe what I give you isn't good enough. You want it all, don't you? Cock *and* cunt."

We're almost out of the airport. You stop for a drink of water and announce that you have to piss. We enter the bathroom together; it's nearly deserted. There's a woman at the mirror contorting her face to apply lipstick, and another detectable only by her feet in one of the stalls; other than that, it's just you and me.

You walk into a stall and gesture for me to follow. "Don't argue with me," you hiss in a half-whisper. "You're feeling like a slut, and every slut wants to be fucked—am I right?"

My trembling has shifted into shaking. After all, it's true. I do want to be fucked. I want to be filled. I want to be wanted.

"Yes, Susannah.' My answer is almost inaudible. I cast my eyes down, hoping that you won't hit me, praying that you will.

"You're not even wearing underwear, are you?"

"No, Susannah. I wanted my cunt to be available for you."

The first slap lands squarely on my left jawbone. "Shut up. Only answer with 'Yes, Susannah' or 'No, Susannah'—understand?"

"Yes, Susannah."

You act as if you haven't even heard my answer, busying yourself with unzipping your flight bag. With a satisfied look, you position yourself on the edge of the toilet and sit down.

"OK, baby, put your leg up here and let me look at your cunt. Oh, yes, you are beautiful. Give me your hand; now spread your lips for me. Ooh, you're glistening. Your cunt is so juicy. How come, you slut? Does the prospect of getting worked over excite you?"

"Oh, yes, Susannah."

You appear totally disinterested as you address my pulsating pussy, directing your comments to my clit. "Good girl—but not yet. You'll get what you need soon enough."

I feel the softness of your breath as you speak, and I push myself forward, silently pleading with you to take me in your mouth. Your tongue flits lightly across my clit, eliciting a moan from deep inside my belly.

"Shut up! This is a public bathroom."

The tug on my hair is enough to bring tears to my eyes and silence to my throat. You return your attention to my cunt, this time plunging your tongue deep inside my damp heat. You squeeze my ass, and I can't help it; my body moves—grinding against your chin, your lips, and your teeth. My eyes are closed, and all I know is rhythm. It feels so fucking good! Your finger has found its way into the tight little hole behind my pussy, and I work hard to keep myself from screaming with pleasure. I slide against the wall in order to hold myself up, wedged between the cold metal and your insistent probing.

Your motions are quickening; you have a finger in each hole now, and you begin to give me the fucking I crave. You are no longer sucking; I can hear and feel your breath, penetrating me through my vulva. As you stand up, I smell the sex in the air. You lean your chin, dripping with my juice, into my neck, and thrust into me with your fingers, your hips, your whole body; the palm of your hand is pressing down hard on my clit. Oh, goddess, it's so good, I think I'm going to come. Oh yes, oh yes, oh no, oh fuck!

Suddenly, nothing. No touch, no motion, nothing. I could cry in frustration. I was so close! I open my eyes to see you bending over, rummaging through your leather bag. You catch me looking at you.

"What are you looking at? Keep your eyes closed!"

You stand up, give me another slap, harder than the last, and another. My cheeks are burning, but my cunt is burning hotter. I'm uncomfortable from standing in heels for so long, and I'm pissed at you for leaving me hanging, but I'm afraid to move and provoke your anger any more. I do as you say, closing my eyes and waiting for your touch. At last I feel your hands on my shoulders.

"Turn around."

I'm grateful for the chance to move; my body is stiff and cold from leaning against the stall.

"Bend over."

Oh, no! You're not going to spank me here, in a restroom at the airport. Suddenly I realize it isn't a spanking you're preparing me for.

"Oh, Susannah, not my ass, not here, please, no."

I want it, but it seems downright nasty to get butt-fucked in a public place. I still consider myself to be a good Catholic dyke.

"Please, Susannah. Be good to me."

"I am being good to you, honey. I'm giving you just what you need. Be a good girl and take it quietly. Or would you rather I spanked you?"

I'm silent. I can't believe you are really doing this. You slip the dildo into my wet cunt, and I sigh in relief and pleasure.

Oh, good, she's changing her mind, I think.

In a flash you are out and pushing the slippery silicone cock into my most tender muscle. Your hands grab my waist, pulling me onto you. Oh, God it hurts, but it's so good; now I don't want you to stop, ever.

"You see, honey, I know what you need. You like it, don't you? C'mon, take it all in. Ride, girlfriend, ride."

I heave my body back to meet your thrust. The dildo is buried in my ass, the tip of it pushing against my belly. The tension builds as you trigger the secret, sensitive places inside my hole, and I work hard for the release just out of reach. Together we move, no words, just breathing, until I feel the sweet beginnings of prickly heat spreading from my ass to my cunt, flooding me with waves of ecstatic sensation. I'm climbing, higher and higher, pushing through the levels, reaching—and then I'm falling, falling into myself, into you, coming with an intensity that shakes my soul. "Oh God, oh God, oh God, it's so good."

I'm spent. I would fall, but you pull out and catch me.

"What a good girl you are," you murmur.

I can't even respond; I lie in your arms like a little child, savoring the last traces of an incredible orgasm. After a while, I come back to the present world and smile at you.

"Thank you, Susannah. You were right. You always know just what I need."

We hold each other close and kiss. The game is over, for now. We rearrange our clothes and leave the stall together. Arm in arm, we walk slowly to the car. I change into jeans and a sweatshirt, and then we're off to start our day.

So, Susannah, what do you think? Are you hard yet? This fantasy should keep us both happy for a little while. No? Well, there's a plane leaving at 8:45 A.M. tomorrow; it gets in at noon exactly.

The Luv of a Filipina Butch

Morningstar Vancil

She was my childhood sweetheart, from our hometown of Cebu, and I was a Marine commander in the Marcos military. The Philippines was still under martial law in early 1980, and my position as an officer afforded me some flexibility and freedom, but as today, lesbians were not accepted.

I was courting her in the traditional Filipino ways with midnight serenades, holding her hand at the movies, compliments for her beautiful eyes, hair, skin, and gift-giving. We kept our feelings secret, though, from her family. My male cousin helped by acting as Christian to my Cyrano de Bergerac. I would meet them, quite uninnocently, while they were on, say, a movie date. I would accompany his girlfriend there and, once the lights were off, we'd switch partners.

My *mahinhin* was a virgin, modest and shy, with good upbringing. She took many risks to be with me. The first time we made love, I led her to a secluded summer beach house. I was the first lover to unbind her silky, dark brown hair, to see it cascade down to her perfect tan ass. Her fresh skin felt smooth to my work-roughened fingertips, and her movements were quick and light—so beautiful that watching her walk was like watching a hula dancer. She took my breath away. I explored her for hours, making love to her slowly with my hands and tongue—making her heart light. She

69

accepted my attention like a good Filipina girl, quietly tolerating my devotion to her body and slowly opening up to my insistent hands. We were both in our early 20s, with so much in front of us.

I loved her.

One day during the rainy season, our base was alerted that an approaching typhoon could affect us. As I looked at the maps during briefing, I realized that her island was directly in the path and became alarmed. I needed to make sure she was safe, but calling her was out; she had no phone. I was young and rash; it was my duty to protect her, so I decided to go to her. Casting around for a way off the base, I rushed to the docks where a fisherman sat mending his nets. I commandeered his boat by pretending to be on official business, which he was willing to buy, but he refused to transport me into the approaching typhoon. After a quick lesson on piloting the little ill-equipped dinghy, he told me I was crazy and offered a prayer, "May God help you," as he helped me shove off.

I needed divine intervention. The typhoon was mounting; strong winds and high, heavy waves buffeted the small fishing boat. I piloted it, poorly but intact, with military determination and a recovering Catholic's prayers, to her island. I walked into my girl's house just as the typhoon hit, and my arrival maddened her. She thought that I was taking too many chances. "You're crazy," she concluded, but she was turned on.

For the next day I was stuck at her shuddering house, her family accepting me as a visiting "friend in need" while she told me her secret desires. Marcos's rule had awakened a latent need; she fantasized of being suspected to be an enemy of the state, of being detained as a rebel, arrested, and interrogated. Her fantasy spiraled at this point. Her captor would take her in every way. These confessions rocked me! My *mahinhin,* my good girl, was kinky—just like me! I confessed that I had the same kinds of yearnings, that I would be privileged to help her live out her fantasy.

For weeks we spent hours discussing her dream, and the level of detail she imagined was full of erotic promise. Her voice saying those words drove me to the edge of reason, and I recruited some of my military butch-buds (fellow officers) to help fulfill them, but I didn't tell her that. We kept talking about her fantasy and making intense love.

One Friday, about two months after the typhoon, I told my girl to be ready Saturday morning. I traveled back to Marine headquarters where the plans for our fantasy were finalized.

The next morning, two butch military police left Marine headquarters, motored to my girl's island, and arrested her on suspicion of subversion against the government of the Philippines. The took her away from her home and family, then sailed with her to an island where there was only one jail cell—a cell I had cleared of prisoners and guards. Two butch-buds agreed to be my lookouts. I was taking a chance that could have had me court-martialed, and they knew better than anyone what I was risking. I trusted them.

Once she was in that cell, her ass was mine. I was dressed in Philippine Marine-issue fatigues and as menacing as any commander, anywhere in the world. I strip-searched her, and after an exhaustive search, was displeased to find that there were no weapons secreted on her body. I then read her rights: She had none. Martial law meant that the military ruled, and she was not military. I was in control. "You're in my court now; for what you did the penalty is death."

She shook in the cool of the cell, but her pale skin was burning hot when I reached out to grab her breast and twist a nipple. "But you're so damn cute that I'll just torture you to death," I whispered into her ear. Once the blindfold was firmly in place, I circled behind her to press my breasts against her back.

With scratchy rope I tied her arms and torso to the bars of the cell. Her back and ass were pressed tightly to the cold, wet metal while her breasts and cunt were at my mercy. I used the paddle, the cane, the belt, everything that had been part of my own military initiation, on her supple skin. I watched her beautiful face become flushed, then tearful, then enraptured. I heard her heavy breathing, her hoarse screams, and the not-so-hoarse screams.

When I slapped her face, she started to break down. I pulled her back by grasping her face gently after each slap, turning it this way and that, to examine her. I'd look into her eyes, hold her gaze to make her remember that she was really with me, that I was still the woman who loved her, that her fulfillment was my only purpose. She got so turned on by all of this that she peed herself. Of course, she was punished after I hosed her down. I interrogated her for hours.

I was so proud of my girl. She never confessed to the things that I accused her of doing; she never admitted to being a rebel.

The final straw, it seemed, was the candles. She squirmed and moaned as the hot, soft wax painted her skin. She was soon begging me to fuck her, making bargains with me. "Take me now please, just take me. I'll confess to anything if you take me now!"

I was so turned on, so impressed by her strength and amazed by my depth of love for her, that I granted her request. She fell on me as soon as I untied, her arms and I barely had time to drag her to the single rough wooden bed on the other side of the cell. There had been a change in my *mahinhin*. She pressed her body into my fatigues until I opened the shirt, but I never had time to take off my clothes— my boots were still on two hours later! She went wild when I slowly licked her breasts; sucking her nipples made her cry out. When my mouth reached her clit, she ripped into my back, through the shirt, with her fingernails. I'd never been more turned on. My modest girlfriend fucked my mouth, raising her hips off the narrow cot and demanding "More, like that, do that again!"

Hours later, when she allowed me to breathe, I dressed her and pulled us back together. I talked to her until she was calm and then summoned the escorts (again, my two butch-buds) who accompanied us back to her island. I carried her from the boat to her bed, wrapped in our partner blanket, and put her safely to bed. My girl had finally come out.

Hannah
Anni Giddings

Hannah was a handsome woman. Kelly watched her Master dreamily, her eyes narrowing as Hannah lifted her coffee cup to her lips. She studied the tendons along her tanned forearms as they flexed from each tiny movement. Hannah's hair was dark and short, with wispy curls that gathered around the nape of her neck.

Kelly fought the urge to reach out and wrap a curl around her index finger as she sometimes did when they were in bed together, but she knew it wouldn't be appropriate now. Hannah's blue eyes were concentrating on her dinner guest. Her thin lips turned up into a slight smile as her guest told a story about losing her luggage on a recent vacation. Luckily, she said, she had decided to take her vacation at a nude, all-women beach.

Kelly's mind was more absorbed with weaving fantasies around her Master's strong arms.

"What are you thinking about, Kelly?" Hannah directed her attention to her daydreaming slave.

"Nothing." Kelly quickly answered, and looked down to catch her embarrassed reflection in her own coffee cup.

"It didn't look like 'nothing' to me." Both women laughed. Kelly continued to stare into her coffee cup while her ears grew hot.

Hannah ruffled Kelly's hair and drew her chin up. "That's what I get for letting her use the furniture," she said good-naturedly. "She gets inattentive and undisciplined." The Master and her slave locked eyes for several seconds, both knowing what was coming next.

"Get on your knees, Kelly," Hannah ordered softly. Kelly was swift and obedient.

Hannah grabbed the middle ring of her slave's collar and tugged it upward. Kelly held her head proudly and stared into her Master's gentle eyes.

Hannah never wanted a slave before she met Kelly. As a matter of fact, until she took Kelly she preferred to drag pretty little boys home with her. She'd never found a woman who liked the type of abuse that she dished out. But Kelly had a sweet, round face, brown eyes, big tits, and a fiery spirit. She wasn't much of a submissive, Hannah quickly discovered, but she was definitely a pain slut. She could be trained. A dog can't change its spots, she figured, but it can be put on a leash and taught to heel. Kelly was a diamond in the rough (actually, a lump of coal was a more accurate description), but Hannah knew this one would follow her in chains for the rest of her days, if she was kept bruised and whimpering.

When Hannah asked her to take the title of slave, Kelly quickly agreed. Visions of perpetual beatings from Hannah's hand danced in the girl's head. She worshiped Hannah's relentless cruelty and was honored by the offer. She would have preferred to play hard to get for a while, but she knew Hannah didn't play games, and Kelly would take no risk of losing her. Hannah never let her forget how easy it was to get a collar around her neck.

Hannah returned to her conversation with her dinner guest while Kelly knelt patiently at her Master's feet. When they rose, Kelly got up and started clearing away the dishes. She heard Hannah's boot steps as she entered the kitchen and approached her at the sink.

"What are you doing, girl?" she asked roughly. The hair bristled on the back of Kelly's neck. Her back went rigid.

"I'm washing—"

"Who gave you permission to get off your knees, Kelly? Huh? Turn around and look at me when I'm speaking to you."

Kelly dropped the dishes in the sink, breaking a coffee cup in her haste, and sunk to her knees. Hannah glared at the girl, debating over whether to add the broken cup to her list of offenses. She decided to concentrate on Kelly's feeble but charming attempt at submission.

"Nope, not good enough. It's too late, my girl." She took a fistful of Kelly's hair and pulled her a couple inches off of her knees. Kelly was trying to get into a position where she wasn't hanging by her roots when the toe of Hannah's boot met her hip at the same time her hair was released. Kelly fell to the ground and clutched her side, then backed against the kitchen cabinet. Her heart was beating in her ears. She was eye level with Hannah's kneecaps and didn't dare look up at her Master's face. She waited.

Hannah's fingers went to the buttons on the crotch of her jeans. She unfastened the top ones so some of her dark, curly pubic hair was exposed.

"Come here, Kelly. Show me how devoted you are to your Master."

Kelly bent forward, tentatively at first. She was afraid Hannah would slap her away, as she sometimes did. She darted her tongue into the soft folds of her Master's cunt and lapped up the warm, sticky moisture. Hannah cupped her hands around the back of the girl's skull and pushed her forward in encouragement.

Kelly took this as her cue to concentrate on Hannah's swelling clit. She thought about her sore hip and the imminent punishment to fuel her passion. This woman whose cunt was enveloping her face was going to hurt her. Kelly rubbed her own thighs together at the thought.

Hannah moved her hips with Kelly's tongue and came. She fell against the kitchen counter as Kelly swallowed her gush of juices. Hannah's muscles relaxed and the walls of her cunt grew warm and soft.

Kelly was pulled from her cocoon by her hair. Hannah's hold on her kept her back arched with her face pointed toward her Master. Hannah's eyes were shining and her cheeks were flushed.

"Go upstairs, undress, and wait for me," she directed. Kelly stood and followed directions. She went into the play-room adjacent to her Master's bedroom, took off and neatly folded her jeans and T-shirt, and settled on a carpeted area of the floor.

She wasn't sure how long she waited. Hannah entered the room abruptly and startled the waiting slave. Kelly rose and stood in the spot to which she was silently directed, and Hannah proceeded to place her wrists in fur-lined, locking restraints. She padlocked the restraints to overhead chains so her arms were stretched but not uncomfortable. Generally, Hannah restrained her victims just enough that they could struggle but not get away. She liked to watch them squirm.

After they were locked in place, Kelly pulled on her restraints to test them. No, she wasn't going anywhere. Hannah smiled at her struggling and stood back to observe her handiwork. She walked to her toy rack and spoke to her slave as she picked out a well-made whip with thick braids.

"Do you want to know how many I'm going to give you?" she asked wickedly.

"Not really," Kelly answered sourly. She hated knowing how many she was going to get. Hannah ignored her slave's show of insubordination. It was best not to encourage her.

"I'm going to start at 50 and proceed from there. If you lose count or if I don't feel you're enthusiastic enough, we will start from the beginning. Do you understand?"

"Yes," Kelly answered sharply. She knew better, but she

glared at Hannah with a look that could freeze water in the desert. Hannah wiped it off her face with the first, fast stroke of her whip.

"One!" Kelly screamed defiantly as it fell across her ass. Hannah stopped and moved to face her slave. Her face was hard.

"Now let's start again, and this time I don't want any shit. Don't fuck with me, Kelly, because I'll leave you hanging there and not touch you until you get that attitude under control. I don't care how long it takes. Is that clear?"

Kelly looked into her Master's stern eyes. She knew from experience that Hannah wasn't kidding. She snapped herself out of it. "Yes," she answered as meekly as possible.

Hannah continued the verbal abuse. "Who's running this scene, Kelly?"

"You are, Hannah," the girl answered with resignation.

"Try to remember that, OK?" Hannah tweaked her slave's chin and marched behind her.

"One," Kelly counted earnestly at the next fall of the whip. "Two, three..."

By 20, she was slurring her words. Oh, God, she hated counting. Counting made her keep her feet planted firmly on the ground. When she had to keep track, she could deny or escape the pain. Hannah punished her once by making her keep count throughout an entire whipping. They had to start over three or four times when she started making mistakes. It was Hannah's guarantee that the whipping would really hurt and the punishment would be effective. It worked well. Hannah only had to do it once. After that, Hannah enjoyed making her slave take as much as possible before giving her permission to give in to her endorphins.

"Please, Hannah, please!" Kelly pleaded between 25 and 26. She braced herself for the next lash but felt Hannah's cool fingers on her hot back instead. Hannah's lips were next to her ear. She could feel her Master's hot breath.

"Make it to 50 for me and I won't make you count any-more," she promised. "If you stop now, though, I stop with you."

Kelly panicked. "I don't want you to stop yet!"

"I didn't think so," Hannah responded menacingly.

"Twenty-six," Kelly croaked in time with the next stroke. Each additional lash until 50 was agonizing, and Kelly cried out the final number with every ounce of determination in her body. Hannah paused and looked at her slave. She was covered with sweat. Her eyes were closed and her hair was wet and matted to her skull. Her back and ass were red but far from wasted, and her tits hadn't even been touched yet. *Yes, my dear, it will be a long night,* she thought. She walked to her rack and picked out a cat with thin, tight braids, and a fiberglass cane.

She laid the cat down on a bench in back of the girl and walked in front of her with the cane. Kelly opened her eyes.

"Good morning," Hannah said cheerfully. She didn't give Kelly enough time to size up her situation before the cane crashed down, meeting Kelly's left tit where the areola fades into the pale, outer flesh. Kelly yelped and didn't even have time to catch her breath before a succession of blows fell across her flesh like a rain of fire. Kelly's breasts were pale white, and the cane turned up bruises and blood like watercolors. The positioning of her arms left her with no way to shield herself from the cane. All she could do was scream.

Hannah stopped the beating long enough to laugh. "Weren't you the one who begged my permission to keep quiet a minute ago?" she taunted her slave. Kelly's head was swimming. She was dazed and looked to her Master for help in her confusion.

"What do you want, Kelly?" Hannah gave her a roguish look, and punctuated the question by slamming the cane across both breasts at once. Kelly gasped and let her head fall backward.

"I want to come, Hannah. Please let me come," she sobbed.

Hannah shook her head. "No, not yet. I'm not ready to let you have that yet. What are you going to do to earn it, my pretty girl?"

Kelly released a cry of protest and rubbed her slippery inner thighs together, trying to create friction.

Hannah kicked them apart. "That's better. Don't make me use a spreader bar on you." She petted her slave's damp pubic hair and Kelly thrust her hips forward and moaned. Hannah chuckled and removed her hand. Kelly started to sob, then stifled it. She was in so much need, but the more she showed it, the more Hannah would toy with her.

"Do you want to take another whipping for me?" Hannah asked her.

"Do I have to count?" she answered timidly.

Hannah laughed. "I won't make you count this time. I promise." Kelly sighed in relief. Hannah always kept her promises.

Hannah picked up the cat and Kelly grabbed the chains over her head for support. She arched forward as far as her restraints would allow to welcome Hannah's whip. This one, because of its smaller and tighter braids, stung more than the first. Kelly grunted and twisted away from it. Hannah anticipated each move from her slave's last. She used the ends of the whip to take advantage of the slick surface of her inner thighs. Kelly yelped but kept her legs apart.

When Hannah whipped the sides and backs of her thighs, though, Kelly could no longer keep her positioning. She danced and kicked and twisted in her restraints. Hannah circled her like a tiger with a trapped animal, prodding and enraging her with the braids of the whip. "Where are you going, Kelly?" she teased as she made her dance back and forth.

Kelly relaxed, letting her chains support her and giving herself completely over to Hannah. She was rewarded with a renewed intensity in Hannah's strokes. Instead of fighting, though, she accepted the pain and let it build inside her. When it was on the verge of becoming too much, it exploded into millions of tiny, airy fingers that spread throughout her worn body. It felt so good. She never wanted it to end. "Thank you, Hannah. Thank you," she repeated between moans. It was Hannah, after all, who had brought her to this state. It was her devotion to Hannah that gave her the strength to endure, and she worshiped her Master for being strong and cruel enough to carry her through.

Hannah laid one last lash across the girl's back. She moved in front of the girl and took her face in her palms. Kelly looked up and found the gift of approval in her Master's eyes. Hannah kissed her girl and moved her right hand between Kelly's legs. Kelly shrieked and clamped her thighs tightly together.

"No, please Hannah, it's too much. I can't come now. Please."

"We're getting mighty fickle, aren't we, Kelly? Beat me," she mimicked, "don't beat me. I want to come. I don't want to come." The grip around Kelly's jaw tightened. Hannah's voice was venomous. "What you want or need is irrelevant, Kelly. You're going to come because I want to watch you come."

Kelly responded by relaxing her thigh muscles and allowing Hannah's fingers to work into her cunt. She fought her orgasm fiercely, though. When it finally overtook her it was so violent that her entire body shook and she screamed until her lungs ached.

Hannah waited until the ripples of pleasure had subsided before unlocking Kelly's restraints. She carried her to the bedroom and lay with her on the bed. Kelly lost herself in her Master's arms.

After a few minutes, Hannah broke the silence. "Kelly," she teased, "do you remember what I whipped you for?"

"Because I got off my knees to do the dishes and broke a

cup?" she asked, safe against Hannah's chest. She didn't know why Hannah had posed such an obvious question.

"That's right. And what would have happened if I had come into the kitchen and you were still on your knees and the dishes weren't cleared, my girl?"

"You'd whip me, of course!" Kelly answered as she looked up sheepishly from Hannah's bosom, catching on to the game. Hannah held her tight and smiled.

Drag Kings Rule

Jules Wilkinson

There was a long line outside the Hardware Club. I ambled past the front in case my mate Mena was working the door, but there was just a bouncer with his arms crossed over his bitch tits barring the way. Traipsing along the queue, I scanned the crowd for a familiar face to save me from the ignominy of standing alone at the end. Luckless, I took my place at the back next to two lovers who were standing in that silent, slightly apart way that lovers do when a compromise has been reached about which neither is really happy.

Removing the rollie I had tucked behind my ear, I stood with the unlit fag in my mouth while I worked two fingers into the pocket of my too-tight leather pants. I remembered to check that the flame was turned right down. In my early drag days I nearly had a nasty accident when a 10-centimeter-high flame ignited the combination of dog hair and spirit gum that had then made up my mustache.

"Can I have a light?"

A short nuggety guy stood next to me holding out a fag. With my best butch action I flicked my Zippo into life again. He nodded thanks and stood for a moment running his eyes from my black bike boots up to my crotch. His gaze made me acutely aware of the dildo I was packing, and instinctively I moved a hand to reassure myself it was still in place. His eyes met mine and he nodded again. I suddenly realized he thought I was what I appeared to be—a stocky leatherman with a luxurious mustache, a slightly patchy beard, and a hard cock.

The unmistakable desire in the man's eyes made my cunt tighten. I stood battling between the fear of discovery and my growing excitement. Then he spoke two words that decided it for me.

"Please, sir."

I nodded curtly at him and turned quickly, striding down the piss-fumed alley behind the car park. The bass throb from the club matched the pounding of my heart and my cunt. Stopping just past some crates and bins I thought for a moment, hoped for a moment, that he hadn't followed me. But he was there in the shadows—waiting and wanting.

We stood as close as we could without touching. I moved against him so that he felt my lips at the same time my hardness pressed into him. Our tongues collided in the cavern created by our joined mouths. He tasted of garlic and beer and cigarettes, or maybe that was me, but he also tasted of something I couldn't define, something that was just foreign. I worried that the heat and spit from our kissing might start loosening my moustache, so I gave him a sharp nip on his bottom lip and moved my mouth across his stubbly cheek to his neck.

His hands, which had been resting on my shoulders, started moving toward my chest, but I uttered a low hoarse "No!" He dropped his hands but then moved them to my ass and pulled me to him. I felt his flesh cock growing hard against me as my silicon dick prodded into his thigh. "Turn around," I growled as I pushed him up against a crate.

My hand moved across his chest—so flat and ungiving. It took me a while, but I finally found the little nub of his tit. Rubbing and pinching it made him groan and press his ass back into me. As I reached down to undo his belt he stretched his arms back to pull me closer. I laughed to myself. Girl or boy, pushy bottoms were all the same. But I was the top here and I would play this scene my way.

His belt slid easily out of his pants, and I looped about half the length of it around my hand. Stepping back without warning, I slapped the end of it across his butt. He gasped in surprise and murmured, "Yes, sir. Please, sir," as he dropped his jeans to ground. I hit his bare ass three, four times; hard enough to raise welts that glowed pink in the neon lights from the car park next door. The slapping of the leather was punctuated by his moans, and the pulse in my cunt quickened.

I rubbed my hand over the welts, across the short wiry hairs of his flat boy bottom and down between his cheeks. His asshole puckered at my touch, but I found it hard to get far with my dry fingers. Luckily the solution was close at hand. I unzipped myself and slipped my hand into my pants. The temptation to touch my clit was too much, and with a few quick flicks of my finger, I came. I withdrew a hand dripping with the mucus of my desire and worked it over and round his tight hole. Soon I was able to work three and then four fingers inside him. Our bodies rocked together as I stroked my hand around the hard ring of muscle that was stopping further entry.

"Wait," I whispered as I worked my free hand into my back pocket. He moaned and pushed back against me. "Wait," I hissed again. "Yes, sir," he whimpered. I could tell the restraint was not easy.

Using my teeth to loosen the cap on the small brown bottle, I flicked it to the ground and put the opening to my nose. I took a deep snort in each nostril, then passed the bottle over to him. I love the hit of amyl when I'm fucking. The top of my head seems to lift off and my brain floats away and all that is left in my consciousness is my throbbing cunt. It also clears my sinuses wonderfully.

I lost track of time, but I think I came again. After a while I was aware that my hand was now completely inside him.

Thrusting deeper, soon my whole forearm was engulfed by his ass. I curled my fingers within him and little shudders ran through his body. He was close to coming. I teased him, pulling my arm slowly back and then thrusting forward quickly with short sharp strokes. I grabbed his hair with my free hand and pulled his head back.

He was gripping the side of the crate for support as his knees weakened with the approaching orgasm. I felt his ass muscles spasm around my arm, and I pushed against him so that my dildo ground hard into my clit. He came with a groan that sounded like he'd been punched and then he slumped forward against the crate. I leaned over him and with a couple of thrusts I came again.

We held that position for a moment, and I stroked the back of his head as I slowly withdrew my arm. He gave a little cry as my hand left him. Between jagged breaths he gasped, "Geez, mate, that was intense." I leaned over him and whispered in my sweetest, dykiest voice, "Yeah, pretty good for a girl."

War Story
Jean Roberta

The once-sleepy village was in flaming ruins. Chloris (as she is known to the Greeks) and I rode between the huts, watching for snipers. She saw the young man aiming at us before I did, and dropped him with one arrow to the chest. Chloris is one of the best shots in the army. I probably rely on her more than I should; being paired with her encourages me to be reckless. I don't like raids, but I do my duty. I'd rather kill than be killed or taken captive. The noble men of Greece offer us no other choices.

A young woman with loose raven hair flowing over her shoulders came out of her hut and stood watching us. The figure of an old man lay in his own blood in the single room they had shared. She had probably been married to him as a girl, and now she was a young widow. Her eyes were dry. She reached up to one shoulder and calmly, without fear or haste, undid her chiton and let it drop to the ground. The gesture was bold and clear. She stood naked in the bright sunlight, her plump breasts standing up like watchful animals. The triangle of hair between her legs was as black as the hair on her head. I could no more fathom her motives than I could gossip in village Greek. I couldn't ask the little widow what I wanted to know. Had her man meant nothing to her? Had he regarded her as his slave, and had she grown so used to such treatment that a change of masters made no difference to her? Did she see us as her deliverers?

Chloris wanted to ride past, ignoring the firm, tender breasts and gently curved belly of the young woman who showed them to us. Chloris wanted to ride past. There was no tactical advantage to be gained by accepting the sexual favors of a foreign woman. The commander had said we would not be taking captives in this raid. We rarely take captives, despite the stories told about us by our enemies; we don't seek to recruit men's women, either as soldiers or as servants.

Standing uncovered in the midst of disaster, the little widow called silently to my heart. I knew that if I refused to answer, her image would haunt my dreams. Knowing how reckless I was, I dismounted and secured my horse to a post. Smiling, the wench seized one of my hands and led me to a small storage hut. Luckily, words seemed unnecessary. I wrapped her in my arms, burying my face in her fragrant hair. She smelled like figs and oil, dust and sweat. It was a rich smell that was strongest in the curves between her neck and her smooth shoulders. Her breasts pressed against my ribs, pressing my heart. I lifted her to feel her weight, and she was lighter than my weapons. She pressed herself against one of my thighs so that I could feel the hot moisture below her belly. When I looked into her eyes, I saw that they were dark greenish-gray, the color of a storm cloud. I pulled off my cloak and folded it for her to lie on. She spread her legs, raised her knees, and invited me with her eyes to worship at her altar. I recklessly shed my war-shirt and pants, then removed the pouch that holds my little bronze wand, the thing we sometimes call "the sword of peace." I showed it to her, rubbing it in my hands, then I let her hold it so it would be warm enough for her flesh. Some women prefer being entered by cold metal, but I never assume that any woman has such taste unless she tells me so. I squatted between my little sweetheart's legs to part the thick black hair and peer into the wet folds within. I kissed the eager guardian at her entrance, and felt it jump in my mouth like a sleeper who has suddenly been awakened. I pulled it gently with my teeth and licked it as it grew. I explored her soft cave with my tongue and found it as hot and tasty as any I have known. The little widow seemed surprised by the touch of my tongue. She reacted to my strokes as though they were an unfamiliar language that she wanted to learn. She responded as though she feared that she would never be pleasured again. I couldn't promise her a long and happy life, but I could serve her present need. She seemed to tremble on the edge of release for a long time, unable or unwilling to surrender. She seemed to be waiting for my wand, which she reached for as though she wanted to use it on herself. Laughing, I kissed it before carefully guiding it into her warm opening. She welcomed it with her whole body. Despite her boldness, the little widow seemed too stubborn or too afraid to let herself enjoy the climax she clearly wanted. I craved the satisfaction of outwitting that part of her that was still loyal to the dead or still committed to resistance.

A simple but surprising move is often the best solution to the problem I faced. I pulled out my thinnest knife, used for piercing, with its silver handle molded in a cunning spiral design. Not having any warm oil at hand, I sucked on this device until it was warm and wet enough for my purpose. I quickly found my little lover's smaller entrance and inserted the knife handle, firmly but patiently twisting it into her to the rhythm of her hips. Her breathing grew louder and her thrusts intensified. Wielding my two probes, I lowered my face to her belly and kissed the guardian at her gate. Almost at once, the little widow cried out, moving in an unmistakable way. I hoped that no one else heard her. My reputation was not the only thing at stake. I was becoming hopelessly protective, and did not want to see her harmed.

I heard the commander's footsteps before she appeared at

the entrance of the hut. She undoubtedly caught a glimpse of my little lover before I managed to wrap her in my cloak. Whether the officer was moved by what she saw, I will probably never know. The commander gave me a look and a gesture, then strode away with a contemptuous swing of her cloak. I hoped I had rewarded my companion enough for the generous gift of her body, because our idyll was over and I could give her nothing more. How bitter it was to know that her heat, her smell, and the light in her eyes would soon be lost to me. I could only look forward to the punishment that might be dealt to me for my lack of self-discipline, since it would remind me of her. The little widow did not seem heartbroken when I kissed her goodbye, but maybe that was a sign that she had more of the officer in her than I do. *If you can hear my thoughts, child of Aphrodite, I pray to your goddess and mine for your protection. If my tribe seems cold or brutal to you, remember that we are constantly under threat from your brothers. If they succeed, we will be destroyed. I can wage peace only when I have the chance, and I treasure my memories of such subversion.*

The Sailor

Diana Cage

From the back she really looks like a sailor. Tight white pants. Broad shoulders, short cropped hair. The uniform fits her well, and I pretend for just a moment that she isn't dressed up in some very obvious costume at a party that feels like the fetish prom. From the front she's very much a girl. Freckles, thin nose, high cheekbones, a decidedly feminine face that I'm sure is the bane of her existence.

The room reeks of propane from the fire show. Earlier, two women danced around each other in a way that was meant to be sultry. They swallowed rubber cocks with flaming ends, made a big show of their tattooed bodies and pretended to fuck each other. They had everything going for them, even enthusiasm, but it was all too staged. They were too black and shiny and clean to be having sex. They looked like a movie, like some teenage witchcraft rip-off straight-to-video bullshit. "Stop trying," I say out loud. "Give it up. Put your rubbery clothes back on and go back to your co-ops." Even the girls on the dance floor in their PVC outfits and bondage gear looked bored. They need rape scenes or foot fucking to get them off. They clamor for murder and mayhem. A little half-assed flaming cock sucking doesn't get anything going for this crowd.

Girls were coughing from the thick greasy air; a few had

passed out on the dance floor like little latex canaries. The beer was gone. The music was bad. I was feeling light-headed and loose, and looking for trouble. For a moment, my sailor disappeared from sight and I panicked, thinking I wouldn't get a second chance. But she resurfaced amongst a group of tranny boys, all huddled together away from the girly girls like little kids at recess. Her beautiful face looked mean even though she was laughing. Looking at her made me feel sexy and I wondered what it would take to get a girl like that to fuck me. Then I remembered that I've gotten many girls like that to fuck me. Everyone just wants to fuck someone.

The club is normally a gay men's porn theater. Live jack-off shows, the works. Tonight it's a dyke fetish party, and latex-clad enema nurses are chatting with Catholic schoolgirls. I came with my girlfriend, Aiden, who likes these parties more than I do. She's having fun, chatting up the cute little girls and boys; all of our friends are here. Every once in a while she brings me a beer, pats my head, kisses me, and then goes back to our circle of friends. Normally I'd join her, but tonight I'm too bored. The beer helps some, but not enough. I've just been hanging around the bar staring at people. I don't feel like dancing.

I head outside and bum a smoke from a group of shrieking, silly girls. A gorgeous redhead hands me a cigarette, but I decline her offer of a light. Instead I go look for some solo leather-jacketed type with a Zippo. Hey, we all have our fantasies. I don't even smoke; I just need something to wrap my lips around, something to do with my mouth and hands. When the sailor walks outside my spirits lift. She notices me, I hold my cigarette up to be lit, but we don't say anything. Up close she's even prettier. Blue eyes, black hair. I'm too tense to flirt with her, so I just look down at my hands.

"Are you having fun?" she says to me as she holds her silver Zippo to my cigarette.

I grasp her hand to steady the flame and she winks at me

in a gesture that's both boldly flirtatious and totally cheesy. "Not really," I answer.

"Seen it all before, huh?" I shrug and we stand there smoking in silence for a moment. Then she stubs out her cigarette and walks back inside.

I feel a foreign sensation as she leaves. At first I can't place it. And then I recognize it as desire.

Aiden joins me outside and I smoke another cigarette. I study her face closely. She's really gorgeous, I can pick em, I think to myself. She puts her arm around me protectively and walks me back through the door.

"What's downstairs?" I ask her.

"Private video booths that show fag porn, and rooms with curtains for anonymous sex."

"You're kidding," I say, and then I realize how naive I must sound. Of course, that's what is downstairs. "Let's go see." She looks at me quizzically and then says, "OK, let's go."

It's cooler downstairs. And quieter. Aiden is holding my hand, playing tour guide. She's telling me about the glory holes in the video booths, but I only half hear her. My thoughts are on the sailor, the way she lit my cigarette, the way she looks from the back, the way she walked away from me. I am dimly aware that Aiden is dragging me into one of the booths. "Let's watch porn," she says. "Come on, baby." She leads me in and shuts the door. "Don't worry, the doors lock." How handy, I think.

She puts some quarters into the slot and the screen lights up. The boys on the screen are really young. I'd guess barely 18. Mainly pretty and hairless, so I pretend they're cute butch girls playing at being boys. One girl is bent over a chair getting fucked. She's moaning. Her cock is rock hard-and she's stroking the hell out it. Aiden slips her hand under my T-shirt and pinches my nipple. I feel the throb in my clit.

My cunt becomes a liquidy place, like my head.

When Aiden and I fuck, I think about her hand in my

cunt. I concentrate on the sensations, the rhythmic circling or the pounding, the feeling of her skin on my skin. I think about how happy she makes me. But tonight I can't concentrate. My mind is too cluttered. I imagine the young boys on the screen. Their asses and hard cocks. I'm overstimulated. Aiden's hand is working me, playing me. She knows how, she knows where to stroke and how hard. She's doing it right, just like she did to me earlier, just like she'll do to me later, but I can't come. I'm not even close. "Come for me, baby," she whispers in my ear. "Show me how much you love me."

Frustrated, I turn away from her and face the wall. She follows me and pushes me down toward the small stool in the corner. I start to protest, not wanting to be on my knees on the floor in this booth where random guys have sucked random cocks, but I catch a glimpse of something through the glory hole that makes me change my mind. My sailor is in the next booth. She's leaning against the wall with her pants unzipped. Not doing anything really, just staring at the screen. I position myself for a better view, and this makes Aiden happy because she has better access to my cunt. I feel her hand run down the crack of my ass before she pulls it back and smacks me hard. She does it again, and this time I lean into it because it's something I can feel.

I can see my sailor clearly. She's staring intently at the screen. I wonder if she's watching the same two young boys I was looking at a few moments ago. The video is still playing. I can still hear them groaning. Her blue eyes are half closed and her hair is slightly messy. She is wearing some sort of binding thing around her chest to flatten her breasts. I am sure for just this moment that I'm in love with her.

She slips down her pants and briefs and slides a hand between her legs. I watch her fingers disappear into the vertical folds of her pussy and reappear glistening, over and over, making that slick tic tic sound. Her face is expressionless, she's just staring at the screen jerking off in the most perfunctory of ways.

Aiden is still fucking me, only now I can feel it. "Fuck me harder," I whisper to herm and she does, taking the opportunity to slide another finger in. She leans over me, presses her body across mine, fingers buried to the hilt in my pussy, and nuzzles my neck. I love her. She's an amazing lover and a loving girl-friend, but right now I'm thinking about the stranger in the next booth and Aiden is just a pair of hands on my body.

Aiden is really turned on; I can tell from the rough raw way she's pushing into me. It must be the porn working its magic. I'm hot too and really close to coming, but I hold on for sailor boy's sake. I can see her hands moving over her clit faster, and I fervently wish I could reach her with my tongue. I groan and push back against Aiden shamelessly in a way I know she loves. My sailor's mouth is open. She flicks her clit a few more times and tenses up, pressing her fingers down into a pussy I didn't get to touch or taste. It's enough, though; it pushes me over the edge and I gasp as I feel the wave of orgasm hit me.

Aiden stops moving momentarily, her fingers still inside my pussy. The sweat that's collected between our bodies has dried, and our skin is stuck together. "Don't move," she says to me. We stay like that for a few moments, and when I look again my sailor is gone.

For the Love of the Fuzzy Cup
Nicole Foster

"Make sure you spread that chocolate all the way into your pussy," P.J. said with a sexy smile and a slur.

The short and sweet (and sticky) gist of it is this: Somehow my lifelong (OK, six-month) dream of getting myself into the SoHo loft of dyke-about-town photographer P.J. Jones had actually come to fruition. For the past two years I'd been scratching and surviving as a waitress in the East Village lesbian restaurant the Fuzzy Cup—something I did to make ends meet so I could spend my free time working on my great American lezzie novel. I'd spotted P.J. around town and at the restaurant sometimes, but she'd always been a little cold—actually she was more like a goddamn iceberg. Whenever I waited on her at the Fuzzy Cup, she'd act like I didn't exist. She'd always return my subtle flirting with a robotic nod, preferring instead to bury herself in the piles of negatives and portfolios she'd have spread across her table.

But tonight I was in P.J.'s loft because the Fuzzy Cup was in dire financial straits, and Pattie and Melissa, the salt-and-pepper butches who ran the joint (who also happened to be P.J.'s best friends) had the zany idea of producing a fund-raising calendar called "The Girls of the Fuzzy Cup," with each month featuring one of the gorgeous dykes from the restaurant posing with a food item. Each spread also had a recipe to go along with it. When Melissa asked me if I'd cover my body in chocolate for the December page and have P.J. photograph me (in the nude!) in her loft, I forsook modesty and practically sprinted to her place from my railroad flat in Williamsburg.

So here I was, Cassie McConnell, a nice transplanted Irish girl from Nebraska, spread-eagle on P.J. Jones's sticky parquet floor. And before I get to the nitty-gritty, let me tell you this: P.J. Jones is no ordinary butch. No, she is a super-hottie. A dyed-in-the-wool butch with messy black hair, freaking azure eyes, and a sneer that would make even George W. Bush run for cover.

"I don't think I can reach this tiny spot," I said to P.J., in a campy but sultry whisper. She'd given me a big bucket of melted chocolate along with a clean paintbrush to access all the difficult-to-reach places—one of which happened to be my vulva.

"Well, I guess I'll just have to do it myself," she said flatly. I could tell by the empty Heinekens on the end table that she'd had a few beers before I'd come over. Which was fine by me. This was the loosest I'd ever seen Ms. I'm-Too-Scared-to-Look-Sexy-Femmes-in-the-Eye.

P.J. got down on her knees next to me on the floor. She dipped a long index finger into the chocolate mixture, then whispered, hot and heavy, into my ear, "Open up, Christmas Cassie."

And open up I did. But then P.J. did something surprising. Instead of applying the chocolate to my swollen lips, she inserted her finger into her luscious mouth and sucked the stuff right off. "Mmm," she said. "Now, I wonder what's sweeter? You or the candy?"

When my eyes grew big as chocolate coins, P.J. knew what to do. She went down on me faster than you can ring a dinner bell. In fact, she ate me out like I was her last meal ever. In between the chocolate and my flowing juices, my pussy was sopping wet. She focused her attention on my hard bud, taking it into her mouth and licking under the hood. "Oh, girl, you are sweet," my hot butch cried out.

She continued to slurp under the hood and around my clit, then flicked it back and forth with her tongue. I ran my fingers through her silky dark curls as she sucked and licked my entire vulva, her saliva mixing with my juices and the melted chocolate.

"I think there's probably a little more sugar deep inside," P.J. cooed, and boy, was I raring to go after that. She slid two fingers into my hungry hole—though, truth be told, I could have taken her entire fist. (Another night, another calendar...)

"Fuck me hard," I whispered in her ear. She was riding my body as she penetrated me, her stonewashed jeans and black tee sticking to the chocolate covering me from the neck down. My entire snatch was on fire as I gazed into those sexy baby blues. As she fucked me, she covered my mouth in sloppy wet kisses (just the way I like 'em).

"Fucking you hard is easy," she told me. "You're a goddamn goddess, Cass." With her left hand she ran her fingers through my long red curls, pulled my head back a little, and nipped me playfully on the neck.

"If I'm such a goddess, how come you never gave me the time of day before?" I panted while she fucked me like a jackhammer.

P.J. said nothing for a moment, then whispered, without looking me in the eye, "Just shy, I guess..."

I guess I'd hit a soft spot with her, because she pulled away a little then kissed a tender, sweet trail down my body. When she reached my plump tits and licked the chocolate right off my hard nips, I thought I was going to explode.

And man, did I explode! A huge, gooey, chocolatey-delightful orgasm traveled through my entire body—from my red-hot puss to my sticky abdomen to my breasts to my quivering lips. "Genius Chrysler!" I screamed out, my body hot and cold and shivering and burning and just plain ol' freaking out.

Afterward, I lay spent on her hardwood floor, a mess of chocolate and saliva and come covering us both.

"So, you think you'll be ordering in more often now?" I chuckled as P.J. ran a gentle hand over my well-worked snatch.

"Oh, yeah, Cass," she said. "I'm sure of it. But I'll tell you one thing: I'm real glad Melissa didn't ask you to be Miss July."

"How come?"

"That poor girl had to do hummus," she said, and we both laughed till we cried.

Marta's Power
Chris Baker

It's the third fight we've had in two weeks. It's never over anything that matters. We both need to be right. On some level I think she likes fighting. On some level I know I do too. But I'm sick of it. Marta's hold on me is making me crazy. She's gone over to her friend Dave's to do whatever it is she does when I'm not around. I have a moment of peace to sit and fume and plot to leave her. She has a key to my place, but this is it, after tonight I'm taking it back.

Each time it happens just like this. Each time I lie awake afterward waiting for the sound of her key in the door, wanting and not wanting to hear the solid switch and clack of metal as the deadbolt slides open. It must be 3 A.M. when I hear her come in. I immediately tense up. I curl on my side; my eyes open, I clench the sheet. I want to punish her for hurting me, for walking out on our argument, for walking out on me when she knows I'm pissed off.

She says my name, and I don't answer. I hear her curse when she trips over my shoes. "You're not speaking to me?" I can tell by the careful, overprecise way she says this that she's a little bit drunk, and it makes me a little afraid. At the same time I feel my pussy fatten up. I realize my clit aches, and has ached from the minute I heard her come in. I squeeze my thighs together. My eyes are hot and dry from crying ear-

lier, and from lack of sleep, and my head aches. Just her near-
ness makes me feel achingly open and wanting.

There was a couple in my high school. One girl was
leather-jacketed and had black hair and gray eyes that made
you feel as though, in her head, it was always winter. Her girlfriend was overwhelmingly in love. She was blond and small
and beautiful, and her eyes never left the face of her black-
haired lover, even in crowds of people. I remember con-
sciously thinking I would like to merge the two of them.
Marta is my synthesis. Lean as a whippet, but sturdy and
dark; sexy as a skate punk but all grown up and dangerous.

I feel her hand lift up the sheet and expose my back and
ass. The cool night air makes me feel more naked. I feel her
eyes on my skin. She strokes the side of my face and my hair,
lightly, delicately. I edge my shoulder away from her, playing
a game I know I shouldn't, but I can't help it; in spite of my
resolve to end this, I want her.

She cups her hand over my ass and strokes it, her fingers
dipping rudely in the crack of my ass. Her palm feels very
warm in the cold room, and she leaves it there for a moment,
letting me feel my nakedness. After a moment she stands up
and the mattress shifts from the loss of her weight. I can feel
her eyes on my back. The absence of her physical presence is
unbearable. And then she is once again beside me, gripping
her favorite cock.

"Are you ready to talk?" She kneels on the bed and slides
her hand up between my closed thighs, grabbing at my
exposed labia that are already slippery. I don't answer. "All
right. I know what you need." She rolls me onto my back and
pulls my thigh nearest her open so I am splayed. She puts her
hand over my pussy, cupping it, and whispers firmly in my
ear. "This," she says, "is mine."

This statement goes directly to my cunt; I can feel it swell
beneath her curved palm and spill between her fingers. I want
her to touch it more, deeper, to spread the lips. I want her to

work my juices around it and over it. My closed lips make me feel like a badly sealed envelope, and I want for her to open me, please just flick it open, work it, but again, I refuse to ask for anything.

She draws my hand from my pussy, up over my stomach, between my tits, to my throat, and rests it there, curved over my esophagus, pressing lightly. She strokes my throat in the same deliberate manner she did my ass. She squeezes. I spread my legs and stare directly upward, my chin pointing toward the ceiling, my breathing short and shallow. I lie under her hand like a grasshopper imprisoned in a child's fingers. She moves her hand down to my left breast and takes it in her hand, lifting, squeezing, then takes the nipple in her hand and pinches and pulls upward. I can't help moaning for the first time; the pain goes directly to my clit, and I can feel myself going a little crazy. "Aren't you going to say please?"

The smell of my cunt is filling up the room.

"Please."

"That didn't sound very sincere."

She squats between my spread legs, the expression on her face distant and in control. I could almost come at the sight of this face alone. She runs her fingers lightly over the gathered surface of my clit and labia grouped in her fingers. I squirm, I can't help myself, I strain upward for more pressure, and she holds my thighs down with her hands.

"Did I say you could move?"

"Please."

"Hold it open."

I do, and she raises her hand and smacks my poor neglected clit, sending shock waves through my body.

"Oh, God. Please."

"That's more like it. Keep holding it open."

Her tongue snakes into my pussy, working into the opening, fucking me slowly. She grabs my pubic hair again and sucks on my clit and labia. All of the blood that should be in my brain is in my cunt. She sits up and holds the cock in front of my eyes.

"You want this?"

"Yes." She holds my lips apart and pushes it into my pussy, working it around the opening at first, letting me feel it entering me. She presses her thumb onto my clit and fucks me, sending pulses into my clit in the same rhythm, and I come into her hand, raising my hips off the bed and fucking back, thoroughly for the first time, fucking her hand, my cunt closing around the dildo like a gripping hand.

Lost and Found

Amie M. Evans

My mother warned me about black-leather–jacketed Casanovas with their motorcycles, tattooed bodies, and tight jeans. My mother said they'd use my body, play with my head, make me feel like I was a princess; then, she warned, they'd break my heart. They were dead-end streets with only one thing on their minds—what was between their legs. My mother also told me if I was lost, a dead-end street was a perfect place to pull in, turn around, and get my bearings. If lost, she advised, find a dead-end street and stay there until you figure out where it is you are going. I always listen to my mother.

I knew as soon as I walked into the almost empty dyke bar that the black-leather–jacketed Casanova playing pool alone was the dead-end street my mother had told me to find if I was lost. And, God, was I lost. I'd been looking for six months for the pig-wrestling paddle artist the tea-leaf fortune teller had told me about. I wasn't sure such a creature existed; I wasn't even sure anymore if I was a princess.

As I walked across the bar to the pool table, I had no intention of letting her break my heart with her tattooed body. As I peeled off my leather jacket and exposed my almost bare shoulders, I was confident she'd make me feel like a princess again. And as I shifted my hip up onto the side of the table, leaning forward to make sure my cleavage showed, I wondered exactly what she had in her tight jeans.

She looked up at me—or more correctly, at my breasts— then, still holding her gaze on me, took the shoot she'd lined up and walked to my side of the table as the balls scattered.

She leaned up against the table, holding the cue out from her body like a staff, and stood there just waiting.

"The place is dead." I said.

She shrugged. Looked me over running her eyes down my body to the tips of my spike-heeled boots.

"Want to play?" she asked.

"Yeah, but not pool," I answered, getting up from the table, pressing my body against hers and cupping my hand over her crotch. Casanova wasn't packing, which was fine since I had my favorite dildo in my purse. My mother also told me a lady needs to be prepared for an emergency. This was definitely an emergency. I was definitely a prepared lady.

Her eyes jumped as my hand made contact, but she stayed cool. "All right," she said as she looked around for where to go. I tilted my head toward the restrooms and took the lead. At the end of the hall was a door that led to an enclosed courtyard used for holding the trash. I'd been here before.

As soon as we emerged into the dark courtyard she pushed me up against the brick wall. The surface was hard on my face and bare chest, her hands rough on my thighs working their way up under my short skirt to my bare ass.

"What shall we play?" She hissed into my ear.

"Hide-and-seek," I cooed pushing my ass toward her. "You hide, I'll seek."

"And what shall I hide?" she squeezed my ass then ran her fingers lightly over my labia.

"Look in my purse—you'll find something to hide."

Her hands left my body and she released me from my position against the wall as she took my purse and pulled out the eight-inch dick. Holding it in front of her, she asked, "You want me to hide this?" She grinned, then tossed my purse and the toy at my feet. "No. I've got something far better to hide. Something that will—let's say—appreciate the experience of being hidden." She grinned as she pulled me toward her, then pinned me to the wall by my wrists. Her tongue licked my neck, starting at my ear and working its way down to my cleavage. Her hips ground into mine as her teeth bit into my nipples through my shirt.

She released my wrist and pulled the spaghetti straps off of my shoulders, exposing my breasts. Her tongue licked, her lips sucked, her teeth bit as her hands forced my legs open. Her fingers were calloused against the delicate flesh of my labia. She found my clit quickly and worked it in small circles. My cunt was dripping wet.

"Fuck me," I ordered. "Fuck me, please," I said more softly, pushing my pelvis against her hand.

She slipped one finger inside my pussy.

"More," I groaned.

She pulled her wet finger out and ran it over my clit then slipped three fingers inside me. She pumped in and out and pressed her upper body hard against mine.

I moved my hips in time with her strokes.

"More," I moaned.

She pulled me down onto the cold dirty concrete floor of the courtyard. She was half on top of me her fingers still deep inside me.

"Fuck me," I told her. "I want you inside me."

She groaned, then leaned forward, her lips sealing over mine in a deep kiss as her last finger and thumb entered me.

For a moment I felt the pressure, the tight pulling of my vaginal flesh as her knuckles pushed to enter my cunt. I held my breath, bore down meeting her gentle inward thrust, and swallowed her fist whole with my pussy.

I exhaled as every nerve ending in my body became electrified. She looked directly into my eyes, and I held her intense gaze. Her fist moving inside me, sending shock waves of intense pleasure throughout my body. She gradually increased the power of her thrusts as I rocked on her arm.

My cunt stretched and tingled, ached, and throbbed. She used her free hand to work my clit as she continued to thrust deep inside of my pussy.

She had my body under her complete control, impaled on her arm, but she also had my soul in those moments she was deep inside me. In that instant, I was in love with her, I'd die for her, and I felt like a real princess.

I came hard; my cunt squeezed her fist as my whole body shook with the overload of sensation.

She pulled out slowly, wiped her wet hand on her jeans, and helped me up. I grabbed my purse and tucked the now-inferior, formerly favorite dildo into it.

"Karen Whitty," she said

"Amie." I smiled

"Just Amie?" she asked.

"No, Princess Amie."

"Well, Princess Amie, can I buy you a beer?"

My mother was correct. Dead-end streets are a perfect place to get your bearings when lost. I felt focused. I felt certain I could find the pig-wrestling artist. My mother was right about the black-leather–jacketed Casanovas. It's true they'll break your heart. Karen Whitty broke my heart, but not that night. That night she made me feel like a princess, exactly like my mother said she would.

Hung Up
Beth Black

I've been doing phone sex for about six months now. This is the longest I've been at any job, and to be frank, I'm starting to get bored. I'm a single mom and a painter, and phone sex is one of the few jobs I can do from home on my own schedule, so I'm trying to stick with it. But sometimes I think if one more guy tells me to tell him how much I love sucking his dick, while I supposedly have his dick in my mouth, I'm going to switch to telemarketing.

That was how I felt until last week anyway. It was Thursday. My son, Max, was at school. I'd had coffee, eaten breakfast, taken a shower, thrown on some jeans and a sweatshirt, and finally called in to the office to let them know I was taking calls. Lorna, the gorgeous MTF who does dispatch, picked up the phone, and after some requisite flirting (She loves soft butches like me—what can I say?) she told me I was in luck.

"We just got a very special caller I think you're going to love," she said. Since this type of comment generally indicates that some gross stockbroker wants me to pretend to be his niece, I wasn't too excited. But I got comfortable and took the call anyway.

"Hello. Who is this?" I breathed in what I hoped was a lusty schoolgirl voice.

"Don't say anything for a minute. Just listen." The voice on the phone said. But there wasn't anything I could say. I was struck dumb because the voice on the phone was no niece-baiting stockbroker—it was a woman.

"I'm standing in front of you. I'm 5-6," she said. "I have short brown hair; I'm handsome. I'm naked except for two items. I'm wearing a pair of well-shined leather work boots, and I'm strapped into a leather harness. My harness is wide and black. It's sitting up high on me so you can get a nice view of my cunt underneath it. If you saw me from behind, you'd admire how my harness frames my nice round ass. But remember, you're sitting in front of me, so what you're really focused on right now is what I've got on in the front. I'm wearing a nice big, black dick in my harness, and I have one hand on it right now. I'm playing with my dick and looking down at you, and your lips are a little open because you are a hungry little girl. You want my dick, and you want my cunt, and you want them bad."

I was floored. I usually feel completely in control of my callers—but this woman was running the show for sure. My pussy was wet the moment I first heard her voice, and I was totally intrigued by the picture of her standing in front of me, showing me her hard cock. I was definitely going to play along with this one, even if I wasn't sure what we were playing.

"Mmm. Your cock looks so good," I told her. "I want to feel it filling my throat." This time I didn't have to try for the sultry voice—I wanted that cock for real.

"Not yet. First I want you to pull off your pants and your panties and take your shirt off. All I want you to wear is your bra."

I couldn't help but up the ante for myself. Instead of just playing along on the phone, I pulled off my clothes for real and sat down in the warm sun of my kitchen wearing only my bra. It was some utilitarian white cotton thing, but I had a feeling she was looking for femme. Call me a transvestite, but I have femme dress-up fantasies all the time, and I wasn't about to lose this opportunity by telling her about my bad fashion sense.

"OK, I'm ready. I'm naked except for my tits. They're pushing out of my tight black lace bra."

"Tell me what big tits you have."

Well, this one I wouldn't have to lie about. "My big double D tits are so full and firm right now, I wish you could see them. My nipples are achingly hard for you. They're pushing out through the lace in my bra." I pinched at my nipple as I talked to her. Each pinch sent a jolt through my wet pussy.

"Nice," she said quietly. I could tell she was turned on. "Now push your tits together and lean forward." I did. "Do you feel me rubbing my dick against your tits?"

"Mmm. Yes-s-s," I hissed as I squeezed and pinched at myself where I was imagining her dick.

"I'm pushing my dick in between your big tits and fucking you. How do you feel when I fuck your tits like this?"

"Oh, I feel so dirty! It makes my pussy so wet!" I moaned.

"Good, good," she breathed. "Now you're going to suck my cock. Do you want my cock, little girl?"

"Please let me swallow your cock. Please, I want your big dick down my throat, I want to feel you fucking my mouth." I wanted it so bad, I was sticking my own fingers into my mouth and nursing them. I could almost feel her dick poised at my lips, ready to force into me.

"Good girl. Now open your lips for me. Do you feel me shoving into you? Do you feel me shoving my big cock into your soft little mouth? Do you feel it?" Her breathing was growing unsteady fast. I could tell she was jacking off thinking about me.

"Mmm-hmm. Yes. Mmm." I moved my fingers from my mouth down to my soaking wet pussy and found my swollen clit and began to rub.

"You like sucking my dick, don't you? You like it don't you? You're a good little cocksucker. Such a good cocksucker."

I propped the phone between my shoulder and ear so I could free up both hands. While I moaned and panted into the phone, I reached three fingers into my pussy and used my other hand to rub feverishly against my clit.

"I'm pulling you off my cock. Do you know why, baby?"

"Please don't make me stop. Please let me suck you." I felt desperate for her dick as I rocked my hands on my pussy.

"I'm pulling you off my cock because you're going to suck my cunt. Can you smell my cunt?"

Smelling my own pussy in the warm kitchen, listening to her firm voice on the phone, she seemed so close. And at this moment, all I wanted in the world was to lap at her juicy cunt, suck her big hard clit, and swallow every drop of her thick, sweet creamy come.

"Please, please! I want your cunt so much, please let me bury my face in your wet cunt!" I was yelling into the phone, fucking my cunt with my fingers so hard that my chair was rocking.

"Eat it. Eat my cunt, eat it, eat it." I could hear her getting close. She wanted to come as bad as I wanted to. She was panting into the phone. Moaning. Barely articulate now, occasionally repeating her demand that I eat her.

Suddenly I felt myself coming. One minute I was fucking my pussy, rubbing the heal of my hand against my fat clit, and then suddenly I was coming and coming, screaming into the phone, "Yes! Yes! Yes!" And as my coming slowed to shudders, I could hear her dimly on the other side grunting as she was getting there too.

"Suck my clit, slut! Suck it!" she shouted, and then her voice caught and she sharply sucked in air once, twice.

My fingers rested on my clit while I tried to recover.

I listened to her, a voyeur, as she finished coming. I waited while her breathing became regular, and we mewed sweetly at each other, "Oh, so good." "Such a sweet cocksucker." We were quiet for a moment and then, suddenly, she hung up.

Sex Hall
MR Daniel

The hallway is narrow. I had expected it to be less bare—
there are no pictures on the walls, which have all been painted dark reds, slick mahoganies, and purples. I laugh to
myself. The colored girls must have had fun checking out
swollen pussies when they were painting this. The lights are
sunk deep into the ceiling and turned down low so it's lit like
a club. A house diva is wailing through the P.A. system,
backed up by an insistent fuck-me-baby, fuck-me-baby
tempo. I feel like I'm in a peep show.

Brown, bronze, and various sun-kissed women move past
me, some with their eyes straight forward, nervous, others whose
eyes seem to burn a path before them. I feel their heat as they
pass. There's a steady pulsing below my skin as I move forward,
the current stopping and starting. I feel the blood push-flow-
push-flow through my neck and fingers, my heart growing, forcing blood into my breasts. I pass the first doorway and hesitate.
The door is open, but I'm suddenly afraid to be caught looking.

Someone behind me stops to look over my shoulder, and
her fingers inquire at my leg. I feel her questions all the way
up and into my stomach. I almost jump into the room, and
there is laughter behind me. I catch my breath, surprised at
my confusion. This morning I was so sure of what I wanted,
what I felt, but now...excitement? Pleasure? Fear?

Didn't I want to be fucked from behind, anonymously?
A voice in my says, "Look forward, baby, or I'll leave."
And, "I know you're wet."
And, "When I remember how you look I'm going to think about parting your bush, how you almost reached behind to guide my hands. But I told you not to move. *Don't move.*"

Hiking up skirt, pulling down panties, the snap of a glove, and a hand between my legs. Fucked in a doorway. Fingers up my cunt, feeling the space in my flesh, pushing deeper and rubbing till there's this cross between a sharpness and pleasure, my muscles filled with blood, taut, filling and pressing until I think I'm going to pee on the floor.

My mouth is filled with stars, and they're burning their way through my vagina. They hurl through my chest, and I can't breathe; sweat collects in the band of my skirt. They light up nerves, sending shocks to my clit and behind my eyelids. I salivate as she works her hand in farther. I pant; my cunt pants for her and the feeling of stars.

I'm high, nipples sharp from the sound of her inside me. I'm straining against damp fabric, pores fucked alert, open, wanting to feel air on sweat and oil steeped skin, as I brace myself in the doorway.

Bodies passing by us go quiet as another finger goes in my puckering ass, tilted to receive, and lips circle my neck, her tongue leaving a trail that ends with a mouth clamped on the back of my throat, kissing, sucking hard, until a half-moon appears. I wanna come bad, but I could stay here forever.

Can you fuck too much? Can you feel too good? Can you be so ripe that you keep bursting and swelling, bursting and swelling until a mouth bites you open again? Her teeth burn into my ass, she whips the hand out of my cunt, and I feel the air leave my chest; my breasts suddenly get heavy and full. Her hand spanks my ass, my skin wet and hot, and enters me again like horses. I swear I'm gonna drop to my knees as the finger in my ass moves back and forth, teasing the rim of my anus. I feel myself coming, raging against the horses, grasping them, thrusting them out as they lunge, push, farther inside. She holds on to me. "That hand isn't going anywhere," she says.

I feel come like hushed spurts, warm like blood, flowing out of me. I'm on my knees; my unconscious fingers take her horse hand, arching as I pull her out of me, and rub her against my lips and clit. I feel like a dog, mouth open and bent over, writhing against her hand, I'm not thinking anymore, just doing what feels good. She doesn't pull away. I come again; air passes through my throat, and I hear a sound like the last breath as you break the surface of water. Doubled over, breathing hard, I pull away from the finger in my ass and pass her other hand from between my legs. I lick my juice from her glove and pull the latex off. My tongue dives for the skin in between her fingers. This is how I will remember her: by her hands. She helps me up from behind, pulling up my panties stretched and tangled in my boots, her fingers spread wide, feeling me up as she pulls down my skirt.

She bites my neck and says, "It's too bad you came early," and rubs her pelvis against the crack of my behind. I can feel her packing. Well, I'm sorry too.

"Next time," she says, her hands firm on my hips, teasing, pressing into, circling against me, slowly. "It's underneath my black vinyl shorts, it peeks through a little cause they're short shorts like the ones the reggae dance-hall queens wear. Zippers up the sides, I only wear them here."

"How do you know you're the only one?" I ask. She can't see me smile.

"Well, if I'm not, we'll find out soon enough," she laughs, and bites the half moon she left before. I listen to her walk away.

Boots, I guess, with heavy soles.

Follow the Sun

Sara Aletti

"Kathy?"

"Yes?"

"Kathy, it's…been too long. I've missed you. It's Judy."

The sweet, high voice, the hesitant rhythm of her speech—I knew it was Judy before she said it.

"It has been a long time." I tried to sound cool. I've never loved anyone as much as Judy—and no one had ever hurt me as much.

"Do you think we could get together? Tonight or some night soon? I'd like to talk."

"Sure." I took down the address, showered and dressed, and packed my dick in an overnight bag. I was ready to make amends if she was.

Happy as I was, I was also wary. We had gone out for a year and lived together for two years. We complemented each other perfectly, sexually and socially. She was a perfect bottom: cute, feminine, sweet-natured. Blindly submissive, she delighted in being on her knees taking whatever I gave her. And I never felt more powerful than when I was fucking her hot, slick cunt.

I wanted to see her again, but I was afraid to admit to myself—let alone her—how vulnerable I was. I hate feeling weak, and when she left me, she made me feel very weak.

But I went, with misgivings.

I was stunned when she answered the door. Even silhouetted by the hall light, I could see that Judy was very, very pregnant. I immediately felt awkward.

"Come in, Kathy."

I walked into a small apartment, furnished sparsely but nicely. Judy always displayed good taste.

"Usual?" she asked. I nodded and she made her way into the small kitchen. She leaned into the fridge with difficulty to retrieve a beer while I sat on the sofa.

"How was it," I asked hesitantly, snapping open the can. "With a man?"

"It was OK. It was kind of fun to play with a dick that squirts. Only," she said, cradling her belly, "this is what happens when they squirt."

She smiled at my discomfort and rubbed my leg. "His dick wasn't as big or hard as yours, though."

"Well, yeah. Nothing short of a couple of minutes in a microwave can make *my* dick limp."

We laughed, and I began to feel more comfortable. It was like the old days. I put my arms around Judy and kissed her, not without difficulty since her belly stuck out so far. I was surprised at the passion with which she kissed me back.

"I missed your tits," she whispered when I took my tongue back. She pulled me hard against her protruding body. "I missed the taste of your cunt. I want them again."

I was taken aback when she grabbed my crotch and began to massage me. Good God, she was horny. Her scent brought back those lazy weekend mornings when we'd lie in each other's arms watching shafts of sunlight crawl from one side of the room to the other. We had a little game: When the sun hit the foot of the bed, I'd start on the soles of her feet and her toes, and I'd follow the sun with my tongue as it moved up her body. It was like a fresh seduction each time—slow and luxurious. By the time I got to her deep, warm kiss, she'd be good and wet, and I'd wrap her legs around my neck and fuck her long and fiercely.

God, how I'd missed those excursions up and down Judy's soft, sweet body.

"I don't feel very attractive," she said in a little voice. She stood and looked down at her feet—actually toward her feet, since I doubt she could see them. "But I do feel stronger than ever. And you know what? I like the feeling of being pregnant."

"It's huge," I said, putting both hands on her belly as she stood before me. "Do you know what sex it is?"

"No, I decided to be surprised."

I had to ask. "The father?"

"He bolted when I told him I was pregnant. Said he wasn't ready. Neither was I, but I couldn't run." She smiled as she sat back down. "Actually, I'm relieved that he left. I might actually have married him. Now I can bring up this baby the way I see fit."

Judy seemed to be taking this pretty casually, but I felt upset, even close to tears. I took her in my arms again. I wanted to help her, to protect her. "I'll take care of you," I sputtered.

Judy looked at me, quizzically at first, then smiled. "You think I need taking care of? That's very sweet."

"You're alone and pregnant, honey, you need—"

"OK. You can take care of me, Kathy. Here's how you can start."

She unbuttoned her blouse all the way and presented me her breasts in cupped hands. They were immense. Her nipples had swelled to twice their size, and turned a dark, luscious mocha color.

I unbuckled her belt and pulled her skirt down around her ankles. I couldn't keep my eyes off of her naked belly. Putting my hand on its bare skin, I realized it was stretched tight as a drum. Her navel stuck out like a doorknob. I kissed it as she eased her panties down. I wouldn't have imagined it, but I found the sight of her swollen belly and bloated breasts enormously exciting.

She pulled me up by the hand and walked me to the bedroom. She lay back on the bed, hooking her arms under her legs to pull them as far out of the way as possible. Her moist cunt lips parted as she splayed her legs, revealing her innermost folds and little button of a clit. Like her nipples, it seemed to have swelled with her pregnancy.

"Eat me," she said.

I quickly took off my shirt and vest and stepped out of my jeans. In the back of my mind I wondered if it would be like it used to be. Could I be rough? Would I be able to snap my belt over those pillowy ass cheeks or ram my dick deep into her body?

Kneeling before the power of her womanhood, I resolved to be gentle. I massaged her ass cheeks while I kissed her sweet, moist sex, hidden like a mine at the base of her mountainous belly.

She groaned and began to writhe under my tongue. I was going to make her beg for it like in the old days, but she forced my mouth violently against her pussy. She bucked up and down and swiveled from side to side. Soon her sopping nest covered my face with a thick sap. Her climax was so violent I nearly suffocated in her muff.

We were both gasping as I moved up next to her. She took one of her big heavy tits in her hand.

"Open your mouth," she said

I wasn't used to taking orders, but in deference to her delicate condition—I don't know why they call it delicate; there's nothing delicate about it—I obeyed. She pulled on her tit and squeezed her swollen nipple hard between her thumb and forefinger. Fascinated, I watched the nipple bristle until it began to squirt milk all over my face. I recoiled at first, but then, instinctively, I latched onto the big, fat nipple and began to suck. My mouth was immediately filled with warm, sweet milk.

"Drink it," she said. I swallowed and quickly filled my mouth with more, getting the hang of the rhythm of sucking and swallowing. She cradled my head in her arms while I sucked on her mama's milk. I had the curiously attractive feeling of being like a little baby at her mother's tit.

When I had milked her I said, "What should we do? I brought my dick...but I didn't know..."

"That's not a good idea. Not at this stage."

I nuzzled her flaccid nipple until her tits and my face turned sticky from the drying milk.

"Let me have your dick," she said quietly. "Shame to let it go to waste. Indulge me."

I was shocked. Had her condition gone to her head? I'd heard of pregnant women's moods, of having to appease them in the middle of the night with ice cream and stuff like that. But to let her stick my own dick into me seemed an awfully big indulgence. I mean, this was the woman who spent the last couple years on her knees, begging to suck my cock, begging me to stick it brutally into whatever hole struck my fancy. Now she wanted to strap on my dick and fuck me?

Keeping her hand firmly on my leg, she turned me over onto my back, crawled over me, and started on my tits. My tits are small and sensitive, and she knew it, so she clamped her teeth down hard enough to make me wince. While I protested, she slipped her fingers into me, first one, then two, then three. I tried to pull away, but she had me locked into her embrace by her arm around my waist and her teeth on my tit.

I couldn't believe it. Judy was working her fist into my cunt. I don't allow much in there—a tongue, maybe a couple of fingers. But I had never felt anything like this: a brilliant, sharp pain at the entrance, and as she slipped her

knuckles past my lips, I felt a monstrously satisfying full-
ness, maybe even fulfillment, like I was a puzzle being completed, a machine with a missing part sliding into place.

I grabbed my feet and hiked up my legs so she could penetrate me as deeply as possible. I gasped—I bet my eyes
bulged—as her hand slipped in with a sigh up to the wrist.
My cunt lips grabbed it and sucked it in until it lodged, from
the feel of it, somewhere in my chest. She spread her fingers,
and it felt like a blossoming flower inside me, like that slow-
motion photography in nature movies...like the fetus swelling
in her belly.

My climax began deep within me, like a pinpoint, tiny
and sharp. Judy was reaching for it, rooting around inside
my body, trying to pull it out of me. Gradually, as she
slipped her hand in and out of my cunt, my climax rose,
like shock waves rising from the depths after an earth-
quake on the ocean floor. It magnified and intensified until
it was ready to break the surface. Gasping and shuddering,
I grabbed one of her tits with both hands and massaged it,
forcing more sweet, sticky milk into my mouth. White liquid ran out of my mouth, into my eyes, and all over my
face as Judy, her free hand twisted in the short hair at the
back of my neck, forced my head back against her breast,
nearly smothering me. I swallowed the wrong way and
began to choke. Finally she grabbed hold of my climax
and dragged it out of me. Long, brutal spasms nearly doubled me up. Again and again I came in waves, as Judy
forced her arm deeper and deeper inside me. I couldn't
breathe. It was like she had hold of my lungs, squeezing
the air out of them.

When Judy finally pulled her hand out of my cunt, I felt
cold and empty.

She rose, waddled over to my bag, and pulled out my
dick. She examined it, smiling, then slid it in and out of her
mouth, its harness trailing like ribbons.

"Mmm," she said, "I can't remember how many times I've sucked on him."

She stepped into the harness and strapped it around her waist. I watched her in mounting alarm, the hanging dick threatening me. I closed my legs and shook my head.

"I don't know about this..." I whined. "I don't...I can't..."

But I was powerless. She easily spread my legs and positioned my dick over my own cunt. I was so wet and open, she just leaned in to fill me. It surprised me how easy it was. She held me by the ankles, putting my toes in her mouth as she began to pump me, gently at first, then with increasing speed and force. The rhythm lulled me and I just closed my eyes, lay back, and welcomed a series of brilliant climaxes that seemed to go on forever.

I fell asleep in her arms, licking at the milk dripping from her nipples.

That morning, the sun rose and slipped over the sill. I stumbled over to the window, raised it and leaned out to breathe in the morning air. It was late spring, and even in the brick-bound city, the air smelled of flowers and grass.

I thought back over last night. Fucked with my own dildo. Fisted by my femme. There might be some philosophical, yin-yang thing about switching, but I wasn't so sure I liked it. I wasn't about to start wearing cute dresses and saying "yes, sir," "no, sir" to dykes, not when I was used to giving orders.

"I'm a top gun," I said to myself, mentally mixing metaphors, "not a bottom feeder." Yet here was my former femme, when she should have been at her most vulnerable, demanding I suck her dry and sticking her fist up my cunt.

I heard Judy stir behind me. I turned to see her. She made such a big lump it looked like there was somebody else under the covers with her, which, in a sense, there was. As she stretched, the covers slid off, revealing her bloated breasts and Tootsie Roll nipples. I felt a twinge in my cunt as I remembered sucking them dry last night, and I wondered if she'd be ready for milking again.

"Come here," she said. "Look at the sun, Kathy. It's reached the foot of the bed." The tips of her toes were so brightly lit they glowed like the Madonna's fingers in a painting.

"Start there," she said, wiggling her sweet toes in anticipation of my tongue. "And follow the sun."

I did.

Confession

Amy Barber and Gina Chopp

Just as I was regretting my lack of resistance about being dragged to church, the priest, forehead beading with sweat, launched into his predictable sermon about the ever-virgin Mary. Not that I wasn't grateful for a homily that strayed from the usual praise of Catholic patriarchy, but I found it difficult to look up to a woman whose unwanted pregnancy was chalked up to the heavens—a celestial miracle. The only miracle I could gather was that Joseph and millions of other "believers" were gullible enough to buy the story. If only it had been so easy to convince my mother that the moans she heard coming from my bedroom when Karen spent the night were bedtime prayers.

If it had been any other Sunday, not Mother's Day, I probably would have refused to come along, much less be coerced into wearing khaki pants and a stuffy collared shirt. I could tell the May heat was draining energy out of everyone in the crowded church. I glanced around at a sea of parishioners halfheartedly fanning themselves with hymnals. At least those were good for something.

Staring past my grandmother and mother to count the panes on the stained glass window for the third time, I noticed a girl who looked as bored and tired as I was. Until then, I assumed I was the only one accustomed to the typical college routine, which did not include waking up early enough for 11 o'clock mass. Maybe it was the knee-high socks and plaid skirt that had initially allowed me to dismiss her as a God-fearing goody-two-shoes. Sorority types had never made for hot fantasies in lecture, let alone eye candy at mass. But the roll of her eyes as they met with mine was the first indication that my original impression was misleading.

Discovering an ally amid the plethora of churchgoers inspired me to test her level of commitment to proper church etiquette. Fingering through the hymnal in my lap, I opened to a random page and remembered a game I once played with my kid sister. Borrowing the putt-putt-size pencil normally reserved for making welcomed last-minute church donations, I searched the page for words that would create an amusing sentence to entertain us both.

"I want this to end." Smiling at my own luck, I slid the book along the pew as everyone knelt for the blessing of the gifts. Soon she was diligently penning a message of her own, and as the congregation stood once more, she glanced at me with a look of triumph and pushed the book back along the pew. The intensity of the organ, announcing the beginning of communion, was not enough to drown out the pounding that was slowly formulating in my chest as a result of her reply. She sacrilegiously had circled "I want to give thanks to your body."

Before I had time to analyze her response, we were waiting in line to receive the ritual intake of the body and blood of Christ, or, as I prefer to call it, spiritual cannibalism. The three-person distance between us was reduced to nothing when my mother and grandmother stopped for wine.

Rounding the corner, she too noticed my position directly behind her, and this miniskirted devil raised the stakes once more. Conspicuously scratching her thigh, she simultaneously lifted her skirt just enough to reveal flesh where underwear should have been. At this moment I found the courage to catch up to her and whisper, "Keep walking," Just as Adam accepted the apple from Eve, she consented to my proposition with a backward offering of her hand, leading me to a temptation that would remain with me for eternity.

She brought me to the last of a series of confessionals and pulled me behind a thick velvet curtain. Immediately, she unfastened my belt as I anxiously slipped each button through its hole on her blouse. I parted the garment with trembling hands, exposing a sea of tanned skin. Her breasts were small, and seeing them with her complexion momentarily brought me back to summer swimming lessons in middle school. Surrounded by the tight glistening bodies of those early crushes, I discovered for the first time that water wasn't the only thing that could make me wet.

The same bashful bliss came over me now as I blessed her exposed skin with moist kisses. She tossed the shirt aside with passion, freeing her hands to unzip my pants. Before it reached the floor, we saw the blouse drape itself over an object in the corner. We leaned in mutual curiosity toward it. Underneath sat a bottle of red wine.

"Apparently parishioners aren't the only ones with sins to confess in these booths," she smirked. Uncorking the bottle, she tilted it gently between her breasts. The rouge liquid ran in slow streams over her hard nipples.

"Not anymore," I replied. The hot pressure of my tongue eagerly lapped the streams back to their origin. I felt her manicured nails dig deep in my back. Ignoring the trails of wine, my mouth made a new path to her skirt. The fingers of my right hand reached up to caress erect nipples, but instead found themselves encased in her mouth. Her teeth and tongue skillfully removed each silver ring.

"Mind if I borrow these?" she asked.

I responded by bunching her skirt above her waist while my tongue caressed the crease made by her thighs and hips.

Falling to my knees, I lifted her leg toward heaven and laid it to rest on the wooden bench. With her spread before me, I could see she was swollen with excitement. Her thighs quivered with anticipation as I leaned in slowly and brushed my tongue along the tip of her clit. She shook, pulling air into her lungs with quick gasps.

Outside the confessional the organ had ceased. The heavy silence made me worry about this girl's potential to be loud. Real loud. I decided to take my chances. I rolled my tongue in circles around her clit, touching it ever so briefly after each swirl, until she whimpered. Her soft whimpering turned to moans as I danced playfully up and down her clit. Her knuckles kneading into my back, she abandoned her will to be quiet.

"Oh, God," she screamed, filling the tiny confessional with her exclamation. "Please," she begged, "please go inside me." Testing my own patience, I waited until the muscles of her pussy pulsed with desire. As she opened her mouth to scream again, I easily slid two fingers past her naturally lubricated labia and watched them disappear to the knuckle. Inside her, I traced the soft tissue with the tips of my fingers, flexing them simultaneously as if I were motioning her toward me. She rocked her hips in time with my thrusts, inviting me deeper. She eagerly welcomed two more fingers, and her excitement increased when I resumed my tongue massage over her throbbing clit.

"Oh, God. Oh, God. Oh, God," she continued, sliding her sweaty palms down the wood paneling. I increased the pressure of my tongue, pushing my fingers harder and faster. She tasted exquisite. My khakis clung damply to my crotch, and just as I was fantasizing about this beautiful stranger returning the favor, the bell in the church tower rang once. Eleven more rings and church would be out. It was now or never I thought, wincing at the irony of mass ending too soon.

Timing each thrust with the subsequent rings, I prayed that the girl would finish. Taking my cue, she held each scream long enough to be drowned out by the next bell. On the 12th and final clang, she baptized my hand with her warm juices. Heaving, I pulled my fingers slowly out of her and wiped the soaking hand along my pants. The shuffle of parishioners could be heard directly outside the velvet curtains. With an ecstatic grin and a few adjustments to her hair and clothes, she was ready to go. I nodded goodbye in disbelief, a bit shy now that it was over.

"Thanks," she muttered, and she slinked out of the room to file in with the crowd.

Stakeout

Lynne Jamneck

The phone's incessant ring tries to force me from my bed—and a recurring nightmare about becoming a defense lawyer.

Could be my current client, ready to fire me because I couldn't catch his star employee in the act of pulling off yet another deal on company time.

I grab the receiver. "Hello?"

"Jaye, is that you?"

The voice is familiar, and I mentally run through the files in my head for a name, some bar code of identification. Then I remembered: That voice had been carefully filed with numerous other little bits in the folder labeled "Leave Well Enough Alone."

Subject: Alison Moore. How ironic that the person on the phone is the same one who inspired that rotten lawyer nightmare that made its way into my subconscious. She also inspired some other ideas in my very conscious mind; thoughts that I immediately told myself were inappropriate and unprofessional.

"Oh, Alison. How've you been?" Really smooth.

"Busy as always, you know. I need your help."

"What's up?"

"One of my clients is up for murder, and his alibi has conveniently disappeared. You're good at finding missing people, and I need this guy found. Fast."

For pity's sake. As if there weren't enough complications in my life already. Like the rent that needs to be paid in four days, I remind myself. This is like manna from heaven, for God's sake, and you want to pass because you can't control your hormones for five minutes? "Give me half an hour, OK?"

"You know the way."

I could almost swear I heard a smile round her very kissable mouth. Already the thoughts of what I'd want to do with her behind (but not necessarily) a closed door was starting to creep back into my everyday conscious.

• • •

Alison was sitting behind her desk, and she motioned for me to come in while she finished a conversation on the phone. I walked over to stand in front of the window, suddenly very aware of her authoritative voice as she finished off her conversation.

It was a bit of a mystery to me why I found her so intriguing; being quite strong-willed myself, I normally didn't find myself gravitating toward fiercely independent women.

Relationships where both parties want to be in control normally don't work out. It makes for great sex, though, I couldn't help but think.

" God damn it. Sorry about that, Jaye." Alison got out of her high-backed chair and, before I could hold out my hand for her to shake, put her arms round my neck and hugged me close.

The professional suits she wore to work hid her magnificently athletic body, and I couldn't stop myself from running one hand slowly up her back to remind myself. Even worse, the white polo neck she had chosen today showed off the curves of her perfect breasts to the maximum. I pulled out of our embrace, for fear of pushing her back into that leather chair and having my way with her.

"So." I raked a hand through my hair. "Who's the elusive witness?"

Alison kept my eyes for a moment, the curve of a smile playing around the corners of her mouth. She knew exactly how to push my buttons, quite an achievement for someone who had kissed only me once.

"Mr. Harold Pincher. Came forward a week ago to testify that my client was with him the night of the murder and has now disappeared."

"Why don't you just put the cops on his ass? "

She smiled. "Cops don't like me, and I don't like them. Oil and water kind of thing. I'm sure, in your line of work, you know what I mean."

I folded my arms, leaned back against the wall coyly, and smiled. If this was what she wanted, I supposed I could play the game just as well. I have a pretty good idea what women like, and I was very aware Alison was encouraging my every move.

"I have a pretty decent understanding with cops, actually. I help them; they return the favor."

Alison smirked. "I bet you drive the girls in uniform crazy. Those moody eyes must make them grab for their batons."

I burst out laughing, not able to wipe the self-assured grin off my face. Damn, damn, damn the rent! Alison was smiling at me, the invitation in her blue eyes teasing me mercilessly. I could have her right here on the desk, and she'd let me. "So OK, I'll see if I can find the elusive Mr. Pincher. Hope he doesn't bite."

"I'm sure you could handle it," Alison added.

I turned on my heel there and then. My body was starting to override my mind on a magnificent scale, and that usually got me into trouble.

"Call me," Alison added as I pulled the door to her office shut.

• • •

After finding out from his landlady that Harold was a "loudmouth Irish nitwit who typically drank too much," I started combing all the Irish pubs within a five-mile radius. It didn't take long at all to find him, hiding in the corner of the bar, nursing a Guinness at the counter.

When he finally left the bar, Pincher drove straight into suburban hell. The retirement-style homes all neatly painted, front lawns still basking in the glow of a fresh cut. I slowed the car and parked two houses down, next to the curb.

According to the luminous gray glow of the car's clock, it was 3:25 A.M. Pincher worked in a bank, so I presumed that he would leave the house around 7:30 A.M.; then I'd tail him to wherever he was hiding out during the day.

Great.

Four hours of doing absolutely nothing except listening to that goddamn guy on the radio who makes lousy jokes and plays way too many '70s tunes.

I reached into the cubby for a cigarette, and as I flicked the Zippo I thought I heard a scratching sound at the back of the Ford. I glanced up into the rearview, looking for any movement, while the cigarette between my lips stayed unlit.

The passenger door next to me opened so suddenly that my nerves jumped to attention all out of sync, making me light the Zippo where someone else might have, say, pulled a gun. I was simultaneously relieved and alarmed to see Alison slide into the seat next to me.

"Aren't you going to light that?" she asked, leaning back to lock the door before looking at me again. "Or are you one of those people who tries to quit smoking by walking around with unlit cigarettes in your overall attractive but at this point very unfocused mouth?"

"Alison! What the hell are you doing here?" I seethed, regaining some of my composure.

"I thought you could use the company," she replied matter-of-factly. Alison's formal tailored suits had given way to a faded pair of Levi's, muddy sneakers, and worn NYU sweatshirt.

"You really shouldn't be here," I muttered unconvincingly. Up until I heard that sound behind the car, I had been perfectly content to sit in the car for the next four hours, smoking and listening to the '70s making a comeback.

However, Alison Moore was like my own private virus; the moment she climbed into my car my body awoke to a new state of consciousness, one I had very little control over.

"So what's Pincher up to?" she asked, ignoring my previous statement. Fine. If she wanted to be here, let her to it. She'll get bored soon enough, I thought.

"Nothing much. Drank himself into a stupor until around 3 o'clock this morning, then came home. I honestly don't know why you felt the need to waste money on a private investigator."

Alison took the cigarette from my hand.

"I want you to kiss me."

I was looking up at Harold's bedroom window when she said this. Slowly lowering the binoculars onto my lap, I looked sideways to see Alison still with that tease around her mouth.

"You think you can just invade my stakeout and make indecent proposals to me at four in the morning? Your firm sure has novel ways of spending their cash."

Alison pointed up at Harold's bedroom window, where the light had been replaced by total darkness.

"Harold's gone to sleep, Jaye. You want to tear my clothes off, and I pretty much want to do the same thing to you. Now, for God's sake, shut the fuck up and kiss me."

"Sure," I muttered and leaned over to firmly open her mouth and taste what I had been thinking of quite a number of times alone in my bed after that first kiss in Alison's office a couple months ago. She took my hand and placed it high up on the inside of her thigh, and I could feel the small involuntary movement of her hips, reacting to the pressure my fingers applied as our kiss became almost violent.

Alison shifted her hips down, bringing my hand to rest firmly against her crotch, and making her sigh seductively. I took my hand away, but she grabbed it and put it back, holding on to my wrist and moving her hips achingly slow, applying pressure where she needed it.

"The first time you waltzed into my office I could see you were trouble," she whispered teasingly. Fighting the strength of her hand on my wrist, I pressed my hand into her, feeling the rough contour of her jeans. She arched her back against the seat, her mouth opened in a silent gasp.

"You come across as the kind who likes trouble," I replied, moving the palm of my hand up and down in slow rhythmic movements. At this point I had to make a conscious effort not to rip open her button-fly's and fuck her deliriously.

"It sure makes for entertaining fantasies when you're alone in bed," Alison replied teasingly, holding my eyes while trying her utmost not to just let go of my hand and let me have what we both ached for.

"Oh? Tell me more."

She moved her hand from my wrist and placed it firmly against my own, pushing me into her, purposefully cutting short the cry that escaped from the back of her throat. She was driving me insane. I knew I could make her come without even putting my hand down her pants, but that would be just too easy.

"Earlier today, after you left my office, I was talking to one of my clients and all I could think about was having you inside me, moving against you…"

She did cry out this time—when I yanked away her hand from between her thighs and pinned it above her head against the seat. She moved one of her legs up between my own, and as her knee brushed against the inside of my leg, I decided that this had gone on long enough.

Ripping open all five of her Levi's buttons with one forceful pull, I slid two fingers inside her white cotton panties, and muttered something like "oh, fuck" as I felt how hard she was underneath the tips of my fingers. I thrust into her roughly, pushing her back into the seat, and glanced up briefly at Harold's bedroom window, relieved that the light was still out. Alison threw her head back and arched her hips up to me, at the same time grabbing me behind the neck for extra leverage.

"That's it," she whispered into my ear with that seductive undertone in her voice. "Get it out of your system, Jaye."

"I think you're the one who needs to get 'it' out of your system," I replied between clenched teeth as my fingers moved in and out of her. The space between the two seats seemed to be adding to our frenzy; it was driving me out of my mind that I couldn't feel her against me.

"Ohmygo—" she suddenly grabbed the hair at the back of my neck, making me wince aloud. I felt a silent tremor rip up through her body, and her grip on my hair pulled even more until finally she yanked down hard, and this time I think I said something eloquent like "Ow—fuck!"

I pressed my hand against Alison's mouth because she was making a hell of a racket, and I didn't want the neighbors to come out with handguns. I glanced up at Harold's room. The light was out, his car still in the driveway. This job had turned out to be so much more than I had even imagined. Visions of paying the rent thrilled me as I kissed her once more until she finally became quiet.

The Mystery of the Perverts

Rachel Heath

It was impossible for me to get my breasts flattened down. My best friend, Delores, helped me when she came over. Wearing just my panties, I put my arms up as she wrapped the bandage around me. Delores was so pretty: fair-skinned, black-haired, with enormous blue eyes.

After I was fully dressed, my hat over my short brown hair, we went into the living room. My stepmother shook her soft bun of graying hair and said, "I don't know what the world is coming to these days. Girls cutting their hair and flattening themselves down to look like boys."

I shrugged and tried not to look embarrassed. (Delores's mother was worse; she had even slapped Delores for wearing makeup, screaming "Fast! Fast!" which was why Delores started living on her own.)

"You girls going to that awful trial again?" she asked disgustedly.

"But, Mrs. Tree," Delores explained, "it's part...we want to see how this country's...uh...system of..."

"Justice," I prompted.

"Yeah," Delores said. "How justice works."

"I think there must be something wrong with you to be interested in murderers," Mama said. "The worst kind of murderers at that." She shuddered, then whispered, *"Perverts."*

Delores and I walked into the warm Chicago morning. "I wish I'd remembered my fan," Delores said as we boarded a trolley car.

"Delores," I asked, "do you think Mama is right? They did such a horrible thing!"

"Of course it was horrible! But that they did it anyway means something has to be wrong with them. I mean, look at them, especially Richard. He is so cute, he has to have a good heart deep down."

A hatless bald man to the side of us commented, "Those boys will hang, no matter what Darrow does."

A gray-haired woman in front of us turned around. "Loeb was led into it by that awful Leopold," she remarked. "You can tell there's something wrong with that boy. His eyebrows meet in the middle just like an ape's."

• • •

Delores and I got inside the courtroom that day. It was all alienists. "The boys had a pact," the skinny doctor named Dr. Healy testified. "Do you want me to be specific?"

"Please do," Darrow prodded.

"If they continued their criminalistic activities, Mr. Leopold was to enjoy the privilege of inserting his penis between Mr. Loeb's legs at certain specified dates."

I felt a sudden rush of fear-filled excitement. Perversion! Delores's short fingernails dug into my palms.

"Your Honor," Darrow said, rising to his feet and approaching the bench. "I don't think this kind of testimony should be taken in the presence of reporters and women."

Judge Caverly ordered, "I want this courtroom cleared of women."

Delores and I looked at each other in shocked disappointment. Other ladies were shaking their heads. "This isn't fair," an older woman muttered.

"Ladies, I have ordered you to leave and you must leave," Judge Caverly reiterated. "The testimony now is going into a lot of things that aren't fit for you to hear."

So the women in the court rose and made their way to the door. When Delores got there, she hesitated, as did several others.

"If you don't leave now, I will have the bailiff escort you out," the Judge said.

Delores and I took the trolley to her place. "That was so unfair," I fumed, shutting the door behind us. "They treated us like we were children."

"Ain't it the truth," Delores agreed.

"Delores," I said, then paused.

"Yeah?" she said.

"Leopold put his penis," I began, "between Dickie Loeb's legs..."

"That's not quite what happens," Delores said.

"Do you know what...two men...?" I asked haltingly.

"What perverts do?" she said. Delores nodded. "Yes, I know."

My jaw must have dropped halfway to the floor. The air seemed to crackle with the excitement of the unspeakable. "What do they do?" I said finally, unable to bear the tension any longer.

"I'll show you," she said. "You pretend you're Dickie Loeb, and I'll be Babe Leopold."

She tugged at my sleeve and gently led me to her bedroom. It had a bed and a chest upon which sat a lamp with a frilly lampshade. A large clear mirror hung on the wall to my right. Pictures of Rudolph Valentino and Theda Bara decorated the walls. She pulled the blanket back and I saw white sheets and a pillow.

Without a word, I lay on my stomach. I held the pillow to my face, which I turned slightly to the right.

"That's the way Dickie would be," Delores told me. I felt strangely proud that I'd guessed it so accurately. I felt her

137

breath along my neck. "Babe might kiss him," she said, and I felt her lips' light wetness along my ear.

"But, of course, to really do what they...perverts...do, Babe would have to pull Dickie's pants down." The words hung there in the air. Then I realized that she was waiting for me to bare my bottom.

I gathered all the courage I had. Slowly, I pulled up my dress. Then my slip. Finally, I pulled down my panties.

"Babe puts his penis—" I whispered.

"Between Dickie's legs." Delores completed the sentence and slipped her fingers between the cleft of my thighs. "That's what the alienist said. But that's not quite right."

Electricity seemed to leap upward from her hand to my sex. I felt a warm beating inside my cunt and my clitoris hardened painfully.

"What he really does," Delores explained slowly, "is put it in here." I felt her fingers tentatively explore the cleavage between my buttocks.

"Oh," I gasped. "But what if Dickie had to...had to...go to—?"

"Babe could give him an enema before they do it," she said. "Perverts do that. I have an enema bag here. Lucky for us, Carrie, I got an apartment with a private powder room."

"Yeah," I said. Could I let Delores give me an enema?

I could. I did.

Although I got her to agree to leave the apartment and return in 15 minutes, I felt embarrassed and afraid that hearing me in the bathroom would disgust Delores. But after I was finished in there I was strangely aware of my internal cleanliness and excited about what was to come.

Delores still had not returned, and I sat on the bed, the bandages still holding my chest flat. The door opened and a pulse jumped in my pussy.

Then Delores lay beside me. She said, "Since the asshole

doesn't naturally make juice like the pussy does, Babe would have to wet Dickie another way."

Her fingers played at my lips, and I opened my mouth to permit them inside. I bit playfully and she giggled and wagged the finger of her other hand.

I shivered as she pried my buttocks apart and began pushing her saliva-wet fingers against my asshole. Slowly I felt my asshole give way to those moist digits. I gasped.

"Relax," Delores said.

I did. And as I did, she began moving her fingers almost out and then back in again. My hand was between my legs, pulling on my labia hood.

"That's right, Carrie. The other man would be rubbing on his peter."

I didn't say anything but kept on rubbing. She kept moving her fingers in and out. It didn't take long—I was so aroused—until finally I came in a paroxysm of violent gasps.

My reflection in the mirror showed a flushed face.

I looked deep into Delores' s eyes. "So that's what perverts do," I said.

• • •

The "assisted-living care facility" I live in is called Breton Ridge. I recently was transferred to an apartment on the first floor, and I like it better here since I have to use a wheelchair to get around.

I was in the dining area when, for some unknown reason, Kay mentioned the Leopold and Loeb case. Kay is a hunch-backed woman with hair dyed a blue-tinged silver. She has a hearing aid in one ear. (I've got them in both.)

"They made another film about that one just a couple of years ago," Rick told her. Rick is completely blind and uses a wheelchair plus a cane in front of it.

"What is it called?" I asked.

"*Swoon*," Rick said. "At least I think that's it. Don't quote me."

Rick was right.

Breton Ridge has an in-house video service. I special-ordered *Swoon.*

The actor playing Loeb was not nearly as cute, in my opinion, as Dickie was. However, the one playing Leopold was cuter than Babe because he wasn't afflicted with those eyebrows. *Swoon* brought back memories—even before they got to the part where the women were forced to leave the courtroom.

By then, my fingers had already found their way to that same warm and very moist place.

The Goddess Bites

Sacchi Green

Rory's ass tingled. She could resist panic, but this utter vulnerability teased her flesh with a sensation oddly close to pleasure. A useful insight, maybe, into what some of her games felt like from the other side—but damn it, this was no game!

She lay in a narrow tunnel sloping upward from a larger cave. Her head rested on her free arm, the only position that didn't put pressure on her trapped wrist. Her numbed fingers couldn't even feel the quartz crystals whose dull gleam had lured them into an unstable crevice.

When the crunch of steps on gravel came at last she thought of bears and flexed her knees, heavy boots ready to lash out. Then fingers of brightness from Gwen's flashlight brushed across her body, to where her arm disappeared into a niche now filled with interlocking, immovable shards of stone.

"You still OK, Rory?"

"Doing just fine," she said, hoping her voice was steadier than it felt. "Find anything useful in the car?"

"Not really. I got the ranger station on the cell phone. A rescue team should be here in an hour or so. They can probably work some kind of blade between the rocks to cut the band of that macho wristwatch your ex gave you—or was it the ex before last? Ex-cubed, maybe?—and probably your hand'll slip right out."

Rory made a sound between a groan and a curse.

"You sure you're OK?"

"I may chew my arm off first!"

Rory felt betrayed by her own mind and body. All right, she felt downright stupid. She was supposed to be able to read stone, its grain, its balance, its faults, and to shape it to her will. She should have known the rocks would shift. Now the same hand that wielded mallet against chisel, feeling the hidden shapes within solid stone beg for release, was immobilized. By stone. And the same hand that could thrust rhythmically into women's deep, secret places, making them beg for a harder beat until release burst forth in raw, astonished cries, was trapped. In the deep, secret places of the earth.

"A fitting punishment," Gwen had said before going to find help. "The earth goddess has teeth!"

It might, Rory reflected, have been a mistake to make Gwen beg quite so hard and for quite so long last night. She'd consented to having wrists and ankles tied to the tent posts, but the tent had barely survived, and her pleading had become edged with fury. It was so damn hot, though.

"Hey, any ranger small enough to crawl in here will have to be a woman," Gwen said in mock comfort. "In uniform. And with a knife. Look on the bright side." She wriggled her way up beside Rory and offered her a drink from a bendable straw stuck into a canteen. "Still, you could be famous as a one-handed sculptor. Legions of girls could make pilgrimages to leave damp underwear at the tomb of your legendary fist."

Rory had a feeling she'd shot her mouth off too much last night. Blame it on the local microbrew. Not that Gwen hadn't, ultimately, appreciated the hell out of that very fist. The thought made Rory's hips twitch.

"What's the matter?" Gwen asked, too innocently. "I hope you don't have to piss!"

"Oh, God!" The sudden, inevitable urge was brutal.

"Sorry I suggested it," Gwen said, not really penitent at all. "Let me get your pants down a little, just in case."

Rory, driven by desperation, raised herself enough to let her jeans slide past her hips toward her knees. Suddenly, her legs were almost as immobilized by denim as her hand by stone. Her ass tingled with vulnerability.

"Maybe distraction will help," Gwen said coolly, but there was nothing cool about her touch or the ripples of moisture spreading and pooling like lava as she stroked Rory's exposed flesh. The savage urgency shifted a few vital centimeters until it was cunt and clit, not bladder, begging for relief.

"Oh, shit!" Rory gasped, glutes tensing as Gwen's finger sank deeper into her canyon.

"Nope, can't have that," Gwen said. "Piss would be bad enough." She withdrew her hand. Rory stifled a whimper. After a few indecipherable movements, the hand—or something—was back, nudging at Rory's asshole.

"Hey!" Then, as her jerking body put pressure on her trapped wrist, "Ow! Damn!"

"Hold absolutely still!" Gwen ordered. Strokes far from soothing went from Rory's cunt to her asshole, spreading wetness and heat. She was distracted all right. She felt utterly defenseless, somehow forgetting that knees and booted feet were still potential weapons. She wanted to shrink away; she wanted to press closer. She didn't move.

The familiar snap of a latex glove resounded off the tunnel walls. "I thought you didn't find anything useful," Rory grunted.

"Just the emergency kit I always keep in the glove compartment," Gwen said complacently, "complete with Big Bad Bear, looking for a den." She grinned wickedly as she held the butt plug for Rory to see.

Gwen probed Rory's back door again, twisted the toy slightly, went a little deeper. Rory managed to brace her knees enough to lift her ass higher—and then she couldn't think at all. By the time the pain had processed into a compelling full-ness, Gwen's fingers were slipping in and out of her cunt, deeper and deeper, playing against the maddening pressure in her asshole.

Rory scarcely noticed Gwen's other hand reaching past her head, back and forth, until something brushed her cheek-bone. Something wet. And pungent. In the dim rays of the flashlight she saw the tip of the drinking straw probe into a chink between the imprisoning stones, withdraw, disappear backward in the direction of her crotch, and reappear coated with thick, glistening moisture. Gwen's musky scent mingled with her own.

"Come on," Gwen urged, "let's see just how slippery can you get!" Her pumping hand went on and on, slurping in and out. "Please, damn it," Rory begged, her voice raw, "please," Until Gwen used both hands, steadying the butt plug and thrusting her fingers fiercely into Rory's cunt while her thumb challenged a straining clit, and waves of pressure from front, back, and deep inside met in a roaring tsunami and crashed in a rush of liquid heat.

It was a while before Rory even noticed that her trapped hand had already slipped free, streaked with thick cunt-juice. It was scraped and almost numb, but when she flexed her fingers they moved.

Then she saw the tube in Gwen's breast pocket. "You had lube all along!" she said accusingly.

"Just in case," Gwen admitted. "Didn't need it, except for Big Bad Bear. We made plenty between us. Besides, shouldn't an offering to appease the earth goddess be all-natural?"

Rory's uninjured hand thrust ruthlessly down into Gwen's pants. "The goddess must be on my side again," she muttered against Gwen's wide grin. "She's just granted me the gift of ambidexterity. And this one's a virgin. Just for you."

The Dirty Sea
Jess Arndt

It was one of those sun-stung days. Blasting hot and full of choke and sweat. Wide patches of wet clung under my arms, darkening my faded T-shirt. I shouldn't have been packing. It was that hot. Under my Levi's the rubber was burning my thighs bold. Down at Ren's bar, in the empty, wasted-out part of town, we were drinking whatever cheap, no-name beer she had to sell us. Still, it seemed like no matter how many I had, I couldn't get drunk. It was a day made for stealing ships. I flipped my hips out of my seat and stood up, nodding to my friends who were too busy bouncing quarters to notice. I wanted to go down to the old docks and maybe swim. Even grimy, city-close water sounded good.

The door slammed limp behind me. Out in the parking lot, the heat was white and eyeball-numbing. I climbed into the old Ford truck I'd had since I was 16 and begged a few coughs out of the engine until it growled. Ever since the day that truck and I met, we'd been telling each other stories about dirty sex against the stick shift and steamed-up windows, radio on low. Stories that somehow never quite made it. But with the sweat trickling slow down my cheek and the warm drag of my foot on the pedal, they started again. Even just simple fucking would do it. The old springs of the bench seat bouncing beneath us, her ass in the air.

I turned out of the parking lot and lit a cigarette. Not that there was an us. Or even a her. But the hot was blowing my mind sideways. As my truck tooled down the old factory streets that wound toward the salt water, dust started to settle along the elbow grease of my arm. My muscles felt all achy for action, out of practice and cranky. The lot by the water was empty. Gutted frames of old cars and the huge hoods of Mack trucks lined the graffitied shipyard fence. I turned off the engine and stared out at the dirty sea. There was a rubbery smell to the air—harsh and burny—and I grabbed a bottle of beer I'd slipped out of the bar with me. It reminded me of this old story I had read, where Poseidon gets so caught up in himself, down under the water, that he becomes negligent and never looks after his oceans at all. Maybe that's why sailors started fucking, just to see if they could get his attention.

I stubbed my second cigarette out on the rearview mirror and was about to jump in the water when I saw a shape moving in and out of the mirror's reflection. There was a girl walking down the road behind me, head down, with a can of spray paint hanging from her hand. I recognized her from her blond hair that curled chin-length and the aloof tempo of her walk. She was the girl who opened up the lonely in me, even though I didn't know so much as her name. I got out of my truck and stood against it as she approached. She looked up and nodded briefly. Her eyes were that kind of green that just loses you. That makes you all lefty inside.

I watched her pick her way, steady, across the small rumple of grass that led to the water, and turn the corner around the broken shipyard fence. Suddenly swimming felt stupid, even though the hot was making my knees weak. I took my warm beer and sat at the edge of the water, where the grass and cement got dwindly. To my right a huge tanker yawned with its ass open to the shipyard. There were loud banging noises coming from the insides of the ship, and a low thrumming that seemed to numb all other sound. I don't know how many minutes ticked by. And then there was a voice in my ear. *Doesn't the air feel like fucking?* she said, and stepped back away from me. I dropped my beer at my feet and looked over at that same girl, but she was staring at the ship's ass too, like she hadn't said anything at all.

I followed her steps along the water's edge, strung up, as if she were some kind of charmed ventriloquist. But yeah, the air did feel like fucking. Like being caught in that hot minute just before everything is splayed open and lost. We passed the place along the wall where she'd been painting, and I saw she had tossed her empty can in the low, scrubby bushes. For some reason my lips were clamped shut. We walked until the small path widened into a flat, cement fill. The tanker rose huge right above us, and the whole place was littered with metal scraps and junk. Sweat was curling under my hat and my stomach was all jumpy, jabbing at my guts. The girl stopped suddenly and I ran up against her back. I could feel the heat of her neck right next to my mouth, where all her little hairs stood fragile.

Under us, on the crackled cement, a face glared up into the blank sky. His eyebrows jutted out in white paint and the dark holes of his eyes pierced up my leg. His face must have been the size of a small car. Under his firm chin someone had scrawled KAFKA in thin black lines. *I come here to think,* she said into my ear. I felt my hand hit her skirt right at the hip-bone, scorching my palm. The thrumming was louder now that we were so close to the ship, and past her I could see the dark cavern of it. Like in a dirty story about sailors fucking behind the huge packing crates. And there, with all the balls of it, I turned my mouth into the soft underside of her neck. Teeth and tongue on her salty heat and her soft smell making me dizzy. She ground her hips into me then, and my Levi's were jumping ship around my briefs. Everything was pucker and warmth, and I played my hands up her back until I pulled off her bra and let her tits fall tight and perfect.

Then gravity hit us and we dogged down onto the cement. Her biting my neck hard into the muscle and my hands tricking past her knees to the bold of her thighs. She laughed into my mouth and said I thought you might want to. She moved her lips just fast enough from mine so I couldn't quite taste her. Somehow we had fallen right onto the curl of his lip and with her ass on the ground like that he was mouthing lewd into her underwear. *What do you think he'd say?* I asked, and she looked at me full on, eyes all greeny. Then she grabbed the back of my neck hard and said Behave. I shivered tight from the crotch up, like a knife in my body cutting through the heat, and kissed her deep before she could turn away. My hand was low against the damp of her cotton panties and I slipped my fingers under, quick like mischief. I could feel the glisten of her move on my hand. There was no one around anywhere except for the moaning of that old ship and Kafka. Like somehow we had found the one forgotten place in the world.

I let my hand hold her there until I could feel her melt loose and achy and then with three rogue fingers full I dove my hand in. She moved down into the rough cement and gripped her thighs around the sweat of my back. Down low on the ground like that it seemed like the water was all around us, with our bodies rowing through the shimmery heat. I pumped my hand and her breathing went quick and suddenly I had four fingers in urgent. I could see a faint line of sweat trail her belly and I licked my tongue rough on it. Then she was fucking my hand so hard it was numb and I was swearing into the cement and never wanted to stop. Not for nothing. I could feel my knees turn bloody on the gravel and I let my hand slam into her hot soft and right at that moment when sex is a taste and a smell and just fucking owns all your five senses and becomes the only word you ever knew ever, she flipped me fast onto my back and my breath came out all hot and jackhammery. All I could feel was her slick and wet through my Levi's and my packing dildo and she moved on me like she owned every bone in my body, moved until I came hard, my back arching lusty like a sailor, and she moaned low and final into my neck as the dust settled around my hips.

I pulled my shirt back down slow over the finger and heel welts she left on my back. The air held sex around us in a hazy breeze. Out against the horizon a ship was tossing all hyena-like and spindly. Across in the parking lot, the round headlights of my truck glared betrayal. Her face, so close to mine, had suddenly become this intimate possession, and I looked quick hot into her stare. She slid her hand from the hollow of my hip up over my small paunchy belly, sending a rush of warm darts under my skin. As I turned back to the growing sea, I caught the sharp corner of Kafka's iron stare. His face was still impassive. *Want to go get a drink?* the girl asked as she lit a sideways cigarette. *I know just the place,* I said, and carefully putting my fist down over Kafka's eye, I kissed her salty mouth while the heat spun cyclones around us.

Sugar
Diana Leigh

Well past midnight a faint clanging registers above the din of the vacuum cleaner. After the third ring I recognize the faraway bell sound as *phone*. In a rush to beat the voice mail, I bloody my shin on an errant CD rack.

Sugar's shaky voice comes through the receiver. She's crying, and I can't make out most of her words through an unmanageable slur. She's had too much wine and one of the mild tranquilizers that her doctor gives her. She suffers from anxiety. She can't sleep. She worries too much about things like aging and rape and racial tension. She cries about turning 30. I suspect she really loves me.

When her outburst subsides, I hobble to the kitchen and staunch the flow of blood from my shin with a dish towel. Sugar whispers into the receiver, "I need to see you, Gwen. I'm lonely." I reassure her, tell her how much I love her, that I want to see her too. She falls asleep while I'm softly whispering to her about what a good girl she is and how much I want to fuck her, push my fingers into her cunt and make her cry.

Sugar loves to lie in bed all day watching old movies. She could stare at the young Ava Gardner for hours. "Look at her eyes, look at the way she wears her eyeliner," she always says. It took me forever to stop trying to imitate the film actresses she adored. During the first year of our relationship I was a platinum Dorothy Malone, a wounded Barbara Bel Geddes, a cool, detached Catherine Deneuve. After we watched *Faster Pussycat! Kill! Kill!* I dressed up like Tura Satana. I ground the gears of the Toyota and sped through the streets of San Francisco looking for necks to break.

I met her on a weekend trip to Los Angeles. I spotted her shoe shopping on Melrose. We shared a mirror at Retail Slut, each of us posing seductively for the other. The straps of my '80s Prince-inspired lingerie slip kept slipping down and exposing my nipples. We agreed that her blond hair and blue eyes contrasted romantically with my jet-black hair and ruby lipstick. I showed her the barbed-wire tattoo across my sacrum; she showed me the ankh on her breast.

We reached a pinnacle of vanity and lust when the sales-girl told us we looked like the vampires from *Daughters of Darkness*. Sugar pulled me into the dressing room and pinned me to the wall. Her height gave her an advantage, but I grabbed a handful of her bleached hair and pulled her head back till she whimpered aloud. The sound made my cunt throb. She pushed up my dress and pulled my G-string to the side. "Please," I said as she slipped three fingers into my soaked pussy. She kissed me softly on the neck and I urged her on with little hip thrusts. She whispered, "Can you come like this?" I answered her by tightening up and digging my short, painted nails into her shoulder. Then I came hard, letting out a high-pitched wail and slumping forward against her chest. The salesgirl knocked on the dressing room door and said, "I'm going to have to ask you two to leave." Sugar smiled wickedly and took my hand, "My turn," she said as she pulled me out of the store.

Her apartment is just off Sunset, behind the Whisky. She has no furniture, just a closet full of clothes, a huge bed, and a full-length mirror propped against the wall. Her bathroom counter overflows with tubes of liquid eyeliner, body glitter, and sparkly nail polish. There are bottles of expensive booze lined up like bowling pins in the kitchen. In the empty living room there's an oil painting: a blond woman with heavy '60s-style pastel makeup, like a young Elke Sommer, reclining naked on a fur rug, her body a collection of exaggerated curves. One breast juts toward the ceiling, a prominent pink nipple perched atop it.

"I want to fuck you with a dick," I said to her as we collapsed on her bed.

"There's a cock and a strap-on in that box." She pointed to a black leather harness and a bright red dick. I pulled it on as gracefully as I could and coolly pressed the head of the cock against her upturned ass.

"Lube?" I asked.

"Under the bed," she whispered.

I felt around and found a small bottle. I drowned the bright rubber cock in it before slowly pushing it against her perfect asshole. When I grabbed her hips she said "Oh, God, fuck me. Oh, my God." We fucked languidly, content to gaze at ourselves in the mirror across from her bed. She ejaculated when she came, gushing all over the sheets and soaking both of us. We fell asleep among the wet sheets and woke up hours later, disoriented and still turned on.

We were crazy for each other from that moment. We saw each other every weekend despite the 500 miles between our respective cities. Sugar hates to fly, so I'd fly down to Los Angeles and she'd drive back up with me. She once drove all the way from Los Angeles to San Francisco with one hand on the steering wheel and one hand in my crotch. In the visor mirror I could see her fingers sliding through the vertical folds, disappearing and reappearing, making a slick tick-tick sound. With one leg out the window of a rented Lexus I came to an extravagant climax. Semis drove by and honked in congratulations.

I hang up the phone and give up rearranging the furniture. The pieces are still in disarray—as if they were interrupted while dancing. In bed I lie awake, fingers on my throbbing clit, imagining the sound of her voice and picturing her beautiful face when she comes.

A few days later, in a fit of desperation, she flies up to see me. When I answer the door there is a tall, slender woman in ridiculous shoes posed next to three huge suitcases.

"I'm sorry, I'm groggy. I took too many Dramamine." She begins dragging in the first bag. "I was crying on the flight. I couldn't stop. When the stewardess came around I said, "I'll have four bottles of vodka." She didn't protest at all; she just set them down on the tray in front of me." Sugar cries all the time. I guess it's part of her charm.

Sometimes she cries after she comes. In the beginning she would beg for me to fuck her hard, harder. And I'd do it. Each time I came when she did, without her so much as touching me. She liked a hand across her throat as she got closer. Not choking her, just resting on her fragile neck like a threat. I never squeezed, but I often wanted to.

Once she gets her suitcases inside, she pulls her movie star sunglasses to the end of her nose, a nose shaped entirely different from the one nature intended. Her big L.A. swimming-pool eyes are puffy and red.

She leans forward and throws her arms around me theatrically. I know she'll stay for too long. She does it every time. She tells me she'll be here a week, and a month later I'll be begging her to book a flight home. For the next six weeks I'll be late to work every day. I'll eat out every night. My bank account will be depleted, I'll buy bikinis at Versace I'll never wear, and I'll have tons of raucous, emotional, and thrilling sex.

After a few moments she does a perfunctory check of my appearance. I'm in a T-shirt and jeans.

"My gawd, what's happened to you? You look so *normal.*" When she says "normal" it sounds like someone else saying *slug* or *sewage.* She stoops to wrestle a pair of high-heeled sandals from her feet. "New?" I ask.

Sugar doesn't work. She shops, spends weekends in spas, goes to yoga classes religiously. She doesn't understand that I have responsibilities. "I think the reason that you and I get along is we both understand the necessity of multiple pairs of black shoes." She's always dropping bits of wisdom like this.

She sighs and says, "I really have to rest, Gwen. The flight left me exhausted," though the flight from Los Angeles to San Francisco takes only 50 minutes.

I grab her suitcases and say, "Take a shower. You'll feel better."

Half an hour later she is naked, leaning over the sink shaving her pussy. One leg is propped on the basin. Her razor is a heavy silver men's model. Her strokes are light, and she runs a hand over the unshaved area to guide the blade. When she turns around to show off a job well done, I kneel down to closely inspect her handiwork. I trace my tongue along the lips of her cunt, teasing her until she's wet. Her clit is large, larger than any others I've seen. I lick it lightly and force her to ask me for more. She grinds against my face in response and want to make her come immediately, but instead I tease her, knowing she'll beg for it. Instead, she pushes me backward with her foot and pins me to the tile. I feel her teeth against my shoulder, and a moment later she bites me so hard it breaks the skin.

"Love me, Gwen. I want you to love me," she says. I feel two of her long fingers slip into my cunt, wet already. It's been wet since she walked through my door in her stilettos. She presses hard against a spot at the top of my pussy that almost hurts, but I don't want her to stop. She fucks me roughly, the same way she likes me to fuck her. The tile is cold, but I'm getting so close, and if I can only get a little bit more, I would come. She feels me open up and slides in two more fingers, but still I can sense the rest of her hand, and I want it inside me. "More, goddamn it," I tell her, and she tucks her thumb into her palm and pushes into me. I scream at the top of my lungs as the widest part of her hand enters the tight ring of muscle at the opening of my cunt. Once inside, she remains perfectly still, simply filling me. I realize my mouth is open and I'm reaching for something, but I don't know what it is, because all I can see and feel is the woman above me, staring at the place where her hand disappears into my body.

Sugar talks me down, cooing warm words into my tingling ears. "You are so pretty, Gwen. Your voice, your hair. I love you, baby. You are everything." When she says these words to me, I melt inside. "We have what it takes, Gwen. We can make each other happy." And I believe her at this moment. Because she is earnest. She means it. I don't reply. I can't. I'm breathless and spacy; I've fallen into the hole in which Sugar often sends me. She overwhelms me. Instead of speaking, we curl up on the cold tile floor and she holds me with an urgency that makes my clit jump.

Later we will eat, shop, sleep. I will roll my eyes at her extravagance and bicker with her over small things. I will want her to leave, to give me back my space and my normal life. But not now. Now I just revel in her naked body and her need.

Special Delivery

Emily Torres

I'd been working at home for about six months. In some ways it was really nice, but much of the time I was just plain lonely. Often I didn't even change out of my pajamas or take a shower. I just got right out of bed, sat down at my computer, and worked. But today felt different. I woke up in a really fucking good mood. Maybe it was the antidepressants, maybe it was the fact that I actually got to sleep at a normal hour, or maybe it was the way the planets were aligned. Whatever the reason, I bounded out of bed and jumped into the shower first thing. I felt like running around the block. I felt like, I don't know, doing something besides sitting at my computer typing. I felt good. And when I feel good, I usually feel horny.

So there I was, gazing out my window, horny and restless. I couldn't concentrate on work—actually, I couldn't concentrate on anything. I was just soaking up the feeling-good vibes and looking around for a distraction when up pulls the big brown beacon of free books, the UPS truck. Writers live a solitary existence, and one of the few perks I get as a freelancer is free stuff. Shivering with anticipation, I wondered if my special delivery was something I would be interested in reading, or was it destined to be sold on a foldout card table on my front lawn?

I watched anxiously as the door to the trunk swung open

and out stepped the most beautiful woman I had ever seen. She had long, bouncy blond hair, like a shampoo ad come to life. She was wearing the UPS girls-of-summer standard-issue uniform: brown shorts, tight around her ass and short enough to nicely expose her lovely long legs. I could just picture those legs chasing down a letter as it was blown out of hand by a big gust of wind. Up top she wore a short-sleeved shirt so tight her ample breasts almost broke open the cheap buttons. The fabric looked hot and itchy, and I wished I could liberate her bosom from the restraining brown material. As she crossed the street, her bosom bounced up and down with each step. She didn't see me peering out the window, or if she did, she didn't let on. In any case, I didn't really care. I had found my distraction.

I ran my fingers through my short, spiky black hair and pulled off the ratty old T-shirt I was wearing, exchanging it for a tight tank top. I'm flat-chested, so it didn't really make a difference, but I live by the rule that more skin is good skin. And in her case, that rule was golden. My heart was pounding, and a pool of anticipation was collecting in my Calvins. I've always been a sucker for a woman in uniform.

I ducked so she wouldn't see me through the window as she approached. I wanted to seem busy and important, not underemployed. Sadly, I regretted not cleaning up after the dog for the past week. My yard was scattered with toxic waste. I wanted to impress her, not scare her away.

When the doorbell rang, I panicked. For a full 30 seconds I forgot to breathe. When it rang a second time, I jolted out of my reverie and smiled. *She rang twice, so she must really want me,* I thought proudly.

"Hello," I said with a smile and feigned surprise, as if UPS had never dropped in unexpectedly on anyone."

'I have a delivery for a...Maya..." she hesitated on my last name, obviously not versed in the lilting language of love, Spanish.

I gave her a look I imagined was suave. "That's me," I told her, my voice nearly cracking from the pressure.

"I have something for you," she said.

And at that moment my gaydar went crazy. I was sure she could hear my heart beating. My body was tingling so much I was worried that sparks might fly out of my fingertips and melt her blouse.

She just grinned at me. She had to know what was going on in my mind. I cocked my hips and tried to use some of the body language tips I had read about in the last lesbian sex book I reviewed.

Slowly she pulled out a long, cylindrical tube.

"Is that for me?" I said as smugly as I could muster.

"Special delivery," she answered, raising one incredibly sexy eyebrow.

I was lost. Putty, Jell-O, chocolate fucking pudding, whatever you want to call it. My knees grew weak and all that good stuff. I wanted her. And wanted her bad. A tiny bead of sweat rolled down her way-too-sexy neck.

"It's hot out," I said, restraining the urge to lick the droplet right off. "Want to come in for a drink?"

Unbelievably, she nodded and strolled through my door, just like in a letter to *Penthouse Forum*. I pinched myself as I locked the door behind her. I went into the kitchen with her following close behind me. As I reached up to get a glass she seemed very close. I felt the warmth coming off her polyester-clad form.

"I would love something wet," she breathed on me.

I nearly choked on my own tongue.

When I turned around, she was right up on me. I barely had time to place the glass on the counter before our lips were locked. We kissed nice and hard. And then she started to explore. Her tongue found the most direct route from my mouth to my tit. It was as if she had memorized the zip code to my heart. She pulled down my tank top, licked a trail all the way down my neck, lingering on my collarbone, then went straight for my rock-hard nipple. This UPS driver was amazing, and she was about to deliver me home!

I reached for her, intending to rip the buttons right off that cheap brown uniform. But she quickly pushed my hand away. Holy shit, the UPS babe was a top! Hallelujah! She pulled off my tank top and exposed my braless A cups to the kitchen air. She then pushed my shorts down around my ankles. I stood there flushed, overwhelmed, and really, really wet.

Her hands were all over me. They grabbed my ass, my tits, and ran up and down my thighs. Not to say that my hands weren't doing some work of their own. They traveled everywhere, explored every highway, every avenue to pleasure. Our mouths were so busy kissing nipples, necks, and knees that we barely came up for air.

The UPS goddess's arms were strong from lifting boxes. She flexed her muscles as she helped me up on to the counter. Her fingers started up like she was typing 2,000 mailing labels. And she was so fast! One, then two, suddenly three fingers inside of me, in and out, over and over, bringing me to the brink of total pleasure. I was about to come when she stopped and kneeled. She licked me like a 50-cent stamp, covering me top to bottom, making sure that I was stuck. I cried out and grabbed her long blond hair, my body shaking, my legs tensing, my toes cramping. I came with a yell. She pulled back and looked up at me, her face glistening with my gratitude. Her perfect pink tongue escaped her mouth and licked lasciviously around those heart-shaped lips.

"Wow," I sighed. "I never realized that UPS really meant it when they offered full service."

"You didn't think we did this job for the paycheck, did you?" she laughed.

When I recovered, I pulled up my shorts and walked her to the door. She waltzed down the sidewalk, shaking her ass and making that uniform sing. She was all the way to the front gate before she slowly turned around, flipping her golden hair over one shoulder, and winked at me.

I ran back inside and got on the Web, ordering as much stuff as my credit card could hold. All to be delivered by UPS, of course. After all, all work and no play makes me a very horny girl.

The Word Nebraska

Tennessee Jones

The men in Vermont usually thought we were boys when they picked us up. A stonemason stopped for us on Route 5, a two-ton slab of marble in the back of his truck, the big wheels almost as tall as my chest. He was thin and dark, his torso covered by a bulky, stained jacket, his hands so huge the steering wheel seemed to disappear between them. His eyes were dark brown, half hidden by heavy brows. I smelled tobacco and sweat when Jake opened the passenger door, but when we climbed into the cab of the truck he yelled, "Jesus fuck! You guys smell like shit; roll down the window!" The introduction froze on my lips. As the truck accelerated he said, "It's all right. I know what it's like. I started hitchhiking when I was 15. I didn't like riding the bus, so that's how I got to school. I grew up around here, and after a while people start to get to know you and they don't mind picking you up. Then when I got out of school I didn't stop for a while. I went all the way to the West Coast." He stopped for a moment. "What are you guys doing?"

"We're going out west too," Jake said to him.

I noticed him looking at me closely as he talked as if he was starting to sense that I wasn't a man. Did he notice the absence of a beard or Adam's apple? Was it something in the scent my body gave off, not as spicy and dark as his own?

After he dropped us off on the side of the road in

Massachusetts, Jake and I talked about dragging him off into the woods, looking into his big brown eyes, and forcing him to suck both of our cocks, feeling his white teeth brush up against our pubic hair. It's funny how queerness seems to spread as our lovers take on other genders, how behaviors like sucking cock become desirable and transgressive. We talked about fucking his ass and leaving him in the dry leaves with his pants down around his boots. Maybe we thought about these things because we were terrified of being discovered, terrified of being beaten by small-town boys because we had pussies instead of dicks.

Jake collars me for the first time in a basement in Louisville, Kentucky. I am skeptical. "After I put this on you," he says to me, "I don't want you to make another sound." I face the gray basement wall and he steps behind me, so close that I can feel his broad chest pressing against my shoulder blades. He places the piece of leather across my throat, drawing it so tight against my trachea that it is a little difficult for me to breathe. I close my eyes as he puts it on, trying to process how I feel about it and what I think it means. He grabs my shoulders and turns me around to face him. "I'm going to tie you up now, darlin'," he breathes in my ear. He has a long length of white rope in his hand. He pulls my wrists behind my back and wraps rope around each of them separately so that my forearms are tightly encased, almost to my elbows. He ties a knot to draw my wrists together and with the same piece of rope ties my feet. "I want to make sure you don't talk," he says, drawing a leather gag through my teeth. "Stand here and wait for me."

He starts walking up the stairs, and I feel panic spread in my chest, tightening the ventricles of my heart, shrinking my lungs. My breath turns hot, as if I've inhaled glass. When he reaches the top of the stairs, he flicks off the light switch and I am left in darkness. First my feet turn cold and then my shins. I discover that boredom is my greatest fear. I can hear him pacing upstairs and then I hear the electric pop of the TV being turned on. White-hot anger flares up in me. The cold spreads to my hands and then stops. I try to move and I cannot. This is a curious feeling. I strain against the ropes and they remain tight. I try to expel the gag from my mouth. I stand for a few moments, long enough to forget that I cannot walk, and almost fall over when I try. I discover I am terrified of falling, terrified of what he would do to me if he found me lying on the dirty concrete of the floor instead of standing.

After a while I feel myself becoming someone else. I am no longer angry. I want him to come back. That desire shuts everything else up. I stop thinking about getting to the interstate the next morning. I stop thinking about myself. I think only about whether or not I will be able to do the things he will demand of me.

Relief mixes with terror when I hear the heavy clunk of his boots on the stairs again. The light flickers on and I discover I cannot look at him. He is tender when he comes to me, holding my cheeks, whispering "honey" again and again softly. He removes the gag and wipes away the drool that is running down my chin. He kisses me slowly, his tongue filling up my mouth completely, my face in his hands, his thumbs digging into my cheeks.

He breaks the kiss and sits down in a gray folding chair. He says, "Come over here, honey." Ashamed, I hop clumsily to where he sits. "Get down on your knees," he says in the same sweet voice. He spreads his legs wide and I see the outline of his cock underneath the thick fabric of his work pants. I press my face into his crotch, the spit from my open mouth staining his pants darker. He grabs my hair and jerks my head back. "Don't fucking touch me until I say you're allowed to." He slaps my face hard, the sting of it spreading to my neck and lips. His gray eyes spark. "You fucking bitch. If you want my cock so much, I'm gonna make you swallow it." He unzips his pants and the big black dick he won in a drag king contest spills out.

I turn into a faggot when I'm sucking his cock. I can envision my eyes closed, my cheeks hollowed out, the perfect curls of my lashes almost disappearing. I look 16, dark-haired, some young boy he's picked up off the street. I gag when he puts his dick in my mouth. This makes him impatient. He grabs my head in his big hands and thrusts his hips so that his cock is hitting the back of my throat. It slams into my throat until I finally open up and let it slide in toward my gut. He has his hands squeeze tighter at my temples to let me know I'm not getting away, that I'm not allowed to breathe until he's done. It becomes a meditation: sneaking in bits of air, finding a way to adjust to the thing that is filling up my mouth completely. I suck him off as hard and fast as I can, the muscles in my jaws and neck aching, the ligaments screaming. I lose who I am while I'm doing this.

I come back to earth after he has pulled my head away. He zips his pants and stares at me. I'm still on my knees, the collar tight around my throat. "You're so fucking pretty," he says to me and takes out his knife. He bends down and cuts the rope off my ankles. "Get up," he says and leads me closer to one of the cinder-block walls. He unbuttons my shirt, the knife clenched in his teeth. He pushes the cloth down to my tied wrists. They tingle with the motion. He rubs his dick against my ass and pushes my naked torso against the wall. My nipples and cheek grind against the rough block. He puts the knife against my throat and whispers again, "Don't make a sound." I feel his other hand loosening my belt, and then my jeans drop down to my ankles. He touches my ass, and his hand is slippery with grease. The knife presses tighter against my throat so that I am sure there must be a thin line of blood trickling down my throat and across my collarbone.

He presses the big dick against my asshole and I shudder; my body bucks against him. The cinder blocks tear at my nipples. He is rough with me, sliding the first half-inch into me viciously. It stops when it hits the tighter ring of muscle inside my ass. He moves his hips in short strokes against me, thrusting a little harder each time. He does this until he stretches out my asshole. I sense the rest of the dick before he puts it inside me, feel him drawing back before he slams into me. I feel like I am losing consciousness when I am being fucked in the ass, the pleasure so great that all I can do is open my throat and howl. I forget about the knife against my throat. He fucks me until my tits are bloody and I cannot speak.

* * *

I close my eyes and see his body spread across the floor, breath ragged, hands splayed out against the carpet. Standing over him I feel that I am six and a half feet tall, the muscles in my arms and shoulders huge and full of venom, as if parts of me are ready to explode. I grab him by the scruff of his neck and pull him up on his knees, my forearm a thick bar across his chest, pressing against his collarbone. I take my dick out so that he can feel it between his thighs. He moans and arches toward me more. My arm slides up and presses against his neck. His throat caves in slightly and he goes limp against me, his labored breath becoming so loud that it clogs my hearing. We sink into this silence together; memories flash across our field of vision that we have never had before: ships sailing, the fear of falling off the edge of a flat world, discovery of new lands. I touch a space that exists in his chest only in these moments. It is just as wide as the plains in Nebraska.

When I let him go he falls back to the floor, his arms wrapped around his head and neck. I loosen my belt and fold the soft leather around my fist three times. The first blow is soft, hardly making a noise against his shoulder blades. I am careful to build the intensity of how I hit him, layering the blows to cover every inch of his wide shoulders.

He is whining softly now, begging me to hit him harder. I want to hit him until I am hoarse, until my voice disappears, until there is nothing but sensation between us. I raise the belt high above my head and bring it whistling down. He screams and I hit him again and again. I follow the movements of his body and strike him in the places that sting the most. I watch his jaws clench and unclench, his eyes tightly closed. I can tell that he has reached a place of absolute trust, that he has given me the right to do anything to him that I want to with the faith that I will not ask too much. I hit him until I am exhausted, until his back is covered with splotches, until his shoulders are black and blue. I collapse onto him, unable to move.

The Sending
S.J. Bryan

This Red Gyal appears straight outta the humid city night right in fronta me. No joke, not even a few seconds ago there was no one even close to where she's standing now.

And I can't say for sure what I'm feeling more her electric blue 'fro or the black lace fan she's waving lazily back and forth, back and forth in an attempt to cool herself.

Brown eyes flecked with yellow fix on me and I stop dead in my tracks. Her words: "You called?" The smile reveals bright white teeth. Arms open and I step to her like this sorta thang happens everyday. Under a street light surrounded by uninterested others I nuzzle her throat. I'm more than a little relieved. Not at all surprised.

See, not even a few days back I filled a glass with cool water, lit a pink candle, laid down a feather, scattered my cowries, and put in a call to any Power that cared. Dared ask to hold a body like mine again. To inhale the crazy-makin' scent of a sista or any She. To hear the way a woman sounds when she really hungers for me.

Been too long and I wanted to be back. For months now I'd been walkin' on the boy-lovin' side'a thangs. For a bit, I was all caught up in it. This intimacy-fearin', game-playin', male-female battling, sista-to-sista competing frame'a mind left me pissed and hurt in places both alien and familiar.

Changed in ways I wanna deny but need to remember.

Now, in the shadows of a nearby alley, I come home.

We don't even bizness with the stinkin' garbage bags or the big-ass raccoon in the Dumpster, busily searching for its evening meal. Cuz this ain't gonna be a cushy bedroom, soft lights and D'angelo singin' falsetto in tha background affair. This is about here and now.

We are frenetic, kinetic. Limbs tangled and connected. Tongues dueling and delving. I grab her hair, sending her down to where my naked snatch hides under a piece of kente too brief to be called a skirt. I spread legs covered in black schoolgirl thigh-highs and begin to ride. But even as I feel my nature rise, I get wise to the fact that this ain't gonna come easy.

Somethin's messin' wit' me. Almost like we got company lurking in the shadows. Suckin' their teeth and talkin' shit...*only ho's and gutter gyals spread for people they just met...but wait, what sort of lifestyle this is here? Gyal pickney, ain't you got no brought-upsy? No fear?*

I bend my knees slightly and grind my cunt into her upturned face. All else fades as she reaches up and takes my womb in her hand. I take in air as best I can and try to not cry out.

If my brothas and sistas, those dark children that look like me but don't know how to juk like me, could see us now, I'd grin and say, *This is who I am. This is why I need to do more than quietly smile and pass and lime then slowly die among you.*

I put this thought to one side, knowin' they'll nevah truly get it. And can I really blame 'em? Red Gyal's teeth on my pussy, expert tongue sliding as she smears my juice 'cross her face is damn near indescribable in our master tongue. But that don't stop me from hissin' encouragements and endearments using every single cuss word I know.

Eyes shut tight, I fumble toward the rainbow side of darkness. An expectant knot tightening in my belly. Lust coiled waiting. Pooni throbbing. Nerves send warning. Her fingers thrusting, teasing. Then I'm exploding, insane.

As I come down, fighting for breath and control, Red Gyal raises herself up and moves into my arms. I expect soft lips and instead receive teeth tearing into my mouth. A precious and courageous gift. I taste my own funk mingled with copper-tinged blood but don't pull away.

I get up behind her, shove her against the graffiti-covered brick and run my hands over clothes that are just getting in my way. With some help I drag blue jeans and black cotton panties past her knees and bury my face in the cleft between cheeks. Her musk is well-spiced, and I feast greedily, bitin' and suckin' as she moans and arches her back.

She turns to face me and demands that I fuck her ass. I slick a hand with spit and work her with as many fingers as she can take. The word *Yes* repeated to infinity is a prayer whimpered in my ear. Her tears and cries are a queer patois I interpret with ease. Her legs clamped tight round me are all the permission I need.

And all the while, there's this look on her face that's messing wit' my mind. Making me bump and grind as if my life depends on it. Making me wish I knew her better. Don't even know her name. Damn! Sure as hell can't hope to ever see her again. But right now I love her. Love her for coming when I called. Love her for being a vision manifested in the flesh.

Primal pussy-to-pussy friction sets the space around us on fire. I hold tight, burying my hand deeper in her and pray for magic enuff to protect us both.

Growls in a bass tone I don't even recognize are punching their way outta me. I'm riding Red Gyal's thigh, legs spread wide, my head thrown back. What little bitta clothes we've still got on are fast coming off. Breaths synchronize and I realize that this vibe has done more than rock us here tonight.

The shades of blood ancestors—tough muthas who survived middle passage horrors, broken ones who passed over

before the ships ever landed, young girls and crones with
folds shut tight who fought and died with *no* on their lips,
sistren who gave it up and lived to kill another day—have
been drawn into the love we've made.

These souls been on ice but ain't quite passed ovah. Their
fate was desire controlled by others. Juicy sweet heat deferred
for survival's sake. Their insistent murmurings, black doves
circling, crying: "Sankofa!" Silken whisperings 'bout a plan:
"Go back to cum forward. The time is right."

To us they offer true emancipation. At last an end to the lies
and the abomination. They open our mouths and our minds to
one strange and forbidden fruit we can safely cherish, savour-
ing it to tha max.

"Sankofa!"

Their spirits mount us and ride our riddim. Sublime con-
juring. Unearthly possession. Touch triggers pleasure centers.
Each loving word is a treasure shared among us in dialects
both living and dead.

This raging continental tide of drumming rhythmic cunt
beats is a freedom train, one helluva ride. They fuck us invis-
ibly. Filling us, full feeling us. Manipulate our clits. Suckle
and bite our nipples. Unseen hands smack and tug and pinch
and stroke.

Their hunger is massive, their thirst unquenchable. From
within and without they push our overheated bodies past tol-
erance, past caring. The staccato slap of flesh against flesh
quickens our pace. We scream and struggle but do not stop.

Even though passersby are no longer simply passing by.
Though our hearts are pounding uncontrollably in our chests.
Though we can't seem to take in enough air. Though deep
purple night is giving way to magenta morning sky. Though
the ground under our feet trembles and shakes and whole uni-
verses of custom threaten to collapse, we can't stop.

A growing crowd of onlookers is gathering not even a few

feet away. But that's about as far as they can get. Some surge forward. Can't say whether they wanna penetrate or interrupt our flow. But in any case they're forced to stand back.

Some shout out their rage. Others tantrum and self-destruct. Others still simply explain in moderate tones that they're OK with what we people do as long as they don't have to see it. But for once the powers that be are fully on our side. And all they can do is watch what we do.

Red Gyal and I are grooving, simultaneously moving toward one hell of a peak. But we are eclipsed by the cries and shrieks of a million dark divinities about to get off.

And when they cum we are deafened by their jubilation. When they cum we are almost crushed in their contractions. When our foremothers finally claim the right to cum all present are washed clean, baptized in the salty sea water of their astral ejaculations.

Then, released, their essence leaves this place for good.

Emptied, spasming, and once more alone in our own skins, Red Gyal and I laugh and cry and embrace. What began in the past has ended in this our freedom time. We are their daughtas—two revolutionary sluts who lust fearlessly and speak in ecstatic tongues.

I open my mouth to ask her name, but the light touch of her fingers on my lips interrupts me. Instead I kiss her sticky palm and promise to remember all. Vow to remember their story, our story, and the place where we all came together.

Untouched by shame, filled with wisdom and the relentless will to fuck, I dress and gather my things. The dispersing crowd parts and I leave Red Gyal in the alley behind me. I don't look back. Chances are, she's already gone.

Personal

Skian McGuire

Everyday this week a bike's been following my truck. I'm finished with my route and headed back to the plant when a black Triumph with one of those rainbow flag plate holders goes by on 91. Just about drives me nuts. Passes me doing something like 80, then pulls in front and noodles along until I got to pass or drop back, and I'm cursing at whoever it is, rainbow or no rainbow. Next thing I know, there's the damn bike again, cruising alongside me, checking me out, black helmet with a tinted visor so I can't see her face. Got to be a dyke. A goddamn crazy dyke; she's turning and looking up at the van window and I don't know how she's keeping the rubber to the road. She's sure as hell not watching where she's going. Jesus! Finally, I give her a palms up and a "What? What, already?" I imagine her grinning maniacally behind the Darth Vader gear. A little wave and she's gone. My heart rate goes back to normal.

Next day, there she is again. For the first time I notice the braid hanging down the back of the black leather jacket, which fits her like a glove. Broad shoulders and narrow hips. Black leather pants. Damned if she doesn't cruise up next to me and throw that tinted visor up. I don't know why the wind doesn't rip her head off, but she's looking up at me in the van, serious brown eyes burning into mine at 70 mph. My palms

172

are sweating. Then she zooms off, and I'm blinking, trying to clear my head. The noonday sun flashing off all that chrome has got me dazzled, that's all.

I'm about to cross into Vermont when I spot her at the last rest stop, leaning against the Triumph, arms crossed. Her helmet's off. She's watching my truck go by.

The third day, I'm half expecting her, and there she is, cruising me, visor up, and poof, gone again. I don't know if she's at the rest stop but I put the signal on. I pull up the truck a few yards past her. My hands are shaking when I slide the door open, then I sit behind the wheel in a sweat. Should I get out? What do I say to her? I like your bike? Christ, I'm too old for this.

She climbs up to the second step and stops, not saying a word. Looking at me. Square face, dark brows, dark hair pulled back, brown eyes locked into mine, not smiling. Her jacket's open; I'm looking at her tits through the white T-shirt she's got on, no bra. Her eyebrows go up. I guess I stop breathing. Everything's gray around the edges.

"Not much room back here," she says from back of the van.

Her voice is low and easy and almost sweet, but it hits me like a cattle prod and I'm out of my seat, squeezing past her, flinging empty trays into a stack in the back against the door. By the time I finish, I'm calm, staring out through the rear glass at the nearly empty lot, the bright warm fall day, leaves starting to turn. I think I can feel her breath on the little hairs at the back of my neck. I guess I'll turn around sometime soon. Maybe kiss her. Is that how we start? It's weird, how happy I am. I don't even know her name.

"I never fucked anybody in a bread truck before," she says.

"Well," I answer, all mellow, "there's a first time for everything."

She's got my hair in her fist, yanking my head back, and the other arm around me, groping for my breast.

"You're awfully mouthy," she breathes into my ear. I

don't know if she's gonna tear my scalp off or break my neck, and I can't talk except for a pathetic little squeak. I'm not calm anymore. I guess she's satisfied. She lets go of my hair.

"Shit," she says, both hands trying to get at my nipples. Impatient, she pulls the uniform shirt out of my pants and pushes her hands up under it, not bothering with the buttons. The sports bra she rucks up under my armpits, and she latches on to both nipples hard enough to make me hiss. She's looking down over my shoulder, at the bunched-up shirt, a faint smile on her face. When she lets go, the pain is even worse.

Her hands find the button of my Dickies, the zipper, she's pushing them down. My underpants are sticking to me with sweat; cotton rips as she forces them down too. Cool air on my naked ass. I'm waiting to feel her hand between my legs, as far apart as the pants at my ankles will let them go.

"Get down there," she says, and pushes me onto the stack of trays, which rattle and slide, and I'm trying to get them steady, trying to get comfortable, still waiting for that hand, when I hear it the slithery sound of a belt whisking out of belt loops.

Not enough room in the van for a real good swing. Out of the corner of my eye, I see she's got most of the belt wrapped around her fist. The first stroke is just hard enough to make me arch my back for more.

"You can say 'uncle' anytime you want." I'm hanging on to plastic, my fingers getting numb, flinching every time the belt lands, biting my lip. Can't remember if she closed the van door.

I shake my head. With a little grunt, she starts again.

And stops. I hold my breath as voices outside get louder, then fade away. When the strap lands again, it's white-hot pain.

"Uncle!"

Her hand is cool on my burning ass. Smooth. A latex glove, I figure out, as her hand slips between my legs.

"You're really wet." She strokes my clit. I sag onto the trays. "You want it, don't you." I groan a yes, and she slides a finger into me. I push backward on her hand, trying to spread my legs wider at the knees with my pants around my ankles. "Yeah," she says, laughing.

Two fingers, three fingers, fucking me. She's on her knees behind me, breathing hard. I'm nearly whimpering when she stops; then cool slick lube is parting my cunt lips. Damn, I'm thinking, she's *prepared,* and her four fingers are slipping into me, pointed, twisting. I can feel my cunt opening up, the base of her thumb pushing in. I want it so bad. I force myself to relax, and all at once my cunt is hugging her wrist. And I groan again.

"Yeah, baby," she says, panting. "Ride my fist like a big ol' fucking Harley." Her hand is turning and pumping. Slow. Gentle. I couldn't get away if I wanted to. "Yeah," she says, as the wave starts deep in my belly. I can't believe how quick. I'm coming hard, clenching on her hand like an iron trap. Before the ripples even stop, she's twisting her fist, and I start coming all over again.

"Please," I'm croaking, my mouth dry. I don't know how many times I've come. "Please." It's all I can say.

"Please, what? Please, more, or please, stop?"

"Stop!" I say, and she twists her hand again, threatening to start it all over again. "Please stop!"

Her hand goes slack. I've still got it tight. "Let go," she orders. I try. I feel her hand uncurl and slip out, and my pussy closes on nothing, sticky and cool as the air hits. I groan, and she laughs again.

She stands up. I turn my head to the other side to see her working her belt back through the loops of her black leather pants. When she's done she leans over me, runs her hands up under my shirt. I push myself up from the stack of trays to give her hands room, but all she does is shimmy my bra back into place. Her turn now? I wonder.

"Pull your up trousers," she tells me, but my legs won't hold me. I'm kneeling on the metal floor of the van, trying to work my pants up without standing, feeling more and more stupid. Any minute, she's going to start laughing at me. But she doesn't.

"While you're down there," she says after I finally get the fly zipped, "you can lick my boots."

Black leather, like everything else but her T-shirt, untucked now. I've never licked a boot before. I get down on my elbows. Until now, I never even noticed how the smell of leather was filling the metal box of the van, even stronger than the smell of stale bread and day-old cupcakes, spicier than the lingering smell of pussy. I think I could get high on it if I smell it long enough. My nose touches her instep. I kiss it and start to lick.

Little laps at first, like a kitten. Pretty soon, big swipes, nuzzling, trying to suck, trying to shove her cuff up so I can get at more of the boot. Then she's got my collar, dragging me over to the other one, smooth and a little salty and that leather smell in my nose like the first morning in heaven. When I start up the leg of her leather pants, she lets me get just past the knee before she hauls me off like a calf away from a teat.

She shakes her head, smiling at the look on my face. "I've got to go." She reaches down, helps me stand up in the narrow space. For a second our faces are right up close, and I think she's going to kiss me, but she hugs me, instead, her warm body, the zippers of her jacket, her small soft breasts all pressing against me, and her smell filling my head. It goes on for a long moment before she pulls back, grinning.

"That was a lot of fun. Makes me want to break my rule."

She's shaking her head, serious now. A little sad.

"I don't fuck strangers more than once." And as I open my mouth she says, "No!" She holds up a hand. "Don't tell me." She's backing toward the door. "You're hot." Her mouth quirks up, half smiling. "But I really like fucking strangers.

Which you wouldn't be if I knew your name. If I saw you again." She says from the step, "It's nothing personal."

No sign of her Friday or Monday. Pretty soon it'll be too cold to ride; not that I expect to see her. It doesn't keep me from looking. Now there's a black Triumph in front of the 7-Eleven, but before I can decide what to do, a paunchy middle-aged guy comes out and throws a leg over. I've got to laugh. It's nothing personal.

To the Marrow

Sharon Wachsler

When your life is at stake, everyone starts to look good, or at least doable. Sex becomes a means of survival. Everything does: vitamins, acupuncture, walking the dogs. You do it and you know it's at least half as important as the amputations and chemo. I fuck, therefore I am.

I met Jessica at my support group. We were the only two not married with a pack of kids. I figured that upped our survival chances right there. At the first meeting she looked at me and leered. She ran her tongue over her lips, smirking, while the woman next to her told how she'd lost her hostess job because her appearance made the diners nervous.

Jessica was vintage punk; a safety pin through her ear, a red velvet blouse with lace at the cuffs, pale jeans she'd probably ripped herself. She was all jagged lines and ruffles. On our first date we dyed her sparse hair pink. It stood out in little tufts and patches, so the color contrast was excellent. She looked like a lollipop—bright and sticky. I wanted to lick her.

Wearing my steel-toed boots, muscle shirts, and black jeans with the key chain on my belt, I looked like a skinhead. Even after my hair came back in, I shaved it off. That's where the "no tits" comes in handy. I freak, therefore I am.

The sex was not the best I've had—it always felt like something was slipping out of place—but it was as an affirmation of being alive and using what we've still got—cunts and fingers and minds.

For Jessica, it went deeper. It was in her bones. Her marrow, in fact. The first time we did it she puked, after. Right in the bed. She'd finished her first round of chemo. "It's all right," I told her, stripping off the sheets like a pro. "I like the idea I fucked your guts out." She screamed like I was the funniest dyke on the block, then covered her mouth and ran to the bathroom. I heard her retching while I put on a CD.

I was in remission, but I had a stash of pain pills from when I should have used them and didn't. I wanted to be awake during it all. And I wanted a way out, later, if I needed it. I even tried to bully the docs into letting me have the surgery without general. I think it made them squeamish, the idea of me being awake while they sliced off my breasts like two bloody custards. The nurses seemed less barbaric. One of them let me flirt with her, even though I could see her ring when she adjusted my morphine drip. I let it drip. At home I took just enough dope to keep going.

When Jessica came back from the bathroom she flopped down on the bed and wiped her pale hand across her face. I was afraid she might fall asleep, so I kissed her. Her mouth still tasted like puke, even though she'd brushed her teeth. That was a nice gesture, because during chemo everything smells 20 decibels higher than it did before. Mint toothpaste stinks about as loud as you can get. I wanted to say something, but it all seemed too corny. So I slid my tongue down her chin, across her chest and belly, and into her cunt. She tasted surprisingly sweet. Like a hummingbird, I lapped at her, my heart beating like hell to keep me there.

I wished she had her period. I knew it was in her blood, her danger. I wanted to taste it. Mine had been removed—slice and sew and the problem is gone. But you can't empty a person of blood and then refill them, like changing the oil in a car. I could get under her hood all I wanted and still not see her problem.

After she came we took some of my pills. I let her fuck me for a while. It felt distant, like my cunt was a thousand years away, but her face was right up close. She had only a few eyelashes. I liked her eyelids bare and swollen, and I kissed them. I liked her nose, her ears, her forehead, stared at them while her fingers fluttered inside my mile-long cunt. When the drugs really kicked in we just lay side by side, sleeping on and off, drooling, like the dogs who flopped across our legs.

I came to before Jessica and found *King Kong* on cable. I could see where he was coming from. I felt like I could hold all of Jessica in one hand. Like my mere presence could make her swoon, with fear, with love, with pain pills, sometimes. Later, of course, I could have held her in one hand. Well, only theoretically, since the family wouldn't let me near the urn. They thought I was sick. The laugh was on them because I had beat it—but for some people, it's not about the cancer. When I met her family at the funeral I understood why Jessica had stayed a punk so long.

Her friends threw her a real memorial, with people talking about Jessica's art and drinking tequila and wearing slutty black stuff from secondhand stores. It made me wish Jessica was there. She would have loved it. We would have dished everyone afterward, in bed, harshed on their haircuts.

On my way home from the memorial I bought three marrow soup bones. I gave one apiece to the dogs and kept the third. I watched how each dog held its bone between its paws and licked out the middle, like an ice cream cone. I got down on the floor with them. Sprawled on the cool kitchen linoleum I sucked out the marrow, imagining Jessica, open before me, tasting blood on my tongue.

Genderbender

Julia St. John Park

You have to understand that men don't usually annoy me. Straight ones, anyway. When I walk down the street, Mexican guys, black guys, white guys—they look straight past me like I don't exist. Not being gorgeous is sort of a gift, I guess, but I must admit I've helped it along. While no one could hold me responsible for the narrowness of my hips—any more than they could the cut of my jaw—I must confess that I had a hand in shaping my wide, rounded shoulders and dense back. My big pecs with nipples that pass for tits are the price I pay to keep my state bench title, year in and year out, against formidable odds. The day I heard some boy point me out to his friend in the supermarket as "Conan the Pre-Raphaelite," that was the day I gave in and cut my hair. Now, so long as I don't wear the long earrings that get me called "faggot," men, as I said, pretty much ignore me on the street. Even in a tank top, I can walk to the bar in peace.

I suppose I don't have to tell you that it's not always worth the trip. Some steely-eyed separatist once tried to tell me that all meat is full of steroids. At the time, of course, I took it personally. But standing at the crowded bar in the Closet, with the air conditioner chilling the sweat on the back of my scalp, I began to wonder if she was right. The women in the bar seemed hard and horse-faced like me.

It was a sobering spectacle that called for another drink. I know what I like in a lady, and it can be spelled out in a single word: soft. Keep your pert, Dixie Cup breasts and aerobicized buns; give me marshmallow titties, long silky hair, squishy thighs on either side of my face, and a bottom that quivers when you slap it. They say people always want what they don't have, and sometimes they're right.

The fat women leaned intimately in corners, buttons straining on their work shirts, while a depressing blond with a ponytail and a washboard stomach danced suggestively at me. At 1 o'clock, just when I resigned myself to going home without so much as a fresh phone number, a male voice addressed itself to the back of my shoulder.

This was, as I mentioned before, an unusual event. I turned around and said "hi" back.

He had muscular arms and kind of a dyke haircut. "Oh, excuse me," he stammered. "I didn't…um…"

"Yeah, yeah," I said disgustedly. "You can still say hi."

His look changed suddenly. Maybe it was my baritone. "I have never said this before in my life," he bragged sincerely, "but I think you are a very attractive woman."

That's because I look like a man, you idiot, I wanted to say. I didn't. Maybe it was because he seemed encouraged by the fact that I didn't punch him out. Maybe, unlike most biological women, I just don't have much experience telling men to go fuck them selves. Whatever the reason, I stood there, guzzling my beer and letting him shout over the music.

I didn't absorb much of his monologue, just that his name was Dave. Obviously, it had been a while since he tried to sweet-talk a woman. He sidled up close, eyeing the veins in my arms, and tried to flatter me by comparing me to a famous East German swimmer who was thrown out of the '84 Olympics—unfairly, he said, for failing her chromosome check. When he asked me to go home with him, I had to laugh.

He ignored my reaction utterly.

"I've got a strap-on," he purred, and placed his hand near the top of my thigh.

I felt my clit stiffen involuntarily. I swallowed hard and looked around the bar. Even the bitch with the ponytail was gone. Let this be a lesson to you: When a guy wearing perfume starts to look good, you've gone too long without pussy.

Dave drove me back to his apartment, which struck me as pretty messy for a faggot's. In his small room I took off my 501's while he held out a menacing contraption for me to step into. It looked like a dismembered forearm being held at bay by a complicated system of leather leashes.

"I'm not touching your dick," I warned him.

"Don't worry about that," he said, eyelids thickening. "That won't be necessary." I stood staring down at the fleshy plastic hose protruding from my crotch and felt a strange surge of excitement. The dildo was obviously too large to be accommodated by any human orifice, and its nature as a purely decorative object delighted me. Dave liked it. He kissed me unexpectedly on the mouth, rolled a large condom affectionately onto "me," and turned out the light.

In a moment, his legs were over my shoulders, and my new plastic cock was violating major laws of physics regarding volume.

"Oh! Fuck my hole! Deeper!" he grunted, as I rammed my six-foot frame against him. The dildo kept crashing through the looking glass of his asshole and reemerging magically. His mounting arousal defied logic. But to my surprise, the base of the dildo rhythmically striking my clit started making me fell hot too. I stopped worrying about his internal organs and tried to figure out how I could stroke my own nipples. Forget it, I finally told myself. This particular crime against nature requires at least two hands for leverage.

"Make sounds like a woman when you come," I pleaded with him urgently.

"Never. Heard it," he gasped.

"You know," I begged, "like in Donna Summer's 'Love to Love You, Baby.'"

After a compliant wince of recognition, Dave made some encouraging high-pitched sighs that drew more blood into my swollen clit. As he neared orgasm, he gripped the enormous toy with his ass muscles, and I was sure I could feel my erect clit being squeezed mercilessly along with it. I continued crashing into him violently until he arched his head back onto the pillow, made an appealing womanly sound, and shot a load of gay come all over my abs.

He threw his arm over his eyes as he caught his breath. "What a pump, girlfriend. You musta hit my fuckin' G spot."

I knelt astride him, cunt throbbing, plastic erection theatrically unreduced, watching him watch the come drip down my taut torso.

"Shall I do the same to you?" he asked doubtfully, as he tossed my condom in the trash.

"No, thanks," I answered. "I don't feel like a trip to the trauma center tonight." I slid off the bed and headed toward the bathroom, where, I hoped, I could diddle my aching clit to a disappointing climax. The artificial dick bounced proudly and ironically ahead as I skulked down the narrow hall to find the jane.

When I did, I saw a crack of light and heard the unmistakable sound of a woman peeing. Before I had a chance to wonder if I was going insane, the door opened, and before me stood a sleepy-eyed, messy-haired, stark naked goddess.

She gave a little shriek when she saw me, and covered her pendulous breasts ineffectively with one hand, her mink bush with the other. The Rubenesque arm over her crotch lay across a rounded, drooping tummy. I gasped and hit the wall with my back.

"Oh," she giggled, looking at the fantastic dildo rising from my mound, "you're a woman." Her arms relaxed.

"It's his," I said, pointing to Dave's room.

"Really?" Then she saw my hunger. She covered her mouth and laughed shyly. Her eyes asked me if it was OK, and mine answered yes. Still chuckling, she advanced the few steps to my side of the hall. She spread her plump thighs and the silky fur of her pussy grazed my naked cock.

In awe, I touched her smooth breasts. She put her warm, dimpled arms around my neck and started sliding her slit over the length of my tool. I looked over her shoulder, and saw her fat ass arching back, forcing the tip of her clit to hit my cock just where she wanted it.

This bizarre turn of events suited me just fine. I spread my cunt lips with one hand and felt her thrusts against me. My clit grew fully erect again in no time, and the dildo glistened with her wetness. I jiggled her heavy breast and fingered the nipple with my free hand as she masturbated to orgasm on my cock, right there in the hallway. She came silently, after some quick, involuntary thrusts.

"Wait," I cried as she padded down the hall to her bedroom. The lower half of me pulsated with unrelieved swelling. "I can't come like that!"

"Isn't that Dave's department?" she asked.

"He's asleep by now. Besides, I want you. For real. Not with this insane thing."

"Oh, I see." Instantly her voice became thick and sexy, the way only a fat woman's can. She shuffled back, and leaned into me. "Dave's not going to lick your pussy, is he? No. And it needs to be licked and sucked, doesn't it?"

I nodded numbly. "Now let's take this off and get some Saran Wrap," she continued as we walked to her room, "and I'll give your poor, sweet pussy something good, before it turns blue."

I lay back on her bedsheets, savoring their toasty smell. She lowered a mammoth breast into my mouth. "Don't suck," she said firmly, "just lie there and let me do you." I let her nipple rub against my tongue as her fingers groped their way down to my battered bush. She spread my pussy lips apart and let me feel the cold air on my burning, wet clit. She forced more of her huge tit into my mouth, and I had to push up against it with my tongue to keep from being suffocated.

I bucked my cunt in the air, hoping her finger would slide into it. But instead she pulled her boob from my mouth, bounced it down the length of my body, and jiggled her nipple around on my swollen clit. I pushed it away, pinching the fat of her wet, sticky breast between my fingers. I longed for her tongue, and didn't want to come until I felt its heat.

She grinned at me in the dark. "Say 'lick me,' " she said playfully.

"Lick me," I complied. "I want you to lick me now." I watched as she exposed her pink tongue and lowered it to my spread snatch. She paused, half an inch from me, watching my face. With her hands, she gently floated a big square of Saran Wrap between my legs. I felt a breeze, and the faintest contact with its surface. I knew I was finally going to get it, and I sighed.

Her tongue pressed onto my cunt, and she lapped me up good—like no one but a dyke can.

"Lick me, lick me. Oh yeah, lick it," I gasped. Her mouth was a furnace, consuming all my energy. She pushed down on my knees, keeping my cunt exposed for her round, cherubic face. Juice bubbled up under the Saran Wrap, and she squished it around expertly, all the while making horny, slurping noises for my benefit. My arms clenched around my chest as an orgasm shuddered through my body.

I hoped she wouldn't notice so she would keep going. No need, though. She tore a new piece of Saran Wrap from the bedside roll and kissed my open cunt softly. Slowly, she began licking again.

Time became meaningless. All I could say was "Oh, lick

it, suck my clit, oh yeah," and it felt like she was never going to stop sucking my pussy.

I cried out and came again in her mouth. Undeterred, she went back to her kisses and started licking again. This time she worked intensely, rubbing her tongue, her chin, and even her teeth into me. She sucked me hard into a final climax as I pressed my solid, flat pussy into her face.

I was numb. I pushed her head away and straightened out my stiff hips.

"Sweet baby all done?" she asked, her face shiny with saliva. I started to cry from gratitude and relief. She told me her name was Sheila. Mine is Ann. Falling asleep was easy next to her safe, luscious body.

The next morning Sheila woke me up. Her breasts smelled delicious and I wanted to kiss them.

"Dave was wondering what happened to you," she said. "I told him he was pathetic." She tossed me a bathrobe and I put it on. It was way too short for me, so I had to tug on the back of it as I crept into Dave's empty room and picked up my jeans and tank top from his linoleum floor.

In the kitchen Dave was making coffee, wearing Air Jordans and a just-fucked look on his face. I couldn't believe he was able to walk. "Look," he said, "we wear the same size."

"I'm sure my feet are narrower," I said, not sure at all.

"Well," he grinned, as he gave me a friendly clap on the back, "you shouldn't mind having big feet, when you've got such a humongous dick."

Despite ourselves, we snickered like a pair of schoolboys, until Sheila came in. Then I looked down and blushed.

Claudine, or, The Devil in Officer Jones

Lynne Jamneck

I knew it the moment she first opened her paint-chipped apartment door to me. There she stood magnificently inviting, dressed in a faded pair of jeans and a tight white T-shirt. Before she had even had the chance to introduce herself, I wanted to fuck her.

She had one hand up against the edge of the front door, the other on her hip as she contemplated the uniformed cop in front of her.

"Right. The car," she said slowly in a voice that had seen too many cigarettes.

"Sergeant Jones," I said by way of introduction.

"Please." She dropped her hand from the door and showed me in. Huge windows lined the one end of the loft's whitewashed wall and looked down on a busy, rain-slicked New York City street. I turned my gaze from the street below, and saw her eyes move over the gun at my side. She was making coffee.

"How do you take it?" I heard her ask. Nuance rose over the clinking of cups.

"Black, no sugar."

"Of course," she smiled. "So then, I guess you'd better ask me some questions, officer."

I took out my notepad. "You say your husband stole the car?" I asked, all professionalism.

"My ex." She lit a cigarette.

Her hand wasn't supposed to be on my thigh, but it was nonetheless. How did that happen?

The sight of Claudine's slender fingers on my uniform slacks made my nipples go instantly hard. With her other hand, she started unbuttoning the buttons on my blue shirt. The hand on my leg squeezed above my knee, making me push back into the couch involuntarily, wary of the fact that I'd be promptly suspended for screwing a woman on a routine questioning.

I wanted to, though; oh, God, I wanted to.

"Why don't you go ahead, Sergeant Jones?" she smiled, her voice still low.

"Claudine—"

She lowered her head and with her teeth started teasing one of my nipples through the fabric of my shirt. "Nobody will come," she muttered, and for the first time I heard a slight crack in her voice, a small infraction of want passing between her lips. It was that tiny breach of control that made me lose what little I had left.

I suddenly became furious at her for putting me in a situation like this, and I wondered how many others she had played this game with on this exact couch.

I was in control, *me*. I'm the fucking cop.

With one hand I shoved her back against the other end of the leather couch.

It squeaked perversely as I moved to lie down on top of her, the weight of my whole body pushing into hers, one of my legs between her own so that our hips pushed eagerly into each other. She moaned as my piece pushed against the inside of her thighs. I grabbed both her wrists in one hand and pinned them above her head, the other hand grabbing her jaw roughly.

Footsteps outside the door, her mouth inches from mine and her breath hot against my cheek.

Keys in the door.

"Fuck me," Claudine whispered urgently in my ear.

"Not yet," I replied, getting off her, at the same time and grabbing my shirt from the floor. I heard a key turn, but a huge pillar in the middle of the room blocked my view. By the time he came walking around the corner, we were composed and I had my notebook in my hand once more. He must have been in his late 30s, graying around the edges, attaché case in one hand.

"Officer Jones," Claudine spoke calmly. "My husband, Ben."

He looked tiredly at both of us.

"No, I'm not the one who stole the car," he finally said, then turned around to pour himself a scotch.

· · ·

The second time I saw Claudine was at a cop bar down East 52nd Street. Black leather pants with drawstrings down the side, black boots that could kick a hole in Johnny Rotten, and a tank top.

I was still sitting at my usual table in a dark corner near the back when she saw me, walked over, and leaned against my table.

"They still haven't found my car."

I picked up the bottle from the table and swallowed the last dregs.

"I know."

We looked at each other.

"They haven't found my husband either," she continued.

"I know," I replied and got up from the table.

· · ·

She wouldn't let me take off my clothes. She wouldn't even let me take off my belt, and she certainly wouldn't let me take off my gun. I pinned her against the wall in the dark the moment we entered her apartment, as I'd wanted to on that first day two weeks ago. Traffic and far-off screams from the streets below filtered through the windows. God it was hot in here.

I slid my hands slowly down the front of her body, starting at her shoulders, fingers tracing the sidelong curve of her breasts, down her ribs and coming to a halt in the small of her back. I started unbuttoning my shirt, meaning to take it off, but Claudine stopped me.

"I want you to fuck me with your clothes on," she said, and I knew by her tone that she was demanding things of me again. It scratched at my cop sensibilities: Do this, *now*, not later.

When I get called out to a scene, I give the orders. I had never been manipulated in my life, and it made me mad as hell. What angered me even more was the fact that I'd been manipulated oh, so willingly. Not by Claudine, really, but by my own desperate need to possess her. The lust I felt for her muffled every single alarm that went off in my head as I lay awake at night, sweating, hand between my legs as I imagined Claudine opening her door to me once more and telling me what a good girl I was.

I'd phoned her the previous night and told her how clever I had been. How I'd managed to make everything look like a sad, freak accident.

Now it was *her* turn to listen.

My hand stung from the tips of my fingers to the base of my palm as it slapped across Claudine's check. It actually caught her off-guard; I could see the surprise in her eyes.

"Tonight we're doing what I want," I said in the voice normally reserved for street trash I loaded into the back of a police cruiser. I felt her hand moving up the inside of my thigh. "Take your hand away," I commanded. She was trying not to show her appreciation at the authority in my voice. I unhooked the cuffs from my belt and in one smooth practiced move had both her hands secured behind her back.

191

Her nipples were rock-hard by now, and I took each at a time between my fingers and pinched them until she whimpered with satisfying pain.

Her jeans unzipped easily, and I found the white cotton panties she was wearing a satisfying affirmation of many a night's lonely fantasies. Claudine was trying to say something through short breaths.

"If you say so much as one word Claudine, I will walk out the door, leave you tied to a chair, and you'll never see me again." I looked into her dark eyes. "Do you understand me?"

She nodded.

"You're such a good girl, Claudine. Just listen to what I tell you."

She nodded, biting on her lip to keep the words from spilling out as I slipped two fingers past the elastic on her underwear. Slowly I reached for her clit. I worked the excited organ, transforming it into a hard, solid affirmation of pleasure. I wasn't sure what turned Claudine on more, my hand inside her panties or the lack of control she was suddenly experiencing.

Within a few moments she was so hard that there was nothing left for me to do but slowly ease three fingers into her, relishing the warm wetness I found there. With her eyes closed, head thrown back, I finally—mercifully—screwed her into the blue paint-chipped door.

This wasn't about sex. But I knew that. It might have been in the beginning, that first day. But that all changed the moment she phoned me and asked me to murder her husband.

Yet I couldn't stop, couldn't keep from giving myself to her, using her, ravaging her for my own personal desire. The fact that she was enjoying it was just coincidental.

Claudine kept quiet right through, and I used her in every way possible; any way my perverted mind could entertain. She did beg, but not with words. She didn't dare.

When I was finally finished I released her hands, chafed from the metal cuffs rubbing against the skin. She stumbled to the couch. I left to pull myself together in her bathroom, and when I came back out there were two uniformed cops waiting for me in the living room. They knew me.

Claudine was gone.

They took me in and asked me questions about the death of Ben Carter. Claudine was still gone. They said they found fingerprints at the scene. I don't know how, because I was wearing gloves. They said Carter was strangled, which I really don't understand. Insulin. He was supposed to die of an insulin overdose.

But to tell you the truth, looking back on the night in question as I sit here in this cell, there's not all that much I can remember. I asked for Claudine. She never came.

At the Almador Motel

Jessie Fischer

Sylvia couldn't believe she'd lived to be 34 years old and had never been fucked with a dildo. She'd been gay at least half those years, and ever since she'd double-fucked those two strippers behind the Denny's in '93, she'd gained a rep among her friends as an insatiable sex fiend, someone who broke all the rules. But that was 10 years ago, and for the last four she'd been living the quiet life with Melissa, in a sweet little home in the suburbs. Then one autumn morning Sylvia had woken up, looked around her, taken in all the "assembly life" crap from Pottery Barn and Williams-Sonoma and Crate & Barrel, and thought, *Who the fuck have I become?* Well, maybe it didn't happen that suddenly; for months Melissa's "Jeanette Sconce With Antique Beaded Articulating Wall Base" in the bedroom had nearly been sneering at her, making her want to dash into the kitchen and destroy all of Melissa's carefully organized back issues of *Martha Stewart Living*.

That was six months ago, and since then Sylvia had broken up with Melissa and secured a loft downtown, which she furnished eclectically. (Her one rule: Nothing could come from a catalog.) When she'd left Melissa, she'd had all sorts of fantasies about women pounding down her door; when word got out that the horniest lezzie in town was single, it'd be nonstop action, right? Well, not exactly: All the women who'd once crawled between the sheets with her on cold winter nights were now crawling between their own 100% Egyptian cotton sheets with their own girlfriends, in their own sweet little homes in the suburbs, making crafty centerpieces and ginger-laced hot chocolate and...babies.

So Sylvia had gone the way of all desperate dykes and placed an online personal ad. Under "Relationship Desired" she had merely typed "Sex." And then the line: "First-timer looking for all-night strap-on action." She knew it sounded lame, but that's what she craved, right? Pure sex. No commitment. She yearned for those days when every weekend meant devouring a new and different pussy, taking in the smells and tastes of a hot femme or a stone-cold butch or whoever the fuck she wanted.

She'd gotten some e-mails from a few duds—women who'd duped her with photos from 15 years ago, women who were really men, women who wanted to watch her with a man, you get the picture. But the babe she was meeting tonight would be the one to rock her world, fuck her to oblivion—she just knew it. Sylvia had only gotten one email from the woman—who went by the screen name "Dil-Master"—and it read:

Tomorrow night. Almador Motel. 9 P.M. Room 203.
I will fuck you to kingdom come.

And attached was a photo of a woman with the most piercing blue eyes, cropped silver hair, and a jawline more chiseled than that of Mount Rushmore's Mr. Jefferson himself.

The following night she spent nearly two hours in front of the mirror, blow-drying her silky brown tresses, applying and reapplying mascara, making sure her lip liner was just right. And then at 8:40 she jumped into her Honda Passport (the one aspect of Melissa's bourgeois lifestyle she couldn't part with) and made a beeline for the Almador. During the drive, she fondly remembered the night she'd driven the then-married-with-two-kids

Joanna Inman to the same ramshackle establishment and turned her out on a scratchy, beer-stained bedspread. Joanna (well, "Jo") was a physical therapist with a flattop now.

The sky was cobalt and a silver crescent moon hung in the air when Sylvia knocked on the scraped lime-green door of room 203, car keys in one hand, pepper spray in the other. (You couldn't be too careful with those Internet liaisons. She'd read that in one of Melissa's O magazines.) The door opened to reveal the woman from the pic, who was even more stunning than she'd appeared in the slightly pixelated photo she had sent. She was wearing a black tee and tight jeans, and a bulge the size of Toledo strained at her crotch, which instantly sent Sylvia's snatch into hysterics.

"First-timer?" the woman said in a sexy, low voice.

"Dil-Master?" Sylvia asked, realizing the cheesiness of it all, but what else could she say? She didn't know the woman's first name. And she preferred it that way.

Wordlessly, Dil-Master (or D.M., as Sylvia had nicknamed her) took Sylvia by the hand, closed the door behind them, and led her to the flowered bedspread. *This place hasn't changed a bit,* Sylvia thought, and as she did a chill ran from her spine straight to her cunt at the image of Joanna Inman flat on her back, her dripping wet pussy playfully pumping into Sylvia's insatiable mouth. But Sylvia was clearly with a pro now, not a virginal closeted housewife. This time Sylvia would be the one getting turned out.

Sylvia took in all of D.M.: her runner's body, her cut biceps, her strong thighs visible through the close-fitting jeans, and gave D.M. an approving nod. D.M. smiled in response, then positioned Sylvia on her back on the mattress and climbed on top of her. Sylvia looked up into D.M.'s steely blue eyes and saw a kind of wisdom there, a kind of experience, surely the kind of experience one can only get from having lapped at hundreds—thousands, probably!—of hot, sticky pussies. D.M. began with gentle licks and kisses at Sylvia's widow's peak, an untamable tuft that had caused her endless taunting on the playground, but which now for some reason drove the ladies wild. *Funny how those things change,* Sylvia thought with a smirk, but not for long because D.M.'s expert tongue and teeth were now licking and biting the tender skin behind Sylvia's left ear. She thought she might come from that alone, but she held back, knowing the best was still to come.

When Sylvia emitted a moan—actually a cross between a chirp and a growl—D.M. pulled out all the stops, quickly slipping Sylvia out of her silk top and leather skirt. Sylvia dutifully assisted D.M. by whipping off her bra and panties. She flung her underpants across the room, and they landed on a wall lamp that looked strikingly similar to her old bedroom nemesis.

Sylvia chuckled under her breath but quickly shut up when D.M. unbuttoned her 501's and unleashed a monstrous strap-on—the biggest, fattest dildo Sylvia had ever seen up close. (Actually, the only one she'd ever seen this closely had been on the Internet.) It was black and thick and long and looked nothing like a penis, for which Sylvia thanked her lucky stars. D.M. reached over to the faux-maple nightstand, pulled out a tube of lube, and greased up the slick cock with the gooey stuff. Just the sight of D.M. stroking her shaft sent Sylvia's hungry pussy into spasms.

With the tip of her dick, D.M. teased Sylvia, moving it in tight little circles around her pink bud, which grew harder by the second. Finally she poked the fatty inside Sylvia's gushing hole; it was just a little poke, like a child testing the pool with her toe, but it was enough to make Sylvia's entire body shudder with delight. *This is what I've waited half my life for,* she thought. *This is what that uptight Melissa couldn't give me. Sex without strings.* When D.M. realized the water was warm and welcoming, she plunged in deeper, thrusting slowly at first, then gradually increasing in speed. The roughness of D.M.'s denim-clad thighs against Sylvia's bare ones was delicious, almost dirty, she thought. They hadn't spoken a word since Sylvia had entered the room, and that was just how she liked it. The last thing she needed was someone asking her if she paid the gas bill through a mouth full of quivering twat.

D.M. was pumping full force now, Sylvia's big brown eyes fixed on D.M.'s baby blues. As D.M. slid her pole in and out of Sylvia's velvety snatch, she found herself unable to tear herself away from D.M.'s gaze. There was something intense there, she thought. Something profound and mysterious. Almost religious. She thought she might drown in their beauty, their wisdom. If there were a place one might find solace or God or Buddha or whoever or whatever holds our answers, this would be the place; Sylvia was certain.

But her pussy was a little more certain, and when she felt D.M.'s thick rod bump up against her swollen clit on its way out, then again on its way in, she closed her eyes tightly, savoring the fullness in her cunt, feeling the blood try to pound its way out of her body. When she opened her eyes again, she was instantly lost in D.M.'s gaze. *Surely this woman is a poet, a philosopher, a teacher, an advocate for the poor and helpless,* Sylvia thought. *How else could she make me feel so good?*

D.M. was pumping like a jackhammer now, and Sylvia's eyes practically rolled back into her head, the pleasure and slight pain driving her wild. Her cunt tightened with each thrust, gripping D.M.'s cock like there was no tomorrow. And just then Sylvia felt herself at the edge, as a million images swirled through her mind's eye and she heard John Lennon's "Imagine" playing gorgeously inside her head and her coming came in long loud waves and everything was perfect in the world and she cried "Yes!" so loudly D.M. thought the filthy wall mirror might shatter into a thousand glorious pieces.

Forget all those one-night stands and back-room quickies I used to have, Sylvia thought moments later, wrapped in D.M.'s strong arms. *What do I need those for when I've got this this philosopher, this teacher, my beautiful silver-fox poet?* Sylvia knew she'd probably spend the rest of her life with this woman. D.M. obviously held all the answers to life's problems in those deep blue eyes; Sylvia just had to figure out which questions to ask.

"So what do you do for a living?" Sylvia finally asked a half-asleep D.M.

"Drive a truck," D.M. said. "For Pottery Barn."

The Fountain

Nipper Godwin

Water in a desert. I cannot turn away from the mirage, even knowing what it is. I know I am dreaming; I will myself to sleep deeper.

You are looking at me with that level gaze that turns my knees to sand. Unblinking, your eyes burn into me, utterly serious. You know what I want, and there is nothing silly or shameful about it.

I am looking into the mirror on your closet door, at my own naked body and at you, regarding me. There is your loft bed in the reflection, the one to which I was bound by handcuff, by rope, by promise, by the sheer force of your will. Well-worn memory, not dream.

Only the object that you hold betrays the illusion, the thing I was too embarrassed to ask for, still too embarrassed to name. You are holding the red rubber hose in one hand, the bag sagging with liquid in the other. You do not leer or scowl or smile or even speak, knowing beyond doubt that anything you want of me is yours. I kneel on immaculate white fake fur on polished hardwood, on all fours, the deep obeisance.

I wait in the cool silence that always prevailed in your house, no music, the noise of traffic muted by the stone and plaster of a different Boston century. In the hush you have commanded, there is only my breathing to listen to. And yours: I feel it on my skin. Then your fingers, spreading me, and the smooth nozzle with its dollop of cool lube, slipping inside.

The liquid that flows into me is nearly blood-warm. My ass is in the air, receiving it, while you stand watching as afternoon light filters though white curtains. Aware of you, every inch of my skin is hot, and I bury my face in my arms to give myself over to your invasion.

"It's only water." I don't know if I've heard your voice or only imagined it. I am more aroused than I have ever been, my clit throbbing, my slick-wet lips opening like a flower. If you laid on the lash, if you stuffed your dry fist into my aching hole, if you only touched me now, I would come. Just when I think the stream will flow into me forever, it stops. Your hand on my hip is white-hot, and I flinch from it, shivering, then lean into your touch like a dog. The tube slips out.

If that was all, it would be enough. But in sleep's disjunctive narrative, we are on your bed. The tiny bathroom is down a ladder, across the room, across the distance of a continent. Your clean sheets. Your mattress. The liquid filling my belly, sloshes, lurches, cramps.

"Yes, you can." Your voice answers my unspoken plea. "I know you can." This time, I know I have heard it, calm and certain, piercing my heart. Nearly waking me. In desperation, I clutch at the wreck of illusion and refuse to be swept upward into consciousness. The light on my eyelids is your city twilight, your bare overhead bulb heating the air around us. You are wearing nothing but that white T-shirt. Your flat abs, your muscular thighs are bare, your upraised knees spread for me. Your fingers twine through my hair and pull me down, back into the dream.

Your pussy. I lower my face into your wetness, trembling. "Yes," you say, "that's right," grinding my face into the coarse thicket of your pubic hair. My tongue searches for your clit, stabs the swollen nub. Your hips jerk and you pull my head away. "Slow," you say. "Easy."

No taste. No smell. The inadequacy of my subconscious teases me; in this, memory has no compensation. You allowed me this only once, the night you tore my back open with a hempen cat and I took every stroke. Your breath rasped from exertion and desire: Sweat and pain blinding me, I listened to your breath. Even when you had worn yourself out on me, I wanted more. You laughed when I told you. You said, "There will always be more."

I listen to your breath, heavy with desire. My face is wet with spit, with your juices; my belly gurgles and aches; my skin is slick with sweat. Desperation drives me; I burrow my nose into your labia, strain my tongue to stroke and lap, purse my lips to seize your clit, your inner lips, and never let you feel my teeth. I am hanging on with every muscle of my body, my sphincter clenched, riding you like chop on the winds of a gale, riding the storm of your orgasm. My triumph.

In semidarkness I stumble to the bathroom, groggy and stupid, and hurry back to bed, numb. I was always obstinate; my willfulness amused you. I reject the coming day, the life I have now, the years that have gone by. Dreams are vapor, but this one waits for me on the other side of waking, something more than air. I sink into the depths of the miracle gratefully.

Rough denim against my naked skin, your thighs forcing my knees apart, the smooth fabric of your T-shirt against my ruined back, your breath on my neck. I remember brown blotches on the white cotton. My blood. It didn't matter, you said, you holding me while I cried, shame and release all in one, me who never cried. You told me I made you proud.

Your fingers part my ass cheeks, push lube into my waiting hole, guide the head of the cock you've chosen, slippery and cool, gliding into me. The slim knobby one, shivering me with pleasure. In and out. It is buttoned into the fly of your jeans, the cloth gritting against me with every deep stroke. Your fingers like fire on my ribs, seizing my nipples, twisting. The cock pumping, my ass opening to it like an anemone, in slow motion heaviness, this amalgam of memory and dream. The moment of stillness, denim teasing my skin, the wave before it breaks. I arch my back. Your breath quick and hot on my neck. Your breath. Your breath.

I wake shuddering, orgasm receding like ripples. I am in my own bedroom in the half-light of morning. The dogs are snoring. Across the big bed, motionless in sleep, is my lover, a good woman, sensible and kind. Not a bad boy like you, you the bi butch slut, "on me not in me," the button that mocked me from the lapel of your leather jacket, reminding me I was not your only choice. You were capricious and cruel as the Father God the nuns told me about, so many years ago, that I never believed until you came, the burning bush, the rock from which water flowed to quench me, a god with tits and cunt and Y-front underwear, whose gaze was as hot and blinding as the sun.

You left me nothing but an image of something I never saw, the twisted wreck of your motorcycle beneath a bridge abutment. Your landlord told me.

For weeks, the woman beside me set food in front of me and picked up books that slid off my lap while I stared at nothing and told her nothing was wrong. She knew that I had stopped seeing you, never why. If her victory was sweet, she did not show it.

You belonged to a place where I could not stay, only make pilgrimage. Desire was a pitiless landscape, unrelieved by any tender thing. I crossed it to drink from you like a fountain. You said there would always be more. You were a liar.

I swore I would never say your name, would never willingly think of you, would not admit to thirst. I would not cry for someone I did not love. Time passed. I never dreamed of you. Until now.

Salt wetness trickles down my face, at long last. Water in a desert.

Butch Flip

L. Nash May

All day at work my mind is full of butches. Big women flexing their forearms around their drink glasses. Butches, hands on hips around the pool table, watching other women walk by on their way to the john. Butches with soft bellies pushing against their T-shirts, protruding slightly over jeans, wearing jeans as only butches can.

I don't want a hard, lean woman with no fat anywhere. Not that I've really got a type; in fact, the girls at the bar can't seem to figure me out. "Her? Who the fuck knows? She's been down with everything but the *Titanic*." It's true, my tastes have been known to run the gamut from these big butches to dangerous-looking girls in full femme regalia, to fashion dykes with trendy hair, perfect clothes, and no manners. I admit, however, to a special predilection for butches—a predilection I intend to indulge in tonight.

How long since the last trick, anyway? Christ, it must be months. I've been working too hard, coming home late and exhausted, sometimes too tired to even make myself come. Tonight I skip out of work early and drive home feeling wide awake—predatory, in fact. I dress neutrally: tailored black pants, red silk shirt, red glasses, big silver bracelet. I look young and intellectual, maybe even a bit innocent. Maybe.

The bar's hired a new bouncer since I was here last, and

she cards me as I walk in. Initially the prospects look dim. To be sure, there's the usual crowd of butches around the pool table, but none of them interests me tonight. They're all busy hiding their softness so deep it's all but invisible, seeing who can outposture whom. I'm not up for it. Well, it's still early. I order an overpriced carbonated water from the waitress who always flirts with me and then head for the john.

I linger in the bathroom watching a beautiful woman re-apply her lipstick; she doesn't look at me. I've seen her here before, and she likes her women taller than I am, and harder.

Eleven-thirty. I contemplate going home; after all, I have to work in the morning, and it's beginning to look like I'm not going to get what I want after all. Having worked myself up for an exploit, however, I'm unwilling to acknowledge defeat, so I linger. For a while I amuse myself by trying to count how many women in the bar I've slept with, but that game can get real depressing real quick.

Just before midnight the leather dykes begin to trickle in. They always arrive around midnight, in small clumps, even when they haven't been somewhere else together. I don't know why this is, but it's true. I look them over, but I don't really know any in tonight's crowd. I decide to leave in 15 minutes.

I'm staring idly at the floor trying to decide if I think he new bouncer's hot or not. Then, she walks in. There's hope for this evening yet. She's tall, with brown-green eyes and the kind of lashes only little boys have, with a little boy's haircut to go with them. Long fine legs, broad shoulders, beautiful hands. She's clearly on the prowl.

She sizes up every woman who walks by with a quick, deft look. Like she can imagine what every breast would feel like against her face, how every curve of hip would fall in her arms, and maybe, I add to myself, noting the keys over her left hip, how each cheek would feel against her palm. She looks like she's probably had just about everybody she's ever wanted, and if the barely veiled hunger on her face now is any indication, I'll bet she can count more tricks in her than I can. But what really gets me is that despite this very competent cruising she still looks soft to me. And smart. There's an ironic shadow playing around her mouth, like somewhere she's watching herself and being amused by her own persona. Something in me clicks into gear.

Trying to look at least passably innocent and fuckable, I observe that she does not take any special notice of the really girly girls, the killer femmes in the high high heels and the short short skirts, although many of them are trying to attract her attention. A dozen people around the room shout hellos to her and motion to her to join them, but like me, she remains aloof. She begins to look slightly contemptuous, like there's no one in the bar who can hold her attention. She hasn't seen me yet.

She has to pass me if she wants a drink, and sure enough, she's heading for the bar. Long easy stride, still giving every woman she passes that detached, thorough up-and-down. When her eyes come to me it is palpable; although I pretend to ignore her, my stomach tightens and my cunt begins a slow burn.

She comes to stand by my table, so close I can smell her, so close I have to look up.

"Buy you a drink?" she says in a voice as practiced as her manner, fully aware of its effect.

"Sure. Beck's dark."

She comes back with the beer and a glass of bourbon and sits down without asking, carefully folding her long legs under the table. I wait for her to speak, hoping I won't be turned off by her first line.

"Do you play chess?"

"Yes." I continue to try to look innocent, to try to keep a smirk of my own off my face.

"Mmm," she says, rolling her bourbon around in her mouth, smiling again, ever so slightly.

"Why?"

"Oh, nothing. Do you want to dance?"

Yes, I want to dance. I know the way I dance makes butches think about fucking me; I dance like I need to get fucked and like whoever I'm with is just the one I need to do it with.

She leads me out onto the crowded dance floor, clearing space easily with her big body. She can dance. She's looser than many butches, more comfortable in her body. The hunger I saw on her face when she first walked in returns. She likes the way I move. She's watching me like she'd like to devour me, a faintly cruel expression on her face. I laugh to myself. Out of her leather jacket, I can see her sweet little breasts, nipples getting hard under the plaid men's shirt. I bet she doesn't like girls to touch her tits; I bet they turn her on too much too quick, make her feel like too much of a girl. I want to take her home.

The music is hot and the dance floor is packed. We are dancing close; I can smell her sweat. She reaches out and pulls my hips toward her. That first touch is a flash of heat. I work my cunt down onto her thigh and do my very best grind. I'm driving myself crazy, getting so wet I worry I'll seep through my pants and leave a mark on her jeans. She looks like she's getting pretty worked up too: Her face is flushed, and her hands tighten around my hips.

By the time the songs ends, I feel positively dangerous. I want to go home now.

"Do you want another drink?" she asks.

"Yes. Let's go have it at my house." Not subtle, but very effective. I've managed to ruffle her composure, if only for a second.

"All right. How do we get there?" She wants to be pleased about going home with me, but she's miffed. She didn't get to play it her way; she's not taking me to her place. She can just ponder that on the way home.

"I have a car. Let me get my jacket."

She sits silently on the drive back to my apartment. The delicate tension between us remains, but there is an added element of uncertainty. I can sense her sitting there, all systems on alert, putting together all the pieces of our brief contact and trying to figure me out. I smile sweetly and hum along with the tape, which just happens to be playing Grace Jones's "When the Hunter Gets Captured by the Game."

We park and get out, and I lead her down a shortcut through one of the quiet little alleys. I let her move me up against a garage wall and kiss me. It's hot, so hot. I want to take her clothes off and fuck her right there in the alleyway. I play slut and push her against the wall while we kiss, secretly assessing her strength. What I find is reassuring. This woman is no marshmallow, but even with her height, she's no match for me. I'm not a tall woman and I hide my muscles under generous curves, but I'm very strong. I have to be. I have a friend who says that threat is all in the weaponry, but I like knowing that I can hold almost any woman down. She takes the pressing as a sign of my wanting her and seems reassured as we walk up the stairs to my flat.

Without turning on any lights, I find her a glass of bourbon while she takes off her jacket and stands admiring my view over the bay. I sidle up behind her and press my breasts against her back, kissing her neck.

"Mmm," she says again, that low appreciative sound like she makes for her bourbon, a sound that makes me imagine how her mouth would feel on my cunt.

Just as she's about to turn around to take me in her arms, I grab her arm and twist it up behind her back. Pinching one of her nipples, I bite into her neck.

"Hey," she says, surprised and no doubt uncomfortable— I'm holding her arm pretty hard.

"What's the matter, big boy, you can dish it out but you can't take it? It's not pretty to have the tricks you use on other girls used against you, is it?"

"No, it's not pretty," she says dryly, "but somehow I'm not entirely surprised."

I laugh a slow evil laugh. "What tipped you off?"

"Oh, I don't know. Girls who want to lie down for me don't usually invite me to their place after one dance and virtually no conversation." There's a hint of a smile in her voice. That pleases me. It's only fun to roll butches if they get into it.

I laugh again and take a firmer grip on her nipple. Just as I suspected, she squirms. "Uh-huh, big boy, you don't want to want anything that bad that quick, for you?" Her breathing's coming a little quicker now, and uneven.

She doesn't answer me, just swallows her drink in one gulp and puts the glass down on the table, her hand unsteady.

"Big butches like you don't want to get fucked, do they?"

"That's right," she says.

"Uh-huh. I see. Well, that's not what this looks like to me," I say, running one hand down to her crotch, pressing the seam of the Levi's against her clit. "No, that's not what this looks like to me at all, you jumping all over the place like any other cunt, like any other common piece of ass." She refrains from comment, but she's straining against my hand.

"You're lying to me. You can't tell me that you don't want to lie down for me, for some nasty girl you don't even know. You can't tell me you don't want my hand inside there, don't want me to rub that sweet clit of yours until it aches. You can't tell me that, can you, big boy?"

"No." Her voice is losing its perfect cool, softening infinitesimally. I want to tear into her, open her up under my fingers, under my mouth. I lead her, or rather push her, one hand still holding her arm behind her back, into my bedroom. I take a firm grip on her hair and turn her around to face me, kissing her mouth and working her tits and clit through the jeans until I'm practically holding her up. She tries to move so I touch her just a little harder. I push her onto the bed.

"Take your clothes off for me, and make it pretty." She can't do it. It's such a girl thing, to take off your clothes for someone who's watching you, enjoying your body—butches are used to women doing that for them. Her face is a mixture of desire and defiance, quite a beauty. I stifle a strong urge to gloat.

"Come on, take your clothes off," I say.

She shakes her head. "I can't."

Slowly, deliberately, I come and lie on top of her. "Come now," I say. "You got those clothes on this morning. You must know how to take them off."

Her face turns red, but she shakes her head again, glaring down at the bed. I pull her hair, forcing her to look at me.

"You don't mean you can't, you mean you won't," I hiss, "and that's very bad. And surely you know what bad boys get."

"No," she says, almost tauntingly, "what do bad boys get?" She thinks I'm going to mete out some punishment, maybe a slap, something she could enjoy. But I'm meaner than that.

"Bad boys," I drawl, "get nothing. Get it? Bad boys don't get kissed, bad boys don't get fucked. Bad boys get left to ache alone in their blue jeans. So either get over it and take your clothes off or get your ass off my bed and call yourself a cab."

She smiles kind of ruefully and starts unbuttoning her shirt, not looking at me.

"There's a nice boy, nice little boy. Make it pretty for me and maybe I'll give you what you want."

Finally she lies there, naked, wanting, and really embarrassed. She wants me to do something, anything, just to stop looking at her.

"How do you like it, boy? How do you like to get fucked?"

Silence.

"You'd better tell me or you aren't going to get it."

"I like it," she says tersely, "on my stomach, and hard."

"Uh-huh. Well then you better turn over and put that pretty ass in the air so I can remind you what this is all about."

She turns over slowly, half-glaring at me over her shoulder. I lie on top of her, wrapping one arm underneath to her breast, running my other hand up and down her legs, circling over her ass and around her cunt. I open her with one slow and deliberate finger, spreading the wet around, teasing her clit. She smells good. I feel like something that hasn't been fed in too long.

"Oh, so pretty," I croon, "and you smell so good too. But you looked so angry a minute ago that I wonder if you still want me." I tease the opening of her cunt with two fingers.

"Yes," she says, "fuck me. Please." She sounds not at all contrite, but shit, I'll give her points for trying. Besides, I need to get inside her. I slide my fingers inside her, working in delicate circles, gentle, teasing strokes.

"Is that good, baby? Is that how you like it?"

"You know it's not," she mutters. She's rocking all over the bed trying to get me to push harder.

"Ask and you might receive, baby."

Silence.

"Now, look," I say, fucking her just slightly harder, "this is no time to pull a strong-and-silent trip. Don't you think you might as well try to get it the way you want it, the way you really need it? You know I can give it to you. But you've got to ask."

"Harder," she says, her voice almost inaudible, "I need it harder."

"Does my big butch need it hard? Is that how you like it?"

"More...please more," she says.

"More what, cunt?"

"More inside me. Please."

"Next thing you'll know you'll be telling me you want my whole hand."

"I want your whole hand right now."

"You do, huh? I'm sure you can do better than that," I say. I smile at her—but also stop fucking her.

"Please fuck me. Please give me the whole thing."

"Make it worth my while."

"I'll make it worth your while. I'll give it up for you so good. Feel how open I am. You could put your whole fist in me right now. Please. I want you."

So she can beg sweetly when it matters. I like that in a girl. And she's right, I could just slide my fist into her and I want to. I just want one more thing first. "Show me you want it now, cunt."

Absolute silence. Absolute motionlessness. Oh, shit. I know she knows what I mean, but will she do it? I have this hideous moment of self-doubt in every fuck where I wonder if I'm really good enough to pull this off, if I'm hot enough to make it worth her while. "You know what I want," I say, all the more menacing for my brief moment of vacillation. I fuck her harder, to give her a little motivation.

She picks herself up onto her hands and knees and moves herself back against my hand. I can hardly help but slide it into her.

"That's right, show me how bad you need it, open it up for me." I reach under the bed for a glove and the lube, work the glove onto my hand and spread some lube on it. She stays right there on her knees, waiting for me. "That's good, that's good." Slowly, so slowly, I work my hand into her. She makes a low groan when I finally get all the way inside her, and as always, I have a moment of sheer amazement at, and almost overwhelming gratitude for the fact that I have my whole hand in a woman's cunt.

"No, don't lie down yet. Hold it up there for me. I want to see you rock around my wrist." I start to fuck her hard. She's wide open, and I have waited long enough. So good, so good. I put my whole arm into it, lose myself in the motion.

She starts to let go, to make small noises, to let her face move when I move inside her. "That's right, that's right, let me hear about it, let me hear how you like it."

I fuck her right down onto the bed and slide my other hand around to work her clit. Almost immediately she starts to stiffen.

"If you think you're coming in the immediate future, you can think again," I say. "I waited long enough, now I'm going to take you for as long as I want. And you're not going to come until I tell you to, got it?"

"But I can't wait much longer."

"That's what you think." I move my hand away from her clit and just penetrate her for a while, a long while in fact. Then I take my hand out and just play with her clit. Either way, it's not quite enough.

I can see on her face when she stops straining and moves only in response to my hands. No more pretensions of control. No more butch trips. All gone. All mine.

"Please. Please don't stop."

I don't want to stop. I want to let it all go, to take her. No more tough-girl lines—now I just want to give her what she wants. "Come for me," I say quietly. "Come for me now."

She makes no noise. She just goes still, so still, and then I feel her cunt grip and release, many small strong times, and she relaxes under my hands.

I sit very still with her, feeling the moment inside and listening to her breathing. I carefully slide my hand out of her, peel off the glove, reach under the bed for a trick towel and come up to kiss her.

She smiles at me. "Give me that towel," she says, comfortable as if we'd done this hundreds of times before. I'm so relieved. I hate it when these tricks get all weird on me afterward.

"Do you mind if I smoke?" she asks after some moments of silence. Her voice has regained its smoothness, its composure.

"Do you want me to get your cigarettes for you?" I figure this is only courteous, since I'm dressed and she isn't.

"Thanks. They're in my jacket pocket."

By the time I come back form the living room with her cigarettes, she's buttoning up her jeans. I knew it.

"Here you go," I say, tossing them to her.

"Thanks," she says again, pulling her light out of her jeans pocket and lighting one. She sits back on the bed to smoke.

"So," she says, all attitude, "did I make it worth your while?"

"You'd still be wanting if you hadn't," I say.

"Can I make it worth your while?"

"No," I say. I'd like to see her try to make it worth my while some time. But not tonight.

She swings her long legs off my bed, puts her boots on, and walks out to the living room. She slides into her leather jacket and comes over and gives me a kiss. "So maybe sometime?"

"Maybe so."

"OK," she says, closing the door behind her. I listen to her footsteps in the hall. Just before she hits the stairs she calls back, "Thanks."

Anytime, I think. Anytime.

Like Nothing Ever Happened

Cara Bruce

"It's time to go." She's leaning against the door frame, staring at me with those intense black eyes. This was the third time she had hurried me, and I could tell she was getting pissed, but I actually enjoy making her mad. Sadistic, yes, but I like to bring her to the point of violence and I know she likes to get there. We've been together for three years, after all.

She looks back down at her watch, doing this on purpose because she knows I don't like to be rushed. I'm up for her little game today. I come up to her, real close, leaning my face just inches from hers; I lick my lips, I look into her eyes. I hover my hands directly above her thighs, move them without touching her over her cunt and I can feel the heat through her jeans.

She emits a small sigh that makes me smile. "We don't want to be late," I say and turn to walk out the door.

Her blood is boiling and her cunt is throbbing until we get downtown. I drive and she sits silently staring out the window. I reach over and rest my hand on her thigh, she looks over at me glaring, and I smile. I can't wait for the makeup sex.

When we get downtown she suddenly becomes happy. She's walking fast, and I get a chance to watch her beautiful ass; she's round and I like that. She has the cutest pooch of a

215

belly; she's wearing a cropped T-shirt that lets her roll jut out. It's so sexy it makes me just want to bite it.

"Kathy," she says, stopping short, "let's go in here."

We go into the woman's clothing store and I can't help but feel extremely butch in my leather jacket and boots. Sarah is holding up clothes to her and asking me what I think. What do I think? I think I'd like to rip every stitch of fabric off of your beautiful body and fuck the hell out of you right here, right now.

"Looks great," I say. She meets my eyes, I can tell by her little smile that I am completely glazed over with lust.

"Let's go," she says and takes my hand. I hate to admit it but when it comes down to it she is really the one in control. I follow like a puppy and the truth is, I'm panting.

We walk in silence down the block. We are supposed to be shopping for stuff for our new apartment. Finally we have moved out of the studio into a one-bedroom and need to take up the extra space. For months we complained of no space; then we get it, and immediately we need to fill it up.

"Maybe we should live empty for a while," I say, hoping she catches my drift so we can just head home.

"No. We need to get a few things," she says.

She is torturing me. Not that I don't deserve it, but she is. Of course it will only make it better when it finally happens.

She stops and gives me a wicked grin. I look up. We are in front of a sex shop. Hee-haw. Have I told you I love this girl?

We go in to this little shop of heaven and I pause by the dildos. Maybe I need a new dick.

"Kathy," she calls from across the store.

I look up; she is holding a pair of restraints. You know, the kind you attach to the bed? In her other hand she has a blindfold. My mouth falls open, I am shocked. I am also soaking wet. She walks toward me, toys in hand.

She comes up close to me, the way I did in the bedroom

this morning. I can smell her sweet breath; her eyes are shining as she licks her red lips.

"So," she says, in that sexy, breathy sort of way, "what do you think?"

I can barely nod my head and she leaves me there, breathing heavily by the dildos. She goes up and pays. My goddess, I think, what have I done to deserve this happiness?

We hurry home. I can't wait to tie her up and get my fingers nice and wet.

I am all over her as soon as we walk through the door. My hands are on her hips, her ass, pulling her close to me. My lips are on her neck; my tongue is in her ear. I lift off her shirt. Her nipples are rock-hard and as soon as I place my mouth on them she moans. I start sucking and nibbling, my hands groping above her jeans.

"Wait," she says, pushing me back. Her voice is throaty, her hands are sweaty.

"Uh-uh," I say, coming in again, shaking my head.

"Our toys," she says, in that don't-be-so-pigheaded-and-listen-to-me tone. I can't help but smile.

She picks up the discreet brown paper bag and takes me by the hand, leading me into the bedroom.

She turns around, lifting off my shirt and unbuttoning my jeans. "What are you doing?" I ask her, slightly amused by this change in our undressing patterns.

"Oh," she says sweetly, "I'm going to tie you up." I laugh out loud; I can't help it. She looks at me, she looks so fucking innocent, and she smiles. "Don't laugh," she says, "I'm serious."

I raise one eyebrow and think that maybe I'll let her have some fun. She gets me undressed and leads me to the bed.

"Lie down," she says. I do but then I grab her and pull her on top of me, I roll her over me and hold her down, kissing her. Then I notice she is not laughing. She pulls off of me and she actually looks sad. I have hurt her feelings by not letting her be the top just this once.

"I'm sorry," I say in my most sincere apologetic tone. "Tie me up, baby."

She looks at me out of those puppy-dog eyes and attaches the restraints to my wrists and my ankles. She smiles at me. Then disappears into the bathroom. Now, I am all about having her look sexy, but I'm dying over here. My cunt is aching, and my nipples are so sensitive they look like you could just pop 'em right off.

"Baby," I yell, "what are you doing?"

"Hold on one second," she screams back, "just don't go anywhere."

I can hear her giggles behind the door.

What kind of a butch am I? I could almost kick myself for not having known better.

She comes out of the bathroom, with my dick strapped to her. My chin drops; I can't believe it. She's going to fuck me with my own dick? I don't think so. I start thrashing around, pulling against my restraints.

"Take that off," I say, "You can't use that."

She just shakes her head and climbs on the bed above me.

"Shh..." she whispers and bends down over my pubic patch. She breathes on my curly hair. She bends down and licks my clit up with her tongue. She moves cunt to clit, her tongue just lapping away. She uncurls her fist, letting her fingers fan out before she slides them, one at a time, into my hole. She's got the first three in there and I arch my back to get them in deeper. Her tongue is tickling me. This actually feels so good I think I might lose it. She wriggles another finger in there. She's going deep with four fingers. She's thrusting and suddenly I want more. I want to be filled, hard and fast and deep.

"More," I whisper.

"What?." she asks, managing to lift her tongue up only for the one second it takes to ask that. "What did you say?"

"Fist me," I say. I can see her lips spreading into a grin

through my black bush. She shakes her head no, and the mere movement of her head is enough to get me going. She keeps fucking me and I want to come. I want to be fucked.

"Fist me," I ask again, almost begging.

Instead she removes her fingers and brings her whole body up. She brings my dick up to me and guides it in. I can't believe she is actually doing this. I am trying to fight the fact that it feels so good, but it's no use. She's fucking me hard and rough, slamming that dildo into my wet cunt and I'm moving my hips against her. Her long hair brushes against my face and her tits are swaying. Her pretty lips are pressed tightly together and a thin line of sweat drips down her cheeks. She looks so beautiful fucking me. I grab her ass and push her deeper into me; she looks surprised for a moment but then goes with it. She pumps me until I moan and quiver with pleasure. My whole body is a huge cunt and hers a big fake cock. I have to bite my lip to keep from crying as the orgasm racks through my body.

Afterward, she unhooks my dick and throws it to the floor. She unties my wrists and ankles and cuddles up inside of my arms. Just like it was me who made her come, just like this was normal, like nothing ever happened.

The Pursuit of Happiness, the Wet Seat of Her Harley, and the Pleasure of Money

Divianna Ingravallo

Nick hired me for my leather G-string, garters, and corset. After my audition all he said was, "You like leather, huh? You can start work tomorrow."

That's how I ended up working in what was known as the best go-go bar in New York City. The prerequisites for working there were blond hair and big silicone breasts, but the sight of my accoutrements blinded Nick, so he ignored my small tits, black hair, and olive complexion.

Nick was Italian. From Brooklyn. His big belly, the gold crucifix emerging out of the hair on his chest, and the ponytail combed out of an almost-bald head made me deny the fact that I was Italian, from Italy, and I said, "I'm from Brazil."

Nick was the persistent type. He wouldn't lay off the subject of leather and screwing and kept inviting me to play in his office. What Nick didn't know was that he was dealing with a dyke from no other place but hell who despised him. This dyke knew that all Nick really needed was to be fucked in the ass with a 12-inch dildo, and how boring, this dyke thought, if I have to be the one to have to show him that.

Besides Nick's strong cologne, crucifix, and sliminess, I

hated working there because I was the only dyke. I know I was. Let's face it, it takes a dyke to spot another one even if she's disguised in a stripper or a nun's uniform.

That's why I was so relieved when Kamala auditioned. Blond hair, so fake it shone from a distance. Real, full breasts, pierced at both nipples, a gold chain connecting the two; smooth curvy hips; muscular legs; thigh-high red boots. And a big personality. Nick hired her on the spot.

Kamala, whose real name was Kim, would ride her Harley to work, looking like an urban cowboy on an untamed horse. Her black riding boots made a statement with each step. Come to think of it, she was a walking statement. Leather jacket with dangling chains, spiked hair, a myriad of buttons with mottos like SHIT HAPPENS or BUTCH GIRLS RULE. But the Kamala who came out of the dressing room was something completely different: true femme fatale out of the cheesiest porn magazine. I loved that transformation so much that I wanted to mold it with my own hands. I wanted to fuck Kamala out of Kim. Sucking the femme out of a butch girl is my favorite game.

The weeks that followed were torturous. Well, at least work was finally spicy. I'd always be creeping glances at Kamala's cleavage, spying on the moves out of her hips, sneaking peeks out of that special place between her legs, where her G-string was just a bit too tight. I became the drooling stripper.

That's why I jumped on her Harley when she finally offered me a ride after work. I squeezed my legs around her hips and placed my hands on her inner thighs. I said, "Drive to the darkest alley you know. My cunt hurts. The vibrations of your byke are not gonna do it for me, baby," and I sank my teeth into her neck to embellish my phranc approach. A tremor ran through her body down to her cunt, which I cupped, firmly, with my hand. Kim followed my order.

She stopped. It was so dark, so hot, so sultry—so New

York. I pulled her leather off, and before she knew it I had her wrists tied behind her back.

"You bitch" slid out of the corner of her lips. I jumped off the byke to finish off my bondage job. Kim knew not to resist. Her Harley's balance was at stake.

Her nipples were instantly hard in my mouth. I pulled her tit's ring with my tongue, twisting it a little, and sucking with my lips, pulled the chain with my teeth. I felt like Audrey, the undulating teenager in *Twin Peaks*.

I pulled her G-string up—it actually slid up for all her wetness—and pushed it against her clit. "Fuck me," she whispered.

"So soon?" I asked, pulling her G-string higher, bringing my knee between her legs. "No, honey. Where's the butch girl gone? In my lesbian manual, femmes get off first." I started masturbating in front of her. Rubbing my clit with one hand, fucking myself with the other. I felt Kim's desire transform into pain. Sweet revenge.

I came and started licking her all over, pulling off what was left of her clothes. She got so excited that a long, warm stream came out of her pussy. I put my hands and face under it, nourishing a thirst I didn't know I had. I felt like a kid trying to drink for the first time at an Italian fountain.

"So," she hissed, "are you gonna fuck me now?"

"No," I said. "I'm just going to lick you." I moved the soaking wet G-string to the side. I pulled up the hood of her cunt by a ring that had mysteriously popped out, and started sucking her, spreading her cheeks open. My tongue became an animal with a mind of its own.

"Fuck me, fuck me now," she yelled.

"You butch girls are all alike," I whispered. And I fucked her with as many fingers as her cunt could take, slowly and then fast and slow again, pulling on her tit chain with my mouth. I would have fucked with my whole fist, but I didn't have the right ingredients.

Kim's toughness was now melting on that byke seat and

it smelled of leather, cunt juice, motor oil, and piss. The residue was between my sticky fingers.

I untied her as if undoing the ribbon of a special present. I told her to drive back to work. She did. Nick was closing up the place. I ran up to his face and said, "Hi, Nick. Let's go to your office. Kamala and I want to show you some kinky lesbian sex." He believed me because my words smelled of Kim's cunt.

Nick followed my order. As I'd suspected, he was a fine slave, a trained slave, in fact. So it was easy to get him undressed and on his knees. I started whipping him.

"You are a bad dirty boy."

"Oh, yes, mistress, I am a dirty bastard." I ordered Kim to blindfold him. The marks of the whip on his ass were the sign of a victory I had been longing for. I shoved a dildo without lube and without finesse up his butt hole and kicked it with my pointy shoe and an exquisite sense of cruelty.

Then we took all the money the club had made that day, which was sitting in the jerk's pants pocket, and left him there. I thought, *God damn it, I'm giving up my favorite dildo*. But it looked so good up his butt that it felt like a small sacrifice. Kim/Kamala and I parked her Harley in her garage and caught the first plane to Rio de Janeiro.

Tanisha Bey

Terry Volpe and Angela Jenkins

"Honey, if you're in that much pain, you really ought to see a doctor."

"I just keep hoping it'll go away."

"Well, it obviously hasn't," Pam says, getting out of bed and heading toward the bathroom.

I lie here, admiring her figure, which, even under a ridiculous, oversize football jersey is impossible to hide. After she leaves the room, I grab my cigarettes. Slowly exhaling my first drag, I find myself praying to any deity who will listen to heal my pain before tomorrow morning.

Pam returns and climbs silently into bed. She's had her say and is content. It's a quality I admire.

"Tanisha, baby, try to get some sleep tonight. If you want, I can take off work tomorrow. You know, in case you need the company."

"Hey, I could get lucky. Besides, it's a really shitty way to spend a day off."

"I know it sucks, but considering your schedule, tomorrow is the best day to take care of it." Frustrated by my stubbornness, she fluffs her pillow angrily. "My offer stands."

"Yeah, yeah," I mutter, knowing she's right. I resign myself to an unpleasant future. "I promise to go to the doctor tomorrow, but I don't want you to miss a day's work. I mean, Christ, it's probably just a yeast infection."

Pam curls up next to me and, placing her hand on my chest, murmurs, "Thanks, little one. I love you."

"I love you too."

I awake to that familiar burning sensation between my legs. Apparently my appeal to the heavens was either ignored or put on hold pending a full credit check. Cursing the fates, my mothers, and the dog next door, I roll out of bed, walk to the bathroom, and brace myself for the pain of that first morning piss.

On the way out of the bathroom, I'm intercepted by Plato, who's frantically mewing for food, water, attention, or the chance to get out and terrorize the neighborhood. I give in and feed him, with one eye on the clock. Is 10:18 too early for a beer? With infinite wisdom and logic (I'm not always this arrogant) I figure that since I'm taking on the AMA today, I need all the false confidence I can muster. I grab a Bud.

Three hours and six weeks later, I'm sitting in the waiting room of the local hospital, trying to gauge the sexual persuasion of every woman who passes.

"Tanisha Bey," the doctor's assistant finally calls.

Reluctantly I tear myself away from an issue of *Sports Illustrated* and walk toward her. She accompanies me through the double doors into the emergency room, assigning me door number 3.

"C'mon, let's make a deal." I receive a blank stare in reply. Either she doesn't get my humor or she's been discouraged from fraternizing with patients. Silently she sticks a thermometer in my mouth and checks my pulse and blood pressure.

"Your blood pressure's a little high. Are you nervous?"

"Yeah, I guess so." I can't exactly tell her that drooling over a color spread of Martina in the waiting room might also be a contributing factor.

With a superior smile plastered on a face wearing too

much makeup, she asks, "What's the nature of your complaint?"

Christ, why do I keep waiting to see Judge Wapner? Wasn't all this shit covered in triage? Hoping to wipe that pious Suzy Heterosexual look off her face, I blurt out, "My cunt hurts. Can you fix it?"

It doesn't even faze her. "What kind of pain are you experiencing?"

"It itches a lot and it burns like hell when I piss."

"Umm."

Now what is that supposed to mean? Why is it that the medical profession, as a whole, manages to make me feel stupid and inadequate? Do they cover it in med school? "Patient Relations 101: How to make your patient feel inferior."

She tosses one of those wonderfully fashionable hospital gowns in my direction. "Put this on. The doctor will be with you in a few minutes."

She leaves without another word, probably to do something terribly important like file her nails or place a call to her long-suffering law student boyfriend.

The "few minutes for the doctor" stretches into 10, 15 minutes. If Pam were here, she use the time constructively, pilfering whatever she could from the examination room. Me, I just here thinking I should've had a few more beers. I can hear voices outside the room. With a sense of impending doom, I stare at the door as it opens menacingly.

"Hello. Sorry about the wait. I'm Dr. Rodriguez."

I return the greeting, hoping she doesn't notice that I'm on the verge of a hysterical fit.

"It's OK to be anxious," she says kindly.

Damn, another illusion shattered. Why is it that when I most need my big bad butch attitude it's on a six-month sabbatical in the Bronx?

"So how long has this been bothering you?"

"Oh, about a week and a half, I guess.'

'Describe the pain to me, please."

I launch into my tale of genital malfunction as she busily jots notes onto a chart. She has magnificent hands. I wonder what they feel like. Ashamed, I look away.

"Is there any possibility that you're pregnant?"

"No."

"Are you sexually active?"

"Yes."

"What form of birth control do you use?"

"I don't."

"Well, then how do you know that…"

"I'm a lesbian."

"Oh." I'm surprised to see her grinning at me. Shocked, I simply stare at her. Her brown eyes sparkling, she says, "The first thing we'll do is get a urine sample. While we're waiting for the results we'll start the examination. OK?"

"You're the doctor."

God, I hate pissing into these little jars. Closing my eyes, I bring to mind the doctor's small, compact frame, quite a contrast to Pam's muscular bulk. I allow my finger to slightly graze my swollen clit. Isn't this just great. Here I am, about to intimately examine by a gorgeous gynecologist and I'm already in a state of intense sexual arousal. How am I supposed to explain this? I suppose I could leave and come back tomorrow. Do doctors usually pull E.R. duty two days in a row? Besides, what would I tell Pam? God, Tanisha, you're not a teenager anymore! Let's just get this over and done with.

Jar in hand and libido in check, I head back toward the examination room.

"I'll take that," says Suzy Heterosexual, Guardian of Mainstream America.

"There it is. Good to the last drop." Handing my sample over, I get a sense of satisfaction from her glare.

Back in the room, a shiver of fear or anticipation runs through me as I stare at the table with its cold metal stirrups.

My resolve to stay coolly objective is quickly eroding.

"Why don't you lie down and we can get started?"

I stretch out on the table, groaning inwardly. Why does it have to be so cold? My erect nipples are evident beneath the thin gown, and I try to rearrange myself so they're a little less obvious. I glance up to see the doctor observing my futile attempts with an amused grin. I'm tempted to ask her what's so funny, but I don't really want to hear the answer.

"Are you comfortable?"

"I've never felt better," I lie, focusing on a cabinet somewhere above her left shoulder. The cabinet holds syringes, something that looks like an enema, and various other instruments of torture.

"Glad to hear it. Now, let's get your legs into these stirrups."

"Do we have to?"

"Well, do you want to get rid of your problem or not?"

Unable to tell the doctor that at this point I have a bigger problem—namely, a powerful attraction to said doctor—I sigh and allow her to help me into the stirrups. Her hand on my calf makes me catch my breath. I wonder what my blood pressure is now. She slips those magnificent hands into a pair of latex gloves. Under other circumstances I might have made some smart-ass comment about safe sex, but now is neither the time nor the place. Grabbing a tube of Surgi-lube, she approaches me with more than a passing glance across my body. Hmm…this could be interesting. Then why do I feel like a trapped rat?

"Just relax, dear. This isn't as bad as you're making it out to be."

"If it's so wonderful, why don't you trade places with me?"

A deep, throaty laugh. "That's not a very good attitude. You came to me, remember?"

"Yeah, well, I didn't expect…"

"What?"

"Never mind." What I meant to say, Doctor, is that I desperately want you to touch me. I'm aching to feel your hand inside me, that's what I didn't expect. Knowing those magnificent hands of yours will soon be touching me in places known only to a select few does little for my state of equilibrium. Closing my eyes, I try to ignore the familiar warm sensation that threatens to completely embarrass me.

"I'm going to feel around your vaginal opening. It looks a little red and irritated. If I cause you any pain, please let me know."

This is ridiculous. This woman is a physician who probably does this kind of thing all the time, and I'm acting like a bitch in heat. Keeping my eyes tightly shut, I try thinking of something, anything other than the beautiful woman standing over me. With the first contact of her hand on my throbbing clit, all thoughts of household chores and term papers to be graded vanish. Involuntarily, my eyes snap open.

"See, this isn't so awful," she says, smiling.

Has her voice gotten deeper, or has my hearing, like everything else, become hypersensitive?

"I'm going to feel around inside now. Just try to relax."

Unable to speak, I simply nod. Her smile widens, revealing a dimple in her left cheek. She enters me slowly, exploring gently, her thumb now resting firmly on my clit. By design? I don't even want to hazard a guess. The movement of her finger inside causes her thumb to move in slight circles. Incapable of stopping it, my hips thrust upward, wanting more.

"Hold still, please."

Inserting another finger, she applies more pressure to the spot where I want, need it most. Something about this "thorough examination" is making me wonder about the good doctor's motives. Still not trusting myself to speak—besides, what would I say?—I remain silent.

"You really must stop moving around like that. It makes it difficult to properly conduct the examination." Her harsh tone is softened by a huge grin.

I mutter an apology, my eyes silently begging for more. As

if reading my mind, she smoothly slides another finger into me. I'm sure more than Surgi-lube is dripping from my cunt. She looks coolly professional in her lab coat, but she has to realize what she's doing to me. She begins rubbing my clit faster. I stifle a moan.

"Everything seems OK so far. How you feeling?"

At this point I realize that the doctor is breathing as heavily as I. Throwing caution and the last of my crumbling inhibitions to the wind, I flash a seductive smile. In response, she slides a fourth finger inside me. In the back of my mind I keep waiting for someone to walk in, but the doctor doesn't seem worried at all. I wonder how often she does this. I can picture it now—dykes lined up for four blocks: "Hey, is Dr. Rodriguez in today?"

"Oh, God. That's so good." Her thumb increases tempo, then suddenly her whole hand is inside me. Her fist seems to hit all the right spots simultaneously. My legs start to tremble as my orgasm approaches. I clamp my hand down over my mouth to keep from making too much noise. Almost before I'm aware of it my orgasm hits. She waits for it to subside, then slowly extends her fingers and draws them out of me. I let out a contented hum.

"That wasn't so bad, now was it?" I just look at her and grin.

"I'll be right back. I want to see if your test results are at the desk yet." She heads to the door. Turning, she adds with a sly grin, "You can get dressed now."

Relaxing in the afterglow, I watch as she walks briskly out the door. If this is her modus operandi for female patients, how does she get away with it? I begin to get dressed. I can't decide whether Pam is going to die laughing or try to get an appointment when she hears about my escapade with Dr. Rodriguez. I finish tying my shoes and sit down to await my fate.

The door opens and the doctor walks in. I was sure I'd have to wait at least another 20 minutes; I thought that was a hospital rule. She must be slipping.

"Well, Tanisha, it seems you have a urinary tract infection." She scrawls something on a piece of paper and hands it to me. After a moment of trying to decipher her handwriting I look blankly at her.

She laughs. "Indecipherable handwriting is a prerequisite for the medical profession. It's a prescription for penicillin. Take three a day for two weeks. If the symptoms don't clear up by then, I want you to come back for more tests. You're free to go."

Gathering my wits and my racing fantasies, I head out the door and get into my car. At home I have just enough time to fee Plato and collapse on the couch before Pam waltzes in.

She stands pensively in the doorway, trying to judge from my expression whether I went to the doctor or decided to blow it off.

"Did you go?"

"You won't believe what happened..."

Winners

Rachel Kramer Bussel

My new girlfriend and I are making a huge public display of ourselves, making out and giggling and generally causing mayhem at the table, but we don't care. Right now we're oblivious to our friends and anyone else, and despite the noise of raucous drinking and bingo numbers being called around us, we only have eyes for each other. Somehow, after a few weeks, public groping doesn't seem like such an oddity to me; in fact, it's a necessity.

But even exhibitionists need privacy sometimes. We giggle as I grab her hand and pull her into the bathroom. We're breathless by the time we get there, unable to hold back or think or do anything but touch each other. My hand edges under her pants, grateful for their looseness and the easy access they provide to her. I press her up against the side of the stall and kiss her, my hand reaching down, down, down until I get to what I'm looking for. Her pussy is hot and wet, the way I remember it, and I scramble to undo her buttons with my other hand so I can feel more of it. Then I slide my middle finger all the way in, and I know that any embarrassment we may later feel will have been worth it for this. She pushes down against me, greedy, and I add another finger, crouching down so I can watch my fingers as they slide back and forth. This is the first time I'm actually seeing her pussy in all its glory; the other times we spent fumbling in the dark, stolen moments that were delicious but much too brief. She leans her head back against the wall, hands clutching the walls, the door, anything she can to hold on as I press down against her, curling my fingers as I press them into her. I start to slide them out, to tease her for a moment, but in a flash her hand is there, shoving me back inside, and I comply, pushing firmly, feeling her stretch and give.

After a while, I stop, taking my fingers out of her pussy and putting them in her mouth, slowly, letting her taste herself. I've been feeding her all night—grapes and cherries, then bits of my dinner as she sat on my lap, ice from my drink and then fingers, one or two slowly pushed inside her mouth when no one was looking. I love the way her mouth opens for me, the look she gives me when she parts her lips, like she'll do anything for me, take and taste whatever I have to offer her. When I slide my fingers in now, I feel her tongue, warm and heavy, pressing against me, seeking out the curves of my fingers, challenging me just as I challenge her.

I remember I have a dildo in my bag, not something I'd normally carry, but I just bought it as a surprise for her. Now it's a surprise for me as I tell her to close her eyes and carefully remove it from my purse. I'm long past the point of caring who else might be in the bathroom with us or what our friends will think about our long absence; this is obviously more important. I tell her to open her mouth, and she obeys immediately. I want to kiss her, but I make myself wait. Instead I slide the silicone cock into her mouth, knowing she won't be expecting it, eager to see the dark purple of it sliding in and out of her pink lips. I tease her with it, my other hand frantically pushing her pants down now and stroking her cunt in time with the cock. She opens her mouth wider and I slide it farther in, testing, teasing. I slide it out and trail it down her neck and chest and she moans as I massage her clit, moving deliberately too slowly for her.

"Please" is all she manages to get out, her creaky voice all I need to hear. I find a condom in my purse and roll it over the cock. She's looking at me now, those beautiful eyes fixed on me so full of love and desire that I am almost squirm, even now.

There's no real graceful way to do this, but we're beyond trying to be graceful. I motion for her to turn around and she does, sticking her pert ass out toward me. I give it a smack, the sound reverberating throughout the room. Too loud, I realize. I bring my hand again to her cunt, slipping fingers in, then out, so fast even I don't know what I'll do next. When neither of us can wait any longer, I bring the tip of the cock to her, thinking I'll start off slow, but she grabs my hand, urging me inside her quickly. For a small girl, she's strong and knows what she wants, and I smile as I slide the purple dick into her. She rocks back and forth against it, and I try to keep up with her hips, pumping back and forth, intent. I can't see her face, but I know what it looks like, face contorted in concentration and need. "That's good, baby, just like that, yeah, I want you to come for me, OK, come hard for me, I want to see that." I have to whisper, but I know she hears me or at least hears the tone of my words. I love to be the one to push her over the edge, to get so wild that she doesn't care about anything except coming immediately. She grunts and pushes back against the cock, and I balance myself by grabbing her ass, squeezing it as I fuck her, sliding the entire length of the cock into her and the holding my palm over the end, pushing just a little more. She bangs her hand against the wall and I move faster, pushing against her as she pushes against me, and when I sense she's right on the brink, I move my hand from her ass to her clit, tweaking it lightly as I press the cock into her one final time and feel her shudder underneath me. She says my name and reaches back to touch my head, and I wish for a minute we were somewhere else where we could curl up against each other. Instead I slide the cock out of her, stand up, and wrap myself around her as she recovers.

We exit the bathroom, unable to keep the smiles or blushes off our faces, and return to our table as the bingo caller yells out "O 69." We haven't done that tonight, at least not yet, but with her, the night is always young, and no matter what numbers are called, we are the real winners of the night.

Having Holly

Thea Hillman

It was so hot. Can I just say it was the hottest sex I've ever had with a woman—practically fully clothed the entire time? As good as the best boy sex I've ever had. Except it was Holly.

Maybe it started when I could crack sexual innuendos and she fired them right back. She was nasty too. Or showing up at her birthday. We were the only women wearing flowing skirts in a room full of argyle and crew necks. Or her room. The pillows on her bed—flushed peach and blue, red—pastel, but not shallow; light. Embracing. A flash of me holding Holly on the bed that was how I realized I was attracted to women. And more specifically, Holly.

So is she going to call or what?

Years of moving around ensue, but somehow we stay close. I come out to her via airmail. She writes back she is, too. She flirts with me over the phone. Goes to a wedding nearby and is too busy to call. She's scared, I think.

I mean, it wouldn't be so weird if we hadn't gotten together.

Another year goes by. Then we see each other. I've changed a lot. She's intimidated. I think, good, I'm not attracted to her anymore. I go to dinner and meet her mom, her aunt, her grandparents. And it's all so innocent that we drink wine, and I make her family laugh, and they like me, and I'm sleeping over.

If only she didn't stroke me afterward, caressing me with so much tenderness.

After dinner, lying in her high school pink ruffled bed, teenage girls at a sleepover, I wonder why we keep returning to the subject of sex. And why when her lover calls and she breaks their date, she lets him wonder what's going to happen that night.

I tell her I'd rather have my hair played with than be fucked.

Cuddling, friends, "nonsexual" of course. She holds me. It's nicer than I ever could have imagined to be held by Holly. She jokes about how beautiful our children would be. My head against her breast. Her fingers in my hair.

Neither of us is taking responsibility.

Excruciatingly, strokes lengthen. Fingers stay close to sensitive ears. Fingers splay open over faces. Hands slip under T-shirts. Hair is tugged. Strokes are held—hesitating—then deepening. Strong hands are complimented. Little moans escape. Bigger moans escape. Bodies shift. And it's not so suddenly that I realize sexual is what is happening with Holly. And the girls who usually have so much to say to each other are silent.

I don't want to be sexual with Holly unless I can knock her socks off.

Years of wanting, denying wanting, unconscious jealousy, and fear fill my fingers as they love Holly. The same love that's always been there, open, that's no longer being mentioned, that's completely different now, or might be.

We scratch, using nails through scalps, down necks.

I can't seem to do anything wrong. Holly moves with every touch, and all I want to do is keep her moaning with my "nonsexual" strokes. Her head is tilted back, mouth open. I'm too scared to make a sound; she might stop running her fingers through my hair, might stop getting closer and closer to my breasts as she rubs my back. The only thing I'm thinking is come on, bitch, touch my breast. Over and over, until finally she does make a move. I tighten my legs around hers and let my fingers dig in.

We don't kiss. That would make it real.

We grind. Rubbing through underwear, boxers. Rip T-shirts off. Don't talk. Grab ass cheeks. Bite, hard. Scratch. Sweat so hard we slide against each other as we clutch and push our bodies as close as they can get. I want her so badly; I enjoy sliding fingers along her asshole. All I want is to make her come. For her to see how hot we are.

She's told me she loves me, but she's never called me "amazing" before.

And she's close to coming. And we stop. Hold each other, stray hairs clinging to our sweat, we laugh. She speaks first, whether you like it or not, you're soft and sweet.

I call first. She says she's happy it happened. She'll call me later on in the week.

Phrases fill my head like you know I'm not expecting anything. I know Holly's track record with women, and it scares me. But she's glowing, and stroking me with so much care that I decide to expect the best from her. I'm just not sure what that is, and I worry because it's clear to me that I could fall in love with Holly.

She still hasn't called.

And I call her. She isn't stressed or upset. I take this as a bad sign. I cook dinner. She makes sure I know she put on lipstick after she got off BART, on her way to my apartment. She brings me flowers and asks me when I grew breasts.

Holly, what is it about you that makes me write?

I think of calling her in New York sometimes. Urgent. Because she might get married at any time. Because I need to tell her how much I love her. Because I am in love with her.

Writing Holly is having Holly.

But I don't. And I can't seem to write to her. So I use her name. Write her. Because in writing Holly I am loving Holly.

Again and again.

The Old-Fashioned Way

Lucy Jane Bledsoe

When I got home, my roommate Erika was hard at work at her typewriter. She sure put in the hours on her writing, I had to give her that. Erika is a 23-year-old sex radical. She hates anything associated with '70s feminism, including Frye boots and flannel shirts. Her favorite phrase is "sex positive."

"How's the single gal?" she asked, ogling me with great exaggeration.

I laughed. At least she had a sense of humor. "Lonely," I said. She raised any eyebrow. "Miss Nancy?"

"Yeah." I missed her a lot.

"I know a good way to relieve loneliness."

"Erika, honey, are you trying—again—to seduce me?"

"I'm not shy."

"I know. But you're young enough to be my daughter."

"Ha! If you gave birth at 13."

"Happens every day.

"I could teach you a few tricks that might come in handy as you started dating again."

"You're that skilled?"

She looked down at the keys of her typewriter, tapped one a few times. "I've been around."

"Whose bed?"

Her head jerked up. "What?"

"Whose bed? Yours or mine? Or would you rather use the stove top? Burners on or off?"

I wished I could have preserved the look on her face just then. A mix of fear and incredulity. That look made me sincere about wanting to go to bed with her. Underneath all that sex radical paraphernalia, Erika was a real sweetheart.

She pulled her image together quickly and responded. "I have some great toys in my room."

I hesitated, then said. "OK." I felt like a coach was about to introduce me to the equipment in a new gym.

"Now?" she asked.

"I might lose my nerve later." I said, playing up to her show of sophistication.

She smiled indulgently. "It won't hurt a bit," she teased. "Come on." She led me by the hand to her bedroom.

"One rule," I warned.

"What?" She adjusted her face so that it was open, accepting.

"No gerbils."

"Get out of here," she said, pushing me onto her bed.

She stood looking down at me and I laughed. I said, "I don't know if I can kiss my roommate, you know?"

"Who said anything about kissing?"

I lay back. OK, this 23-year-old kid wanted to run the show. Fine. I was tired.

Erika stripped off her oversize jeans and lumberjack shirt. She wore no bra or underpants. I saw a bit of silver glinting through her pubic hair. I winced at the thought of her pierced clit. What if I snagged the ring and tore it off or something?

I didn't make any moves to take off my own clothes. This was Erika's show. She sat on the bed and ran a hand from my throat down to my belly. I wished the touch had given me some kind of buzz, but it hadn't. She unbuttoned my shirt quickly and pulled it off my shoulders, then unzipped my jeans and left them on me.

Next Erika opened a drawer by the bed and started pulling out "toys." I closed my eyes and listened to the appliances clank as she tossed them on the bed. *Please don't tie me up,* I thought. I really didn't want to be tied up. What was wrong with good old-fashioned sex? Did it really take her cabinet full of high-tech appliances to get off?

"Can I undress?" I finally asked.

"Sure." Erika stood back to watch. I undid my black lace bra and dropped it to the floor. Erika swallowed. I raised my hips to pull my jeans off my butt. My panties came with them. Then I posed for her, propping myself up on one elbow, extending one leg straight out and crooking the other leg so that my vulva opened.

"You're beautiful," she said, her voice croaking. For the first time, she didn't sound as if she were speaking from a script.

"When are you gonna stop readying your tools and get to work on me?"

She swallowed again. "Close your eyes," she said, so I did. She sounded like she was saddling up a horse. Finally she said, "OK."

I opened my eyes. First I looked into Erika's eyes, which were hot green and defiant. She held her mouth, with its very full and red lips, in a snarl position. Her hands were planted firmly on her narrow hips. "My God," I shrieked, bucking straight up on the bed. "That's a whale sticking out of your pussy."

"That's right. I'm gonna shove this whale up—"

"Oh, no, you're not," I interrupted quickly. "A lavender whale up my vagina is not my idea of—"

"Loosen up, Liz," Erika said, climbing onto the bed with me.

"E-liz-a-beth," I said, feeling very tired. "My name is four syllables long."

"To me, you're just my whore, my sexy trashy little whore."

I moaned with disgust, but Erika took it as pleasure. "Oh, yeah," she went on in a growly voice that was entirely different from her regular high voice. "You're a cheap piece of meat to me." She placed her red mouth on my neck like a sea anemone.

"Wait a second," I said, utterly unmoved by her attempts at talking dirty. "Could we just, you know, touch a little first?"

"Relax," she said. "Just let your mind go. Your generation spent so much energy taking back the night, you gave up your own pleasure. Try imagining I've just paid $300 for your gorgeous body. You could get that much, you know."

I laid back, too polite to tell her that I had no problem with talking dirty. I longed for Nancy's trashy mouth. But it's got to come from the heart. Dirty talk had to come from real passion.

Erika reached under the bed and produced some wrist restraints. She kept trying to talk dirty but it sounded more like she'd memorized a bad porn script. I let her tie me to the bed. I let her climb on me, twist my nipples a couple times, then push that lavender whale up me. She pumped away on the dildo, muttering, "I'm deep in your ocean, baby." I bucked my hips for her, but I wasn't going to go so far as to fake an orgasm. She didn't come either.

We lay there for a while, me tied to the bedposts, and didn't talk. The lavender whale flopped to the side of her dildo harness. At first I felt embarrassed. Then I felt sad for her because she hadn't transformed me into a liberated sex machine like she said she could. Finally I felt angry. Erika and her friends really believed they'd invented hot sex and radical politics. Like, what did they think women had been doing for the last 3 billion years we've been on earth? Waiting for the 1990s when the sex radicals would show us how it's done?

I broke the silence saying, "I bet you're really thankful for the Catharine MacKinnons and Andrea Dworkins of this world. They keep sex good and dirty for you."

"Antisex prudes," Erika muttered, missing my point.

"I'm gonna whisper 'Catharine MacKinnon' in your ear while I fuck you and see what happens," I said.

Erika got a funny look on her face. She knew I was mocking her. Her ears reddened to match her lips.

"Erika," I said, more gently now. "With all this apparatus in the bed between us, I feel more like a lab animal than a woman having sex."

"Loosen up," she snapped. "You're just too uptight to allow yourself to feel good." She shifted her whole body into a pout.

"It seems to me that being able to get off with half a hardware store in your bed is more indicative of a loser state of mind than needing all this crap. Believe me, my orgasms are superb with a hand or a mouth. What gets me off is the, oh, maybe you could say the essence of the other person. I don't need props. Come on, clear this bed out and let me show you the old-fashioned way."

That sweet look of fear crossed Erika's face again.

"Come on, girlfriend. We've tried your way. Now try mine," I whispered. Then I swept all the gadgets onto the floor.

"Watch out!" she cried. "That stuff costs a lot of money."

"Sorry," I said quietly as I started tonguing her outer ear.

"You just have to control everything," she said, still petulant.

"Mmm, probably so," I said. I scooted down the bed to suck on her toes, one at a time. I reached a hand up under her ass and stroke the crack. I could feel all her muscles tense. I wondered if she felt naked without her toys. I moved my mouth up her thigh and encountered the lavender whale. I used my teeth to undo her dildo harness. Each time she tried to help with her hands, I bit them. I heard her sigh a couple times. I didn't know if it was annoyance or the first stages of relaxing. Once I got the harness of, I licked her clit ring, but not her clit. I circled around and around her labia, licking her thighs, stroking her anus, but not touching her clit. I wanted her to get so desperate she had to ask me.

She started moaning when I put a lubed finger up her anus. Then gasping as I put three fingers in her vagina. I moved the fingers, all four, in and out of her very, very slowly. She hauled her knees up as far as they would go and held them with her hands. Her head tossed back and forth, and primeval sounds came from her throat.

Finally, she begged, "Oh, God Elizabeth just do me please." She even got my name right, for once. Still, I waited. I wouldn't touch her clit, but I fucked her harder and faster with my fingers. She had to scream first. She had to scream before I'd touch her clit.

Then Erika did scream. "Oh please, oh please, oh please," she hollered. I touched her clit lightly with the tip of my tongue, then sucked her until she came, wailing and bucking. The old-fashioned way.